ROBERT CLAY ALLISON
Requiescat In Pace

Robert Clay Allison

Requiescat In Pace

James. S. Peters

SANTA FE

Book design by Vicki Ahl

Sunstone books may be purchased for educational, business, or sales promotional use.
For information please write: Special Markets Department, Sunstone Press,
P.O. Box 2321, Santa Fe, New Mexico 87504-2321.

Library of Congress Cataloging-in-Publication Data

Peters, James Stephen.
  Robert Clay Allison : requiescat in pace / James. S. Peters.
    p. cm.
  ISBN 978-0-86534-560-7 (pbk. : alk. paper)
  1. Allison, Clay, 1840 or 41-1887–Fiction. I. Title.

PS3566.E75525R63 2008
813'.54–dc22

                              2007047988

WWW.SUNSTONEPRESS.COM
SUNSTONE PRESS / POST OFFICE BOX 2321 / SANTA FE, NM 87504-2321 /USA
(505) 988-4418 / ORDERS ONLY (800) 243-5644 / FAX (505) 988-1025

To Clay, Monroe, John and Saluda.

*Photo: Marriage photograph of Robert Clay Allison and America Medora "Dora"
McCulloch, Circa February 1881, Mobeetie, Texas.*
Courtesy West-of-the-Pecos Museum, Pecos, Texas.

...and behold a white horse:
and he went forth conquering,
and to conquer.

—*Revelation 6: 2*

ROBERT CLAY ALLISON wearily drove his loaded wagon north on the second day out of Pecos, Texas. He was headed toward his ranch that abutted the New Mexico state line. It was mid-afternoon on the third of July eighteen hundred and eighty-seven, and he had perhaps ten miles to go. The pair of horses towing him labored on in their same boring clop along the dusty road, plodding faithfully as ever in their only mission in life, to make someone else's burden easier. He had looped the reins around a small post to let the beasts have their way as he often did. They knew the route as well as he, and needed no urging or guidance. The broiling west Texas sun fried away savagely, and he leaned back and smelled the stink of booze and sweat and grime the glaring orb cooked out of his body.

He was drowsy from drink, drowsy from the sun, drowsy from the monotonous sway of the vehicle. He was forty-five years old and would turn forty-six in two months. If I lived that long, he snorted cynically. The passing years meant nothing to him any longer, he mulled: it was only what it all added up to that counted. He snorted again, wondering why he was getting so philosophical of a sudden these past few months. Must be going loco. On these supply hauls back and forth every month or so of almost fifty miles one-way he found himself brooding more than usual. Pondering and replaying old memories like intently read newspapers yellowed by time, wrinkled from overuse. Sometimes he would become angry with himself at the dredging and digging, wondering what in hell for, and wishing more for loss of memory than lucid recollection.

There just wasn't any enjoyment in his life any more, not even that small pleasure of satisfaction he got after finishing some mundane chore which earlier would have given him a smile of accomplishment, the patting himself on the back for a task well done. And his marriage was shot, too. Forget the handbasket. Not that he was ever a joyous personality, but everything in his life had come down to nothing more than constant labor and endless pain. He had no regrets, he was too ornery for that, he had only a bunch of anger. Seems like everything was going to hell.

His leg was throbbing again, and had been more so the last few weeks. Reaching for the whiskey quart squeezed next to him on the seat, he up-ended it greedily, letting the warm rye pour freely down his gullet like a waterfall, hoping it would lessen the pounding in his right tibia and foot. The hurt leg was from an old break when he was twenty-seven which never healed properly, and the mangled foot the result of a self-shooting accident a few years later. Down the years he eventually became so crippled he couldn't even sit a horse any longer, let alone ride one, for the mere hanging of his leg from the saddle ripped his entire body in excruciating agony. It filled him with self-loathing to see healthy men galloping and loping easily day after day, something he took for granted until the privilege was suddenly taken from him. Now he was left in embarrassment at his limping limitations, feeling like an old woman towing a damn buggy behind a pair of nags. And to twist the knife he had to follow a road or worn pathway. No more cutting across the plains with the freedom of a Comanche. No more galloping with the wind just for the joy of it. He wanted to curse God, but was afraid. It seemed it was the only fear left in him.

Where did it all turn sour? Why was he so grumpy of late? Offhand there were three times he could look back and see where he was truly happy as a pig in slop, where he felt relatively content and carefree, when the world was a wondrous place before him, and nothing was impossible. The first came to mind each time he crossed the wide shallows of the Pecos River just south of his ranch, when the remembrance always returned to him of playing along the banks of the Tennessee River as a child. His home town of Clifton, Tennessee sat on its eastern shore, and as he rode across the Pecos he swore he could hear, see and smell the swift, deep waters of the Tennessee where with his brothers he fished, swam and skipped stones. It seemed an eternity ago, but he was suddenly right there. Sometimes he had to shake his head, wondering if he was losing his reason. But they became such grand memories he always looked forward to crossing the Pecos on his trips back and forth to town.

Christ, was he ever so young, or relatively naive? There was his younger brother Monroe, jumping up and down over a caught fish, and little Johnny excitedly pointing and yelling about another big steamer plowing by. Sometimes his baby sister Saluda was with them, playing in the mud, or just sitting in a little pool of water smiling and giggling, happy as a lark. Of the seven offspring, they were the closest. Their older brother Jesse was hardly with them, more the stern disciplinarian. He seemed cut from their father's cloth, a twin, echoing their father's rule-the-roost personality. As a result Clay, Monroe, and John warily kept a distance from him. All along the river there were thick woods, as well as scattered forests throughout the county. Good hunting, fair farm land, and a paradise for kids to hike and roam about in; to play Indian or outlaw. But soon young Clay's dog days were at an end, when at ten, eleven and twelve he became just another hand on the family farm from sunup to sundown. He learned to hate each morning he woke, for it meant a long day of grubbing in the dirt, as he called it. Many a time he caught his father's wrath and was switched or belt-whipped for either dragging his butt when he should have been toiling, or laughing and playing instead of bent over a chore. And if his taskmaster father Jeremiah, demanding as any biblical prophet, weren't there to keep a hawk's eye on him, older brother Jesse's no-nonsense sternness stood over him like a long, threatening shadow. Clay began to feel warped justice taking hold, that his punishment lay in overkill. Soon arguments and fisticuffs broke out between the two, but the younger, shorter, lighter Clay was no match for towering, taunting Jesse. A meanness began taking hold of pre-teen Clay, and it burned within him like a hot iron. The "get even" syndrome. Brother Monroe was a sympathetic ally, for Monroe's first name, Jeremiah, "Jerry," named after his tyrant father, was hateful to him. He favored his middle name which in his adult years he claimed thankfully, completely eradicating Jeremiah from his signature forever.

His second recollection was his time in the Confederate cavalry during the Rebellion. He and Jesse and Monroe first joined together in an artillery outfit. The war had been going on for six months but the old man needed the boys in the field. "Never mind the war," fumed the old man. "This is where you are enlisted." But soon practically all the able-bodied men in the county answered the call to arms, to whip them damn Yankees for trying to tell them how to run their country and their lives, to crush states' rights. Never was such a swarm of bees so wrothy at having their hive kicked. But the old man began feeling uncomfortable at keeping his sons on the farm when most males in the vicinity were off doing battle. "Well," he announced one morning to Jesse. "It's September and most of the work is done for now, so why don't you take Clay and Jerry in the army with you? It'll be over by spring anyways, and after the Bluebellys are beat to hell you all can come back and pick up where you left off."

Twenty-year-old Clay and seventeen-year-old Monroe were delighted to be delivered an excuse from the wretched farm labor they detested, and they yahooed and thanked the old man for the chance to knock off a few Yankees. "Kill them bastards good, boys!" Jeremiah shouted to his three sons as they strode off to enlist. "Kill them! KILL THEM ALL, GODDAMN IT!"

While twenty-two-year-old Jesse stayed throughout the hostilities as a wagoneer, army life didn't much agree with Clay and Monroe. A year later Monroe took sick and was hospitalized. Soon as he felt strong enough for a long walk he abandoned his bed and AWOLed all the way home, remaining hid on the farm whenever soldiers passed by, Confederate or Union. Clay too saw the army as a bunch of crap, feeling that a man afoot was no man at all. Fed up, he feigned mental illness with a few epileptic fits thrown in, and his desperation for removal made him a good enough actor to earn a medical discharge after three months service. But the old man was in no mood to appreciate Clay's rejection of army life and took the news unkindly. Finally after eight months and a session of hot words with his daddy, Clay rode off in anger to rejoin the Confederate military just days before an exhausted Monroe turned up to further add to their papa's hellish mood of mind.

But this time Clay chose the cavalry, because he was damned if he was going to walk and fight. Here he discovered his deep penchant for battle and bloodshed. His unit fought with General Nathan Bedford Forrest's cavalry, who was also the top cavalry leader in the Confederacy, if not the entire North and the South. Aggressive with a killer's instinct, "Get there first with the most men" was his motto. A lithe and powerful six-feet-two hellion on a horse, he ran circles around the Union, whipping them throughout the war left and right, much of the time outnumbered. He had a terrible temper to go with his natural talent for strategy, and once killed one of his own officers in an altercation, later admitting he had to do something about his short temper.

Of course Forrest was Allison's hero and role model, as was proper, for who wants a wimp in the front lines? In Forrest's words, "War means fightin' and fightin' means killin'." It was whip, stomp and kill the enemy, and to the last man, if possible. Yankee and Rebel both followed those jungle rules. The law was survival at any cost, and Clay found a natural talent for it. He often recalled those renegaded years as the finest years of his life, shooting, knifing and slaying his Union opponents by the droves, and as a memento of those times he sported a Vandyke, ala Forrest. He lived for the numerous cavalry raids and fights, relished it when he could thrust and twist his Bowie deep into the gut of an enemy, horseback or afoot, especially when staring into his eyes inches away, spitting into his face, cursing him as he slid to his death. Now and then, aground, he and a few of his comrades would come across a few straggling Yankees, surprising them, and beat them to death with rifle butts. Few line soldiers on either side knew what a prisoner was. "What's them Bluebelly's got their hands in the air for?" one asked after a fight as four Union made their way toward them in surrender. "Beats me," laughed Allison. "Maybe they're asking God for a quick death." "Wale, shit, suits me fine," chortled a crony as he opened fire. In moments all four lay dead.

Rocking in his wagon beneath the blinding sun, Allison took another long pull from his quart, feeling thankful for the numbness that covered his ruined leg. Oh, God, he sighed. His two and a half years with Forrest were the best. Pure heaven. Nothing to do but ride, raid, fight and kill. Absolutely nothing like it. Such unbridled freedom he would never know again. Yanking the reins he pulled the team to a halt so as to take a leak. Dismounting on the left side of the wagon in order to favor his good leg, he nearly tumbled off the vehicle. Once on the ground he steadied himself by gripping the sideboard with his tight hand and unbuttoning his fly with his left. Swaying like a reed in the wind he realized he was in bad shape. He had gone on a two-day binge in Pecos while his wagon was being loaded from a list he made up, then half-snockered rode off just after sunrise while it was still cool. He wished now he had slept it off in a hotel before leaving. He of course couldn't return home drunk as he was, Dora becoming disgusted with his drinking, treating him more and more with silent contempt. But he needed the booze for killing his leg pains, and he never showed his ugly self when at home or around her. Yet he knew he probably didn't set a good example for their daughter, and the smell of liquor on him came to infuriate Dora no end, although they never had a word of anger between them. Yet the silence was just as bad, and in the last few years it festered as a deadly virus which ate away what good feelings they had left for each other.

Clinging unsteadily to the side of the wagon he emptied his bladder in the road, puffs of dust rising as the thick yellow stream struck the powdered earth. As he swayed and lost his balance a moment, urine splashed on his boots and trousers. "Goddamn it!" he snarled. "Can't even piss straight."

In June eighteen hundred and sixty-one, two months after the start of the Rebellion, Tennessee was the last of eleven states to withdraw from the union. Although earlier it had rejected secession by nearly four to one, on a final ballot it voted overwhelmingly to secede. Regardless, the state remained divided, with east Tennessee still sympathetic with the North, denying both, slavery and secession. Wayne County, in south central Tennessee where the Allisons resided, was overwhelmingly anti-secession by a bit over two to one. Yet, of twenty-two military companies organized, eleven were Union and eleven Confederate. There was very little slavery or slave owners in the county, it being poor and mainly a farming population with families working their own farms. But there were fanatic adherents for and against both, slavery and secession, and it would broil again locally for a time after the war.

Following the official bloodletting, Allison returned to Clifton but it was not to continue on as a farmer. He was a changed man, certainly not the same twenty-year-old who left to escape farm work for what he thought would be a brief lark in the military. He had seen and experienced his share of constant and seemingly endless brutality and slaughter, and was one of many veterans on both sides who returned home at loose ends, aiming to make some sense of their lives. His father let him be, and Jesse mostly ignored him, all continuing about the farm as if the Rebellion had been but a small botheration. Restless and impatient, curt and dissatisfied, Allison was a man wondering what to do with himself, and the area was going through changes he couldn't tolerate. Reconstruction was working its way throughout the South, and a branch of the Yankee's Freeman's Bureau put in its appearance. Regional bickering and factional fighting between Union and Confederate diehards erupted, with occasional confrontations and bloodbaths in the county. The KKK soon made its presence known and added to the flaming atmosphere.

Being born in, bred and conditioned by a white supremacist slavocratic society, Clay didn't much concern himself over the black man's dilemma. Hell, he argued, niggers weren't even counted as full human beings in the first place, but listed with farm equipment and stock, such as cattle, cows, horses, hogs and sheep. Send them back to Africa, for all he cared.

Their family was too poor to own any slaves anyway, and farmed their own land. Who in hell do the damn Yankees think they are anyhow, trying to tell us how to run our country?

Before a month was up Allison made his decision. He packed together a handful of possessions, mounted his horse and galloped westward. It seemed scads of post-war humanity was headed across the Mississippi, especially for Texas. And it was to Texas he headed. He heard the cattle trade was becoming a big thing down there, so thought he'd look into it.

In west Texas he fell in love with the vastness of the country. It was his third impressed memory and it was like the opening of a new world. The state's expansiveness filled him with an electrifying sense of freedom, the exciting feeling of endless, unhampered elbow room his persona sought, needed and fed upon. Having no problem finding work as a herder, he set out to learn everything he could about the cattle trade. Bursting with confidence he took to the work avidly, for he enjoyed it immensely, finding an innate talent. He saw his future as the owner of a large ranch and a great herd of cows, of every year shipping off thousands to market, and yoked himself to the dream. It was the heyday of the cattleman and he would be one of them. It was there for him; he could see it, feel it, taste it. This is what he would work toward and was his driving ambition, day and night, awake and sleeping. To be a renowned and respected cattle baron. Down the road he would find a chunk of open range and make his mark. Yessiree. That's where it was and that's where he wanted to be. One of the conquerors of this new land.

Soon he was so capable he was made trail boss by his employer Marcus Lafayette Dalton and ram-rodded one of the first herds over the Goodnight-Loving Trail to New Mexico in June eighteen hundred and sixty-six. He brought a few more herds over for others, including the stock of Lou Coleman and Irwin Lacy. On several of his drives he ended up in the lush, creek-laden Vermejo area of northern New Mexico and decided this is where he would make his start. The place was already filling in with ranchers, farmers, miners, settlers and squatters, and cattle, horses, sheep and goats were everywhere. News of a gold strike in eighteen hundred and sixty-seven was the principal draw for the bipedal incursion, and every ilk of humanity followed. Before long the region reflected the appearances of many other primitive frontier societies with the usual diverse collection of humans out to make a buck off the strike. Bankers, speculators, merchants, butchers and carpenters jostled with politicians, lawyers, gamblers, gunmen, thieves and whores in an attempt to squeeze what they could from the land and from each other. All juggled for survival in their individual scrambles toward the top of the economic anthill. Early, there was no law to speak of, except the somewhat rough hempen yardstick used by a handful of pseudo-moralists. Before long the struggling settlement celebrated the birth of its first child, a girl named Elizabeth, and the citizens, seeking a patina of civilized atmosphere, christened the community Elizabethtown, which became the county seat of newly formed Colfax County.

Allison stared down the long dirt lane ahead of him, buttoning up his carelessness and wiping off his hand. He lit up a cheroot and stood gazing at nothing in particular, feeling heavy and tired. Waves of heat curled from the earth all around him, giving the countryside a warped, wavy look. Colfax County, he muttered, shaking his head in disdain at the memory, undecided as to whether he should cry a river or scream a stream of curses. I wish I never saw the goddamn place.

On Allison's last drive of the Lacy-Coleman cattle he was paid with the loan of two hundred of their cows, the calves of which he jump-started his own herd. With unspoken foresight, the brand he adopted was the squared-circle. But casting about for open free-range in the area was impossible, and for several years he grazed his growing hooves on the pastures of his ex-bosses.

Frank Wilburn was more bullheaded than independent, and this trait caused him some trouble which vexed cattleman Charlie Goodnight, and later brought upon his head Clay Allison's wrath. On the trail he was in the habit of riding alone and ahead of the men, and Goodnight had firmly cautioned him often to stay within the group. "If you get into any Indian trouble, Frank, you'll be on your own, for I won't spare any of the men to rescue you from your foolishness."

"Hell," he replied, ignoring intelligent information. "I can take care of myself."

On a return trip to Texas along the Pecos River near Horsehead Crossing, sure enough, they were jumped by a half-dozen warriors. Wilburn, alone and ahead of the riders as usual, panicked and lost his head, frantically whipping his horse which began frenziedly racing in a wide circle. But he did pose a humorous sight to Goodnight, and he couldn't help but smile broadly at the bouncing manikin on the confused mount. Wilburn's beast eventually completed its wide circular route and headed toward Goodnight, finally slammed into him and nearly knocked his horse off its feet.

"They, they," stammered the wide-eyed Wilburn, "were shooting at me!"

Observing the panting horseman's burned forehead and split crown of his hat from a bullet, the cattleman replied dryly, "I believe they have." Wilburn glued himself to the group thereafter.

Allison had briefly met Wilburn once, and was put off by his air of pompous self-importance. Later, hearing of his behavior on the trail he was further disgusted, for he knew the inane antics of one could put all the men of a traveling party in peril. Allison despised bullies, detested abusers of authority, and loathed those who refused to follow sensible instruction. He was a stickler for discipline on a drive, that much he brought back with him from the army.

Still doing work for Lacy and Coleman after their final drive from Texas, they assigned him to collect several debts. The men who owed the herders were Tom Stockton and Frank Wilburn, both of whom were on the initial drive on the Goodnight Trail. Wilburn drove a small herd of his own, and later joined with Stockton in a few cattle ventures. More of a cattle dealer and investment promoter than a drover, Wilburn was at times dangerously short on cash.

With the two Allison bided his time, for Stockton was busy building his two-storied hotel-restaurant-bar called the Clifton House, while Wilburn continually pleaded for more time. One night, Allison, his patience over-stretched and his repugnance for Wilburn expanding, especially after hearing comments of his unreliability, deliberately sought him out. After visiting four waterholes in his odyssey, he came across him in McCulloch's hotel-saloon. Already well-oiled, Allison was in a fine mood to play debt collector, and approached his quarry from across the crowded room to the bar. Ordering a glass of bourbon, he turned to the man and asked, "Frank Wilburn?"

"Why, yes. May I help you?"

"You sure as hell can. You owe a sum of money to cattlemen Lacy and Coleman, do you not?"

"Yes, I do. And may I inquire of what business is it of yours?"

"Just this." Without another word Allison drew his Colt and pushed the end of the barrel against Wilburn's nose. "I'm Clay Allison and I work for them as a bill collector. You will pay what you owe them to me immediately or I'll blow your useless ass away right now." Thumbing back the hammer he added, "Which is it?"

The man froze, realizing that his lifespan may now be measured in seconds. Amazingly, even to himself, he coolly stared across the barrel into Allison's ice-blue eyes and replied, "If you kill me, the debt owed them will go to the grave with me. Tom Stockton and I are in the middle of a lucrative cattle deal, which you can certainly check out with him, and before the week is up I'll be able to pay your employers in full."

After some long, quiet seconds, Allison rasped, "If you're lying, you're a dead man. Understand? Far as I'm concerned you're a mouthy, fat-headed four-flusher, and it would pleasure me greatly to pull this trigger."

"Ah, Mister Allison, I understand and agree with your incisive assessment of me to the full. I have attempted for years to correct my personality flaws, but alack and alas, I am afraid I have come away empty-handed, and must remain a part of this imperfect vessel for the rest of my life, although it appears I may not have long to wait."

Allison was dumb-founded to face another who was so indifferent and blasé toward impending doom as he, especially with the barrel of a cocked six-shooter rammed up his nose. He couldn't help but feel a certain amount of admiration toward him, wondering too whether he were drunk or just plain crazy. "Wale, shit," grinned Allison as he uncocked the hammer and holstered his weapon. "You are one nervy bastard, whatever else you are, I will certainly grant you that. Let me buy you a drink. Bartender, two more here!"

"Thank you, Mister Allison. Mighty hospitable of you."

"I will check with Stockton in the morning, and if your story is as worthless as cow shit, you had better be a long ways from here."

"I sincerely thank you for your sterling trust. You will find Tom most agreeable to my tale of temporary economic woe, and your employers anon will be completely compensated."

"You certainly are a smooth one, Frank. Are you sure you haven't cornered the market in snake-oil in this county?"

"By God, Mister Allison," laughed Wilburn. "That's a good one! But an excellent idea. I'll have to look into that."

Shaking his head Allison could only laugh with him, liking the man's gall, and was glad not to have shot him after checking him out the next day with Stockton.

Before too long Allison began leaving his mark in the county, feats of deviltry and fits of violence over the next ten years which would add to the myth and legacy of the man. Standing shoulder-deep before a bar one wintry night in Elizabethtown with a handful of cronies, the liquored conversation turned to Charles Kennedy, who had been tried that day for a shooting.

"So Charley done got a hung-jury decision," commented Gus Heffron sourly. "Reckon that means he'll get off scot-free."

Kennedy was a thirty-one-year-old carpenter from Tennessee. For extra income he also rented out a few rooms at his house in town where he lived with his Mexican wife of seventeen, Gregoria, and year-old son, Sam. But he was an unsavory character who rubbed too many people the wrong way, and made not a few enemies, which was something akin to euthanasia in frontier society. He had been tried for a shooting that afternoon.

"Yep," agreed Allison. "That lawyer Mills is slick as snot."

"Where's Kennedy now?" inquired Davey Crockett, who claimed a kinship to the famed one, evidence seeming to be his lantern-jawed physical replication.

"They got him chained up in the butcher shop, dummy," replied Allison cuttingly. Mollified and hurt, Davey whined, "Ain't no call to insult me, Clay. I was only askin."

"Goddamn, I done told you all night, at least a dozen times. Or can't you remember?"

"Oh, yeah, uh, I recollect now."

"You recollect now," snorted Allison. "Wondrous. I think you're a dummy like the original Davey. He had to be one to let himself be trapped by a bunch of barefoot greasers."

"Aw, Clay, that ain't no way to talk of my hero kin."

"Shit. I don't believe you're any kin to him. Only a coattail-grabber is what you are."

Davey slumped in dejected silence, downed his glass and asked for another.

Allison eyed him a moment then guffawed as he slapped him on the back. "C'mere, you little fart," he grinned, wrapping an arm around Davey's shoulders and shaking him in camaraderie. "I don't care a damn who you are. You can carry all the tales you want, but you're still a friend of mine. Barkeep, give us all another round, here!"

The dingy, dimly lit hovel roared on into the night with an admixture of laughter and curses in between an occasional disagreement or fight. The fights were brief things, mostly drunken swinging that would terminate when two or three howlers would leap onto and pummel some solitary flaying fool. The patrons in the main were herders freshly off the range, or miners having quit their shift, all tired, gritty and stinking after a long day's labor, and the stench in close quarters could be chopped with an axe. But daily showers and baths was a rare phenomena on the frontier, and where sometimes even the water wasn't fit to drink. The brothers Port and Ike Stockton, part-time gunmen and full-time cow thieves, were among the Allison crew. They too had come to New Mexico with the Lacy-Coleman herds, were long-time Lacy employees, plus Lacy kin.

"You know," spoke Port. "Gus is right. Kennedy is gonna get clean off."

"Hell," grumbled Gus. "I think he should swing. Besides being guilty of that shooting, he's a liar, a con and a thief. Owes me money over six months, and just laughs when I ask for it."

"Hell, yes," chortled Davey. "Let's rope 'em!"

"Let's do it then," echoed Allison. "Enough of this damned jawing."

The handful of men filed into the gelid night and trudged through the deep snow until a few dozen houses later they came to the butcher shop. Breaking the lock they shuffled into the unlighted interior. Kennedy snuffled half-awake in confusion. "What?" he mumbled. "Who?" He felt himself grasped roughly in the dark by what seemed a disconnected collection of hands. Yanked to his feet, he felt a rope suddenly squeeze around his neck as he was hoisted to a beam. When he stopped his kicking, choking and gasping, the men turned silently and waded through the snowdrifts back to the saloon. Further into the windy icy night they continued their carousing, celebrating a job well done. "To justice," saluted Allison, glass held high. "Aye!" echoed the others. "To justice, goddamn it!"

It was the previous winter that Allison broke his leg. Stepping down from his horse he lighted on a patch of ice and slipped, twisting his limb beneath him. It was a stupid but not uncommon accident and he laughed about it later, after the pain and setting. Doc Longwill tended him at his office in Cimarron where he was driven in a wagon by Lew Coleman. Allison was using Lew's pastures at the time, still seeking a place of his own. His reputation as an industrious and knowledgeable cowman who worked hard and played harder took hold in the vicinity, also that he was a man of strong opinions and not shy in expressing them. But because of his playtime he was increasingly avoided by many of the more sedate ranchers and settlers, hearing the stories of his erratic behavior while drinking. Booze was never kind to Allison's brain, nor any human's for that matter. But unfortunately for him the commercial chemical produced a more disastrous result. So, regardless of his cordial and courteous behavior in daily society, the more conservative folk gave him wide berth. Even with his drinking companions, the rougher crowd he gravitated toward, and of which he soon became undisputed leader, he could be rude and rash with, such as his ragging of Crockett. His targets of course were mainly when he was in his cups, and although principally verbal, the dark undercurrent of his feral behavior would sometimes surface in murderous acts. Many sensed two personalities in him. Over the years several lawmen came under his verbal thrashings, good friends who gave him unusual slack. But often when the unwelcome twin began emerging, the majority of his companions would suddenly find a reason for a change of environment. Yet he was a considerate man, and a kind one too, such as when an incident which occurred a few weeks following his leg-breaking accident.

He was pulling up in his horse-drawn wagon before Lambert's hotel and saloon one afternoon when he noticed a woman and two children in obvious anxiety. Climbing out of the vehicle and adjusting his crutches under his arms, he swung to her side, doffed his hat, and asked, "Good afternoon, maam, Do you need some kind of assistance?"

She had just been dropped off after a ride from Raton and was from Texas. Her husband had died a week before in Raton enroute to some friends in the region, but being new to the area and not knowing anyone, she was at a complete loss at what to do.

"Well, what are their names? Maybe I know of them, having lived here a couple years."

"The Mills family."

"Mills? Uh, by any chance any relation to Melvin Mills, the lawyer?"

"No, afraid not. They are farmers, mostly."

Relieved at that, he asked, "What line of work was your husband in?"

"We had a small farm in Crockett, Texas we sold. He was in the Thirteenth Calvary in the war, and we decided to get away from all that Reconstruction trouble. He took ill on the way and never recovered."

Hearing that the man served in a Rebel cavalry unit was all the clincher Allison needed to give her all the help he could render.

"Maam" he addressed concernedly, clutching his hat before him. "My name is Allison, Clay Allison, and I too served in the Southern cavalry, in Tennessee. Reconstruction stuck in my craw too, and is one of the main reasons of my own shifting west. Let me suggest something, and see how it fits with you. I don't know the Mills people you speak of, but if they're hereabouts we'll find them sure enough. Meanwhile you and the children are welcome to stay with me until we locate them. Free food and room long as you need to. It's a small place with a shed I can put up in while you're here. Only thing I will require is you do the cooking. I haven't had many good home-cooked meals the last few years, and certainly would be gratefully indebted to you if you would accept my offer."

"Why, Mister Allison, I do thank you, and hope we will not inconvenience you in any way?"

"Good heavens, no, maam. You would flatter me most highly by accepting."

"Then I accept, Mister Allison, and do so thankfully. My name is Martha Matthews. This is my son, Joseph, and my daughter, Addie."

Shaking hands all around, Allison then hoisted the two bags of Mrs. Matthews' worldly possessions into the wagon bed, and all proceeded to his abode in the Coleman pasture.

It was ten days of fine eating that Allison experienced, and when her old acquaintances were eventually located it was a rueful day for him. He thoroughly enjoyed his time with the children, practically taking them over like a mother hen. It gave him a needed break from his own problems, especially of wondering if he would ever find free-range. Of late he had been thinking of moving, possibly in a southerly direction. He toured with the kids all through the countryside, sometimes taking them on his rounds, making sure they each had a pony to ride. He loved their innocent excitement at every little thing, no matter how silly, and was as protective of them as if they were his very own. They gave him a fatherly feeling and he realized that something important was missing in his life. He also didn't drink a drop over those ten days, and absolutely didn't miss his boisterous companions a bit.

One afternoon after dinner while the children were taking turns riding a tired but patient mule back and forth in a field, Clay asked Martha, "Where were you originally from?"

"Illinois. I was an only child and my mother died shortly after my birth. My father was a professor from New York and stayed in Illinois after they married. He taught school and enjoyed it so much he never returned east. Besides me going to school, he taught me at home, and I had such a love of books I didn't mind the extra lessons at all."

"I can believe that," he smiled. "Just to hear you talk is an education for me. This town could use a good teacher."

"Well, I do have a teaching certificate and eventually want to start again somewhere."

"Hope you decide to start here. Is your father still teaching?"

"No. He died while I was finishing college. Shortly after I graduated I went down to Dallas, Texas to visit some cousins. That's where I met John, my husband. We couldn't stand being apart a second, so ran off and got married before the week was out. The heat of youth, you know," she laughed lightly. "He was such a grand man."

"I must say, with your permission, Martha, he couldn't have chosen a finer wife."

"A month later we moved to his hometown of Crockett, and while there we had Joseph and Allie. I taught when I could, but mostly I taught John, who hadn't a day of schooling and was embarrassed over it. But he had a natural intelligence; had no trouble grasping things and parsing them out, and was lightening fast in his head. It was such fun watching him grow with ideas practically every day. We were doing so well, had a small farm, a few dollars put away, all of us happy as a covey of quail, and then the war started. I didn't want him to go, but there was no way he was staying home while all his male friends ran off to fight. He was an advocate of secession because of state's rights, although he didn't approve of slavery."

"I didn't care about slavery either way. All I wanted to do was get away from farm work."

Voice slightly tremulous, she continued. "He was gone for the better part of three years, but in not much fighting, thank God. Mostly patrols in Texas and Louisiana. Was in the hospital two, three times, ulcers they said, which finally took him. When he came home he was mostly silent for nearly three years, so changed, just purely locked up inside. Absolutely ruined."

Allison sat silent, letting her talk, knowing there were things she had to let out.

"Finally one night he said what it was. They were taking some Union prisoners back to camp when one sixteen-year-old Yankee walking along side my husband's horse looked up at him and called him a nigger slave owner. John, shocked and puzzled both, stopped and just looked down upon him. Now, my John was the most kindest and gentlest of people. In fact, many a time I have seen him catch a fly in the house in his hand then take it to the door and throw it out. We'd both laugh over it, but he enjoyed doing things like that. If he ever caught a rattler, he'd sack it, then ride off with it miles away where he'd let it go into some rocky region hardly anyone ever bothered to go to. So John looked down at that young man and asked, "What?" thinking he may have misheard or misunderstood him. 'I said you are a slave owner,' he hollered. 'ALL you damn rebels own niggers and should be hanged!'

'Young man,' addressed John. 'You are sinfully in error of your accusation. I know a lot of Southerners own slaves, but also many of us don't. I for one don't because I don't approve of slavery. And besides, I couldn't afford the outrageous luxury of the purchase of one anyway.'

'You are a yellow-bellied liar of a slaver, you are!" he shouted, not heeding my husband's words. 'A coward! A dirty lying coward!'

"John was shocked at the stranger's unjustified rage at him. 'Why in the world did he accuse me of all that?' he asked me, 'calling me names and all. And especially calling me a liar after I explained myself in such detail to him. I was flabbergasted and embarrassed too, with all the men around me laughing at the entire scene.' After the seeming tenth time that the frothy young man called John a lying yellow Rebel slaver, he said he just suddenly got numb. He looked down at him and said, 'Young man, you are an ignoramus of the lowest order, or you would be humiliated at the mere idea of giving expression to your accusations. You are an unforgivable cretin, sir,' and he drew his pistol and shot him to death."

"I have seen many a man shot for a lot less," Clay commented gently.

"But John never got over it. Killing that man killed something in him, and he couldn't come to terms with what he did. All he could do for years is chide himself for murdering a man who merely called him a liar. 'Why did I do such a vile thing?' he would ask. 'Kill him over such a trivial reason? He had no right to do so, true, for he did not even know me. But good lord, all I had to do was ride away, ignore him, leave and never see him again. Yet no, I drew and put a bullet through his head. He was unarmed and no threat. Only an ignorant child. We weren't even in combat. Why'd I do that over a stupid, inane insult?' Her eyes shined with a light film of tears.

"It was probably a natural instinct he couldn't control, Martha," sympathized Allison. "And the man had no right to curse your husband so severely in the first place, not knowing him."

"But it killed him, Clay. He was a walking dead man after that. It ate him alive, carrying the guilt of killing him in cold blood. Like the mark of Cain. He was always such an outgoing, happy-go-lucky person. Forever doing something for somebody. So full of life."

Allison reached over and lay his hand over her two clasped ones on the table. "War is a heartless equalizer. I agree on that."

"Have you ever killed anyone, Clay?"

The question and the entire mood of the conversation thrust him suddenly back into the old memories of war and personal combat. He could clearly hear the pistol and rifle shots clattering through the ranks, the screaming howls of both sides, the roaring Rebel cannon and the echoing booms of the Union's, hear the thunderous beating of thousands of hooves rumbling over the broad rolling countryside, all blending together in war's cacophony as bodies and horses fell everywhere by the dozens.

"I said, have you ever killed anyone, Clay?"

"What?" he asked, brought back to the present. "What?"

"Have you ever killed anyone in the war?"

"Yes," he rasped. "And it was truly awful," he lied. "Just plain awful."

Two days before they moved on he took the children to Raton for a photo shoot. It was something more than a mere souvenir picture for him, and he kept a copy of the photographic memory forever. Flanked by the brother and sister, he sat with his wrapped leg crossed, crutches over his lap, staring at the camera in soft sternness. The girl stood solemnly, the boy more with a contented proud air, his new hat in one hand at his side. His other hand gently rested on Allison's shoulder, a silent connection of male comradeship. The boy had found a father for ten days.

One afternoon in a local saloon while on a liquid tear Allison got into a disagreement with "One-armed" Bill Wilson, Charles Goodnight's long-time trusty herder and range manager. Goodnight and Wilson were in the area briefly to pick up some cows from a delinquent Elizabethtown butcher. Bill was one of four iron-mean brothers Allison had become acquainted with earlier when trailing herds from Texas, and all being natural hell-raisers, found sympathetic souls in each others company.

"Goddamn it Bill, you're wrong!"

"Naw, I'm not, Clay," replied Wilson in a good natured manner. "The liquor's just got you by the head, or you wouldn't say that."

"What? You saying I can't hold my liquor?"

"No, no, pard, only that you're mistaken in what you said."

"I oughta cut your ear off to make you hear better, that's what," retorted Allison as he drew a long knife from his belt scabbard.

"Whoa, now, hoss," spoke Wilson as he stepped from the bar, his one hand palm up before him. "Hey, ain't that Charlie Goodnight coming through the door?" he added, motioning with his chin over Clay's shoulder.

"Where?" asked Allison as he turned and scanned through the cluster of men behind him.

Wilson then made a swift and diplomatic exit, not caring to continue their "discussion," seeing where it was headed. Clay was a damn good man with a horse, cow and gun, understood Wilson, but sometimes his social graces with people were a bit testy. Especially when lathered up.

When Allison turned and saw Wilson gone he felt insulted. Angry, he looked about the room and saw County Clerk John Lee standing against a wall conversing with Lawyer Melvin Mills. Walking toward him he called, "Hey, John!" As Lee turned his long duster billowed out a shade, and from a few yards away Allison flung his heavy knife to pin the edge of the coat to the wall with a loud "thunk!"

"Oh, my God!" howled Lee as he tore away and fled out the door.

Undismayed, Allison picked up his blade from the floor and looked for another target. As he grabbed Mills to push him against the wall for a repeat performance, the lawyer broke from his grip and left as fast as Lee before him. Everybody laughed and roared at Allison's antics, remarking that it was a bad day for clerks and lawyers. Returning to the bar Allison downed his drink, had another, then left. Climbing aboard his mount a touch unsteadily, he walked his horse slowly down Cimarron's one main street. Suddenly before him appeared Doctor Longwill. He had just spoken to Mills in his office who related his barroom experience, when Mills fled in panic out the back door as he looked through the window and saw Allison riding in their direction.

"Mister Allison," scolded the doctor somewhat facetiously. "You've been behaving badly."

"Hell, I don't mean any harm to Lee or Mills. But I'm looking to find Wilson so's to collect his ear, by God!" And with that he rode off on his vain hunt.

One balmy evening in April, Allison, with cohorts Crockett and Heffron, rode to a corral in an outlaying pasture on Crow Creek and stole a dozen Government mules. They immediately jockeyed them eastward to the Texas Panhandle where they found eager buyers.

It was such an easy and profitable venture they decided on a return engagement months later in the fall. But it all went awry. When Allison stepped to open the gate with gun in hand it swung out of his grip and slammed his fist, discharging his cocked revolver. The bullet drove through his booted foot and exited his sole. "Arrrrgh!" growled Allison, dropping to the ground, twisting and writhing in agony. The men ripped off his boot and fashioned a tourniquet with a belt, then wrapped his wound best they could with torn pieces of blanket.

"Listen, you two," gasped Allison. "Run them damn mules to Texas while I ride off to Doc Longwill and get this foot tended to! Now git!" Clay then raced off for Longwill's in Cimarron.

Allison could not have picked a worse time or place to plan his dream of a free-range cattle empire. Colfax County of late had been swallowed up by the Maxwell Land Grant. Or rather, since the grant was there before the county, in the formation of it the county gulped up the grant.

Either way, it was a real estate meal that gave everyone in the county connected with it, land thief and settler alike, an unhealthy dose of indigestion. It was the squatters and homesteaders who settled on the grant before the county was formed who stood to lose the most.

In eighteen hundred and forty-one the Mexican governor in Santa Fe granted land to Charles Beaubien and Carlos Miranda. A few years later a hunter-trapper-scout, Lucien Bonaparte Maxwell, married the young daughter of Beaubien, fourteen-year-old Luz, and soon after moved onto the grant. For some years Maxwell enjoyed his self-adapted role as a benevolent (sometimes not) despot and land baron, leasing and selling acreage here and there, with the Mexican and Anglo farmers, homesteaders and ranchers paying their rent in crops or livestock. It was an idyllic setup and satisfactory to all, and the bucolic atmosphere somewhat reflected an early European fiefdom which satisfied the Napoleonic streak in Maxwell's ego. But just after the Civil War, gold was discovered on the land and Maxwell's Eden practically overnight became a miserable hell. A bursting population gradually took away his control and threatened the domination of his holdings. After taking his share of gold out of the ground the fallen fief sold his grant in eighteen hundred and seventy to a group of speculators, then made a grand exodus with his wife, children, servants and livestock to Fort Summer, one hundred fifty miles south.

The new owners put the squeeze on all who settled within the grant boundaries, whose borders were to be disputed for many years, charging rent on the miners, squatters and settlers, and served eviction notices if they did not pay heed to the new demands. It was the end of any thought of free-range in Colfax County or the grant. Big cattle ranchers were encouraged and welcomed to buy or lease, while many of the smaller herders and squatters were told to move on, and sometimes given a token remuneration for their improvements. In anger anti-grant organizations formed, miners struck, and many squatters refused to unsquat. Midnight raids against the recalcitrant began, shootings started, and the Colfax County War commenced. The bitter battle would go on for thirty years, and be fought in and out of the courts with bullets and law books.

The power behind the grant was the Santa Fe Ring, a collection of politicians, lawyers and financiers working out of Santa Fe, led by politicos Steve Elkins and Tom Catron, who voraciously saw the vast piece of real estate as a wondrous opportunity in speculative investment. There was no true map of the grant, and its boundaries were as flexible as Maxwell's imaginative calculations, and the man wielded a supple protractor and compass. By Mexican, and Spanish, law, the two original owners had a right to roughly ninety-seven thousand acres. Yet Maxwell liberally extended it far as he saw fit, north even onto the bottom edge of Colorado. The new company hired its own surveyors and drew up a plat of nearly two million acres, ironly solidifying the ex-fief's nebulous claims.

To add to the profit-seeking mix, Colfax County had its own handful of speculators, and since the grant was in Colfax County they felt it belonged to them to do with as they saw fit. So the Santa Fe Ring was at odds with the Colfax Ring, each maneuvering and jockeying for control. Although a smaller group, the Colfaxers had two advantages: the grant's location was in their county, and the coteries were separated from each by a mountain range, the Sangre de Cristos.

With the growing hostility against the Maxwell Grant, and especially the Santa Fe Ring, there was also a growing boldness in some of the homesteaders which the Ring could no longer tolerate. So a few of the corporate heads got together and decided they needed a field operator to carry the word to the more stubborn. A thug-enforcer. They found one in Charles Morris, and his usual methods were nighttime visits with several cronies. After riding across properties, knocking down a few fences, shooting chickens, dogs and occasional livestock, and blasting through doors and windows with rifles or six-guns, a number got the message. Sometimes a few needed a personal interview which carried with it a pistol-whipping or two. In many instances it worked miracles, and the Ring was pleased when a settler or squatter packed up and moved on.

But then one sunny afternoon in July eighteen hundred and seventy-two in a local bar Morris got into a verbal fracas with another thug, John "Chunk" Colbert, and he shot the unarmed Morris to death. Hardly eighteen months later, on an icy wintry night in December eighteen hundred and seventy-three, Chunk cold-bloodedly slew another man which would eventually lead to his own demise by a bullet from Allison.

At a dance in snowy Trinidad, Colorado, across the state line from Raton, Colbert put an end to a dispute he was having with another drunk, George Waller. While Colbert's crony held the argumentative Waller against a wall, Chunk drew and put five bullets into him. He then headed south for New Mexico. He stopped at Dick Wootton' s stage station at the border for breakfast. A younger gunman happened to be present also breakfasting, the short-tempered Port Stockton, a twenty-year-old killer people normally gave a wide berth to. Sharing a few words with Colbert, who snarlingly bragged about his latest notch, Port then left and quickly departed for Trinidad to inform the law, who of course knew of the shooting but were at a loss as to where to find killer Chunk. Stockton would have done society a favor apprehending him on the spot, but realized he was out of his class, so chose withdrawal as the better part of justice. In Trinidad, after the law got the word, Port insisted on joining the eight-man posse because he was a friend of Waller's, and desired to be in on the kill.

Galloping down to the Clifton House, a hotel-bar-restaurant on the outskirts of Otero, New Mexico, twelve miles south of Raton, they tied up their weary mounts and entered, discovering their quarry was in the same building. Getting his room number, the men quickly presented themselves at the door and flung it open. Several men were sleeping, and as one sat up wondering at the sudden commotion, Port instantly shot him to death. But he happened to be a new waiter for the restaurant, John Cañada, a few days on the job the second sleeper informed them, who was the cook. Embarrassed at their blunder, and further discovering that Chunk was staying in another building about forty yards from the hotel, the posse sent the cook to verify his presence. The cook clumped through the deep snow and entered the room facing Colbert's Colt and quickly explained about the posse. As Chunk dressed, he instructed the cook to disrobe and take his place in the abandoned bed, told to stay, then exited the area. The manhunters returned to Trinidad empty-handed.

But Colbert brazenly remained in the region making a pest of himself and defying the law and anyone else who might be foolish enough to challenge his comings and goings. Three weeks later, on a balmy January afternoon at the Clifton House, he met a sometime acquaintance, Clay Allison. Chunk was in the company of a crony, Charles Cooper, who was sporting a bandaged hand. It was the result of a cut from a bottle shot out of his hand by Colbert who was demonstrating his marksmanship skills. Allison had a strong distaste for Colbert, regarding him as a low-life thug and back-shooter. He now saw his chance to take care of Port Stockton's uncollected debt, of his failure to kill Chunk for slaying his friend Waller. Allison gladly took up Stockton's IOU.

"Goddamn, Clay, you gimping galoot," laughed the inebriated Colbert. "Where the hell you been? Ain't seen you in a coon's age."

"Right here for hours, you toad," returned Allison. "I hear you been on the prod lately."

"You got that right," boasted Colbert. "Mostly just cleaning out my gun barrel."

"Didn't you snuff out Waller up in Trinidad a while ago?"

"Thass right, cowboy. What of it?"

"Wasn't he a friend of Port's?"

"Right again, and so what?"

"Just making conversation, stud. Nothing personal."

"That punk snot, Stockton. He's the one run to Trinidad and cried to the law about where I was. If he was such a bad 'un, why didn't he speak up at Wooton's while we was breakfasting? Where can I find that yellow snake? I want to settle his hash. Where the hell does he hang out?"

"Hell, he's all over the place, but I haven't seen him in over a month."

"I hear he's good friend of yours, so next time you see him tell him

I want to put his yellow ass belly-down over a horse. Got that?"

"Yessiree, stud. Message is good as delivered."

"Wonnerful. You a good delivery boy, gimpy."

Allison's blood ran through him like cold ice. "By the way, stud," he asked. "Didn't you waylay Charley Morris back-aways?"

"You bet. Another dummy I enjoyed plugging. I hear he was a friend of yours, too."

"Yes, he was. And I always told him never to argue with an armed man. Especially whenever HE was unarmed."

"Hell, I told him to go get a gun, but instead he made a grab for me. What could I do but defend myself against being man-handled?" He laughed until tears ran down his cheeks.

Allison laughed with him mirthlessly and ordered them another round.

The three drank and gabbed in feigned camaraderie for near an hour when Allison groaned and said, "Hell, all this gabbing is making me hungry. How about you fellows joining me for something to eat? We can get some tasty Mexican food next door at Mrs. Gonzales' place."

"Hey," agreed Colbert. "Good idea. But I'd like some oysters. Wouldn't you, Coop?"

"You bet," replied Cooper.

"Well," settled Allison. "Let's buy a can or two here, and while you two scarf up the oysters, I'll have some chili and tortillas."

Agreeably the three men shuffled off half-drunkenly to the small jacal next door.

The three were the only ones in the room and sat at a table facing each other, Allison on one side, Colbert and Cooper on the other. Allison knew this was the moment of truth, so to speak, for just before sitting he noticed Colbert's thong-strap was off the hammer of his Colt, with his hand hovering near it. After Allison gave the woman his order, he handed the cans of oysters to her with instructions to heat them up. As she left Allison smiled and stood and said, "Excuse me for a few minutes, gents, but I must answer nature's call and piss out some of this alcohol."

Colbert's blood-shot eyes caught Allison's and saw too late the beady focus of intent, and in a clumsy clawing draw his barrel hit the table edge, going off. Prepared, Allison was already on top of the situation and triggered off a round into Chunk's forehead, throwing him backwards to the floor, chair and all. Cooper sat stunned and wide-eyed, paler than pale.

"Let's go, Coop," ordered Allison as he grasped him by the wrist and pulled him out the door and onto his horse. A handful of citizens who had no desire to be a witness to slaughter scattered like quail. With Cooper's reins in his hand Allison galloped toward the open plain south. It was cold and dusk and Allison had no mercy for the only witness to the murder of Colbert. Before an abandoned adobe ruin he pulled Cooper off his horse, dragged him inside and put a bullet in him. There were old discarded mining tools about, rusted and broken picks and shovels, and he grabbed a handleless spade to scoop away the sandy soil a yard deep. Dragging the corpse into it, he covered him then scattered sand about. Just like the war, he muttered business-like. Just like the war. After brushing the topsoil with broken bush branches, he left, taking Cooper's mount with him. He would give it to the Stockton brothers to take to the Panhandle with their next handful of cows. Or they could change the brand for all he cared, long as it disappeared. Port might even like it as a souvenir.

"Greetings, Mister Allison," smiled Doctor Robert Longwill as he approached Clay's table in Lambert's saloon.

Allison looked up from his newspaper and returned the smile with his own grin. "Howdy, there, sawbones."

"Mind if I join you?"

"No, not at all. Have a sit."

"I have here a bottle of special medicinal rye I'd appreciate sharing with you."

"Well, by God, let us not hesitate. I bid you a medical welcome, dear physician."

Longwill poured them both a glass, set his bowler on the table, and sat. "To your health, sir," he toasted.

"And to yours, sir," echoed Allison.

"How's that foot coming along? Any trouble?"

"It goes where I go and I can't get rid of it, so I keep dragging it along after me. Actually I don't know what I'd do without its wondrous twisted shape now."

"Oh?" puzzled Longwill with raised eyebrows. "And why is that?"

"Well, to shamelessly confess, I get more pleasurable attention from little old ladies who almost go teary-eyed at the sight of this galoot limping pitifully. They practically help me into doorways and up steps. I adore the attention."

"Why you old rascal. I had never suspected such ego needs."

"Just don't tell the fellers, or you will hear from me directly."

"No, no," laughed Doc, palms elevated in supplication. "Your secret is safe with me."

"Good," he chuckled. "Nah, the foot is as good as it's going to get. Just a little sore in the winter time, or in rainy weather. Been giving it a good hot soak now and then like you said, and that appears to soothe it some. I can't thank you enough for saving it."

"You'd never guess who I got a letter from yesterday."

"Not being a good guesser, I'll have to ask."

"Your old boarder, Martha Matthews."

Allison's eyes visibly lit up. "You don't say?"

"Yep, and a rightly nice one, too."

"Hope all is well with her and the young ones."

"Just dandy. Her and that Mills fellow she married moved from Trinidad to the Indian Territory. She has another little boy now."

"She was good people, Doc."

"I'll never disagree with that. She wrote to thank me for tending her sick boy, Joseph. And she said to especially thank you for your concern in bringing him so quick to me."

"P'shaw, Longwill. She is making something out of nothing. I just wanted to make sure the hacking cough he had weren't anything serious."

"She thought awfully highly of you, Clay. And the kids too. Especially Joseph. That boy thought the sun rose and set on you. She says he still can't stop talking about you and the good times you showed him."

"Wonderful boy," softened Allison. "Smart as a whip."

"He says when he grows up he wants to come work for you on your ranch."

Allison laughed lightly, shaking his head slowly. "I'm afraid he'll have to wait some for that ranch. But tell him I'll certainly give him the news when I'm ready."

"That Martha was one rare specimen. I enjoyed the short time I talked to her when you brought them in. And the boy too, for that matter."

"I had thought she mainly went to some university, she has such a fine mind," spoke Allison. "But her father, a professor, addedly educated her himself."

"Do tell? She is a gem, that's for certain."

"How's Joseph doing?"

"Can't get enough of school, and brainy as his mother. But, ah, there's something else."

"What's that," worried Allison.

"That western hat you bought him in Raton? Never takes it off. Even takes it to bed with him every night. Tells everybody and anybody that it was a special gift from, 'Mister Allison, the New Mexico rancher!' "

"Good grief, Doc!" laughed Allison. "Some tykes just don't have any good sense at all!"

"Here's her letter, you're welcome to read it."

"Thanks, Doc."

As he read the two pages he warmed over at the memory of the three of them melding so close and naturally, like old kin separated for years, then rejoined. Her last lines touched his heart. "Please thank for me, and the children, Mister Allison for all his unselfish concern and kindness toward us in our time of difficulty. He is a wonderful human being, and I will forever be indebted to him. Most sincerely, Martha Mills."

"On that last page is a drawing," noted Longwill. "Take a gander."

Allison raised the third page before him and widely grinned. "Well, bust my britches. Look at that."

The sheet contained a pencil portrait of a man with a Vandyke, staring toward the viewer.

Above it was printed, "My Friend, Mister Allison." Below, it was signed, "Joseph Matthews Mills."

"That kid's got talent, Clay. The likeness isn't bad at all, don't you think?"

"It's a good sketch, really is. Would it be all right if I kept the drawing, Doc?"

"You bet. Why don't you copy the address and drop them a line? They'd be tickled to hear from you."

"No, no. I'd just like the picture."

"Well, if you ever change your mind, I got the address."

Allison reached inside his jacket and withdrew his leather wallet and opened the flap. "Here, Doc. Had this photo taken in Raton of the kids and me." He handed it across to Longwill.

"Well, now," he chuckled. "What a trio of bandits we have here. You should have got the mother in this, too."

"Wish I did now, but didn't think of it then."

"Joseph really took to you, didn't he?" commented Longwill as he returned it.

"And me to him. Ever I get married, my first boy will be a Joseph."

As they sat in silence Allison stared a long moment at the photo. "Good kids, Doc. Rare as hen's teeth, and then some." He neatly creased the drawing into several folds, inserted the photo within, slipped them into his wallet, then returned the wallet into his jacket. "I wish them all the best."

Longwill refilled their glasses while speaking somewhat somberly.

"Mister Allison, you done missed the boat on this one."

"What?" he puzzled. "How's that?"

"Listen. I know I'm sounding like an echo chamber, but Martha thought very highly of you. She was drawn to you in the strongest way. A word from you would have cinched it."

"Oh, c'mon, Doc. She was practically all set up for a marriage soon's she found those family friends."

"No, no, Clay, hear me a moment. Her friends didn't know of her husband dying until she found them and told them. Later one of the Mills boys took a shine to her right off the bat, so asked them to intercede for him in getting married. He wasn't a bad looking fellow, hard working and straight-arrow as they come, so she said yes. What else could she do? Widowed, broke, no kin, two kids to raise, no family to turn to for help. And I heard they seemed very agreeable with each other's company. I'm only saying if you had stepped up and said a word or two, well, I just know she would have looked kindly on you."

"Aw, Doc, I'm afraid you're stretching your case a little much. What would she want with a struggling herder with not even a pot to pee in? Hell, dollar-wise there was just no future for us."

"Well, maybe you're right. Yet there's a lot of people in this valley struggling from day to day, and happily helping each other do it. But when you and she and the kids walked into my office that day together, it was like I saw a family with strong concern for each other, and comfortable with it, too. Anyway, by God, I raise a glass to their happiness."

"By golly, I'll join you in that."

After a long pull at their glasses they lit up a fresh pair of cheroots and sat back with a sigh.

"So tell me, Clay. Have you any prospects for some range any time soon?"

"Not only no, but hell no," came his sour retort. "You know the grant is pretty well sewed up unless you're a big rancher with a passel of dinero up front. I just have a handful of cows I keep shifting about like a nomad. I'm about fed up with this place anyway. Thinking of pulling out and dropping south of here, maybe the Roswell area."

"Actually, Clay, I've been looking to talk to you about something. In fact, ahem, I come as a messenger of good tidings."

"Oh, boy, now I'm in for it. Beware of Greeks and doctors bearing gifts, I say."

"Well, this is not a Trojan horse, believe me."

They both laughed lightly and leaned back in their chairs, drawing quietly a moment on their smokes. Longwill leaned forward, pensively knocked the ash from his cigar, and refilled their glasses. "Seriously, Clay. I've been asked to make you an offer. No hard feelings if you turn it down, either."

"Sure. I'm listening."

"The Santa Fe Ring would like to hire you on as their enforcer."

Allison's eyes narrowed as he started to raise from his chair.

"Now Clay, c'mon, wait. Hear me out first, please."

Allison froze a moment, then leaned forward with both hands on the table, pinning the doctor with his boring gaze. "All right. But this better be good." Then he sat.

"Clay, I know you don't like my Ring connection, and I'm not apologizing for it. We all have our individual methods of survival in life's jungle, and this is mine. It may not be honorable to travel with dishonorable people, but at the moment this is the best I can do. Maybe next week I can turn over a new leaf, until then I'll accept the minor political leavings that's left on my plate."

"Yeah, I know all that, and it's no skin off my nose, but both those scabby rings that have this county tied up should all be roped by the ankles and dragged though the state behind a horse. It just galls me to see a likeable and intelligent fellow like you tied in with them, that's all. But, like you say, and I can't argue it much, it's survival."

Allison's and Longwill's friendship was looked upon by some as a strange one. Although from opposite ends of the social spectrum in background, education and professional strata—the doctor a medical graduate from Virginia, and Allison a thinly-educated son of a Tennessee dirt farmer—the two hit it off in their basic outlook on life. Longwill's intellectual cynicism jibed with Allison's personal cold-blooded experiences in the war and on the trail, and although neither embraced a doom-and-gloom outlook, they shared the philosophy of survival of the fittest. And of course their definition of the "fittest" meant that if you survived you were fit, no matter how much of a lunkhead you were, and the loser be damned. Both being from the South they shared a commonality, and their age difference of three years, Allison the younger, gave them a generational agreeability. By the long shot of chance in this frontier settlement of such a diverse range of humanity they were at first thrown together by circumstance— Longwill setting Allisons' broken leg, then doing what he could to save his bullet-shattered foot—then, by similar personality traits. They enjoyed each other's company immensely and the exchange of ideas on a range of subjects, especially the possible and potential future of the Maxwell Land Grant question.

"Anyway, there's a nice section about twenty-five miles east of town on the bank of the Canadian. In fact, it straddles it a bit. Good grass and a shed or small barn of some kind on it. The Santa Fe people would be glad to deed it to you down the road for your services. They'll furnish the lumber and a handful of laborers to restore or add on to the building some, and even wire-fence the whole shebang. Also throw in a few cows now and then to add to your small herd, fifty head to start with. Plus all the guns, ammo and horses you need for whatever men you have."

"Them's pretty good wages for a guard dog."

"Dog or sentinel, I'd have to agree."

"Those pricks," came Allison's harsh retort. "Why me?"

"Obviously your sterling reputation," grinned Longwill. "They know you don't take any shit, and know how good you are at handing it out. They like what they hear about you. They like your firm decision making. You're a fighter, Clay, they respect that. And they need a fighter."

"It's nice to feel needed, Doc," he replied sardonically. "But I'm no gunman. I like to refer to myself as a shootist."

"They've heard that, too. And they call you a civilized shootist."

Allison's eyebrows raised in surprise. "They seem pretty informed."

"All you need to do is urge the feet-draggers to speed up their departure. I imagine a little night riding would do wonders."

"I remember Charley Morris doing some of that for the Ring just a year ago. Before he met with his misfortune."

"Ah, yes, good ol' Charley. Talked to him a few times and liked the man. Not too bright, but had a good sense of humor."

"One of your recruits, I heard by the grapevine."

"Well, yes, now that you mention it. Not one I'm proud of though. It was not too bright of him to argue with an armed thug while he himself was unarmed. Got killed for it."

"Yeah, I remember," commented Allison. "Knew them both. Charley Morris and Chunk Colbert, tin-horn gunmen, although I think Morris was the better man. Just took one foolish chance too many was all. I loved nailing Chunk. He was a mouthy turd."

"I'd never met him, but what I heard chilled me."

"So why didn't the Ring make him an offer?"

"Not a chance, Clay. He was a crazy killer, and the Ring would never pick a hyena over a shepherd. Just plain logic."

Allison sat staring at Longwill, knowing the silly chess game they were playing. Never a good chess player, Allison still loved the game. It's infinite, convoluted tactics intrigued him. Now here he was, exchanging moves with Longwill. Or rather, the Ring. He would be just another pawn to them, although he liked to fancy himself at least a knight. But he knew that a knight by any other name in this real estate game would stink the same. Enforcer: hired gun. Shit, did it all come down to this? The section of land they offered in the game was a gambit, the tempting play for me to reach out for. But a gambit is not a capture, damn it all. And they still own the game.

"I still can't figure you coming to me for this job."

"Listen," spoke Longwill, lighting a fresh cheroot, then pouring a dash more rye into their near empty glasses. "It's true, like you say, I earlier recruited Charley Morris. He was dependable, but sadly, careless. And this being a small town a few people know who his riders were, local rowdies, small herders needing extra money, or a few gunmen passing through looking for a stake so as to move on. It's known you rode with him a few times, and so I just thought I'd ask if you would consider the position."

So there it was, mused Allison. "A touch of arm-twisting?" he snorted.

"Good grief, no," laughed Longwill. "Let's just say it's your work history. An informal recommendation of sorts. And a promotion."

"To play the landlord's evictor."

"I'd say manager. Hell, why don't you think on it? Take a ride out, look the place over, let me know in a couple of days. Here's a rough map." Longwill rose, drank the dregs of his glass, then set his bowler at a rakish angle with a lop-sided grin. "I've had all the liquidation I can handle, so I'd best make for my office. Keep the rest of the bottle, Clay. Good talking with you."

"Thanks, Doc. See you in a couple of days."

A few minutes later Allison corked the bottle, drank the leavings of his glass, then went to the bar. "Lambert, I'd like to leave this with you for a future time, if you wouldn't mind. Half a quart of choice rye."

"No, not at all, Clay. It'll be here for you."

"Thanks. Have a taste or two for your trouble."

Allison limped across the barroom and out the door. Preoccupied, he mounted his horse and walked slowly out of town, trying to picture the land in question. He was tempted to ride out then, but it was getting late, near three, and he wanted a daylight inspection. Too far for the hours left, so he decided on the next day. He'd spend an hour or two going over its square mile. Good Christ, the landlord's manager. He wondered what in hell he was coming to.

Eight the next morning he moved out at an easy lope from Coleman's pasture with some sandwiches and canned goods in his saddle-bags. Longwill's drawing was easy to follow, and hours later he was walking his mount eastward across a field of thick, high grass that gradually and gently sloped toward the Canadian, which flowed north to south. Riding south along its bank he saw it as swifter and probably deeper then the Pecos he had crossed years ago. The river meandered through the eastern third of the section, leaving a portion of the land across the river. It too rose slowly from its bank, steeply here and there. Scattered juniper bushes and cottonwoods flanked the river now and then, feeding from the fast flow of water. He'd have to make sure where it would be safe and shallow enough for his cows to traipse back and forth. If he took it. He about-faced and retraced his route north to the end of the section, then turned west to follow its northern edge. Completely traversing the western portion of the property line, he liked what he saw. He spied the shell of a half-finished rock house and behind it a caved-in wooden shed. They appeared a couple of years old, probably one of the first of the squatters to move off, or to be run off. They left nothing behind but a few broken jars, a rusted pot, some rotted harness, and the ragged remnants of a garden where a few anemic stalks of stunted corn attempted regrowth.

Leaving his horse to contentedly graze on his own, he limped through the grass for a time, enjoying the mild April afternoon breeze, the smell of the soil, the flitting and chirping of the varied avian, the flushed pheasants and rabbits. Along the Canadian he glimpsed several young deer, a rare sight now this close to the settlements, civilization having pushed much of the natural tenants back upon themselves on a continuous retreat. He wondered how Monroe and John would like this place? He had written home to them every few months, telling them he was on the prod for a decent ranch, and asked if they would like to come out and join him when he found one. They were immediately hot for it, and awaited his summons.

For the past year Lew Coleman had been corresponding with Clay's sister Saluda. Earlier, Coleman had been living with a young Mexican woman who bore them a son, then died as a result. He shipped her body in a casket to her parents in Santa Fe, assuring them in the near future he would visit them with their grandson. Six weeks later their son followed her in death. It was a terrible blow for Coleman who was depressed and uncommunicative for months following their demise, and not comfortable to be around. He shuffled about in constant gloom, mumbling over and over how so many dreams are left unfulfilled. He badly missed his lost son. Buried on the property, the boy's stone carried a simple salutation, "Louis S. Coleman. One month fourteen days." The bereaved father was constantly hovering over it, silent, mute, red-eyed and shaken. Allison did all he could to pull him out of his doldrums, finally getting him and Saluda to exchange letters. And now that the two looked forward to a marriage, Clay could not be happier for them.

Seeing Coleman resuscitated by new plans for his future lent Allison's own thoughts in that direction, fulfilling his own aching dream of a ranch, herds of cattle, and he a thriving cowman on the rise. Well, if he wanted one it was under his nose, right where he was now standing, and by God it felt exciting just thinking about it! Looking all around him he saw nothing but his dream coming to fruition, the wondrous fantasy he envisioned when he first hit Texas five, six years ago, and he had clung to it since, hoping and dreaming. If he let this go he knew it would be the end of his potential in the area. He would have to get out, try his luck elsewhere. If he stayed he would be just another horseback laborer, and there was no future there, pushing someone else's cows. Of course he could throw in with Coleman, and the two could have a small but secure business with a chance of increasing their holdings according to their profits. But, no, he wanted to do it all himself or not at all. He was too bullheaded about that. He wanted his own ranch and under his own terms. He wanted to show he could do it himself, with no one else's help or input of any kind. Christ, all he had to say was "Yes," and this was his.

He remembered his father's last embittered words to him the day he rode off for Texas. They had argued again, his father wanting him to take an interest in the farm. Short on patience and long on expressing his opinions strongly, Clay roundly cursed farming and anything to do with the farm. Insulted, his father fumed and said coldly, "You will never amount to a damn thing," and strode off.

All around him he could see and hear his cows. There was John and Monroe sliding between a bunch, cutting out a few for market. Young Joseph Matthews Mills was with them, wearing that hat he bought him in Raton, loping about as salty as any bronc rider. His ranch house with a barn and corral faced the river for a fine view, and there was Martha and her daughter Addie, standing in the doorway waving and calling them in for lunch. Her husband had died as a result of an unfortunate wagon accident and she had returned to Cimarron with his body for burial. Clay happened to meet the funeral group and joined them. He nodded to her and she returned his gesture, while young Joseph, wearing that hat, clambered out of the wagon and ran over to Allison to shake his hand. Clay looked down from his mount and addressed with a smile, "Good to see you, Mister Mills." Joseph replied, "Good to see you, Mister Allison." One thing led to another, and in his imagination they were together again, this time as a family, and he married to Martha.

"Yes," he said to Longwill, "yes. It's a fine section, and I'd be insane to turn it down."

"Glad you approve. It's really a fine spot."

"I'd like it wired in."

"No problem."

"I'd like the stone house finished and the barn rebuilt."

"You've got it."

"Who's paying the taxes until I get the deed?"

"It'll be taken care of. Once you get the deed the expenses are of course your responsibility."

"When do I get the deed?"

"I honestly have no say in that. But I imagine in a year or two, depending upon the effectiveness of your service and how stabilized the grant company is by then."

"Longwill, if I am short-changed or screwed in any way, I want you to tell Tom Catron his ass is grass. I will responsively hunt him down and will personally put six forty-five slugs up his fat ass."

"No need to talk like that, Clay. Tom is a man of his word, crooked as he is."

"Well, he and his Santa Fe Ring has the rottenest reputation this side of the Mississippi, and I want you to deliver my message. Verbatim."

"Good as done, Clay."

"In a little while I have to leave town for a few weeks. Soon as I return I'll start my eviction process. While I'm gone I'd like the Ring to begin fencing and rebuilding those structures."

"They will start first thing in the morning. By the time you return you can move right in."

Allison and Coleman took a stage to Pueblo, Colorado, then a train to St. Louis, Missouri. Disembarking in St. Louis they were astonished by the huge population that confronted them. At the station they had to switch trains, and felt as if they were moving through a mass of swarming humanity which threatened to engulf and crush them if they dared stop for even a moment.

"Good lord!" exclaimed Allison. "This is worse than any stampede of longhorns I've ever been through!"

"By God, I ain't never seen anything like this either, except maybe at the excitement of a lynching or two!"

"Maybe that's where they are headed for," yelled Allison over the noise. "Think we should ask for an invite?"

"No, no," laughed Coleman. "Let's just quick grab that next train and get on out of here!"

Fortunately their timing was propitious, and before an hour they were seated and on their way south toward Jackson, Tennessee, on a line completed the year previous. That too was a timely historic railroad event, for it saved them a dusty stagecoach trip of at least three hundred miles in the hot month of April. But from Jackson, where they dismounted for a jaunt east to Perryville, it was a coach ride for fifty miles to the Tennessee River. There they grabbed a steamer for their final leg to Clifton, a pleasant and peaceful glide on wide rolling waters which gave them a cooling relief for the last thirty miles.

On the entire trip Allison was antsy as a child on Christmas Eve, and nervous as a man about to be lynched. While eagerly looking toward the family gathering after eight year's absence, a part of him thirsted to boast to his father and older brother how he had finally found a perfect ranch for the herd he had acquired. He craved to brag to them of his "success," and flaunt his role as a cattleman on the way up to these dirt farmers. Thus far only Longwill knew of his pact with the Ring, and that he was actually only able to pull himself up by "his" bootstraps through their courtesy. He had told Coleman little more than, "I might have a financial partner with whom a piece of land would hopefully be worked out in the near future. I'm not one-hundred percent certain as to what may happen, but on my return to Cimarron I'll know." He had too much respect for Coleman to reveal the truth, was sure he would not approve his riding shotgun for the Ring. Well, he'd have to wait, and when Coleman discovered who Allison's "financial partner" was, he'd just have to hope he'd understand. Just thinking of his ranch waiting for his return gave him an emotional charge beyond belief, and that's exactly what he would do, share his elation with the family. And of course, echoing in the back of his mind were the parting words of his father, which still stung as sharp as a hornet's bite. Yet while he savored the moment of throwing it in his face he felt childish at such a cheap tactic, unmanly even, knowing he should act the adult and put away the old anger both had so often expressed verbally in the heat of their disagreements. Too, there was a touch of guilt, knowing the successful-rancher image was a lie, a dishonesty gained for the sake of his ego-saving vengeance.

All these thoughts burned into his brain and ate at his conscience.

It was like a bad case of indigestion he couldn't rid himself of. Lying was a thing he was never comfortable with and he avoided it like the plague, feeling that honesty is what counted, to let the chips fall where they may in all matters through candid, straightforward say-so's. So he constantly seesawed between the roles of prodigal son and grim avenger, relishing neither perception.

At the landing were the family, and Allison could not deny nor hold back the lump in his throat at seeing them clustered together to welcome him. Saluda and John were the first upon him, and the two, John, now twenty and a strapping six-footer, and Saluda an adult of twenty-one, boisterously engulfed him and sent him back a few steps in their enthusiastic embrace. His parents, Jeremiah and Mariah, took him in their arms, and his heart was moved at the words, "Welcome home, son." Monroe, now twenty-eight and a school teacher, gave him a warm abrazo, as did Jesse, who was there with his wife of six years, Francis, and their four children. After a time of happy chatter and laughter they climbed aboard a wagon and made for their parents' home.

Lew and Saluda's wedding and party was well attended by relatives and friends from miles around. Clay made certain of his conservative behavior by his iron resolve not to indulge in any alcoholic imbibing whatsoever, and was completely successful in giving the impression of joining the constant toasting and salutations with his vessel filled with juices and other virtuous liquids. He realized what alcohol did to him and resolved not to embarrass or insult the matrimonial festivities a whit. He never grew to despise juice so much and silently vowed a purging of his system of it on his return to Cimarron.

Yet the two weeks at the Allison home was pleasantly anti-climatic for Clay, in that his past resentments and need to assert his self-importance melted away before the genuine family solicitude toward him and his related tale of prosperity in the cattle business. He spoke no more than he had to of his ranch, nor embroidered on it as it came up occasionally, merely sitting back in modest understatement and let others comment on the industry and his potential future in it. He continued feeling qualms of conscience in his somewhat dishonest pose, wishing he could relate aboveboard his bargain with the real estate promoters. But what could he say that wouldn't demean the impression he desired in the first place? How could he tarnish the dream in his heart he painted for others, even though he came to accept the reality of his economic limitations which guided him to his pact with them? Hell with it, he said, let it go. They wouldn't understand. Once back in New Mexico he would do what his agreement called for, and the family would be no wiser to the bogus image. For a week he even worked in his father's fields, hoeing, digging and plowing as if he were back to farming again. He found the exercise refreshing and the penance therapeutic.

Clay noticed Monroe and their father seemed to have buried the hatchet, or maybe since Monroe had divorced himself from laboring on the farm via education and getting his teaching credentials, it had removed the sore point between them. They were quite cordial now, both father and son serving as freshly accepted members of the Cade Grange, an agricultural association of the county. Looking upon them they seemed two different people, the harsh antagonism gone between them. It left Clay astounded, but very glad.

In four months Clay would turn thirty-one, and during this visit he felt a kind of change in him, or the wish for something more within him, like perhaps something was missing. What touched him was watching the family and their interplay with each other; his father and mother and the soft subtle actions of concern they held for each other; Jesse and his playfulness with his kids and wife; his brothers and sisters ragging one or the other, and next giving tender care for each's welfare; the natural atmosphere of filial regard between all had touched him. It was family, he realized, as it hit him. The special closeness of a family of his own he wanted and wished he had. Watching them all in their different displays of affection moved him considerably. It wasn't mawkish sentimentality that surged through him, but the genuine emotion of the desire for a meaningful connection for another human being. Someone to grow with. To love. The words of Doc

Longwill came back to suddenly jar him: "Mister Allison, you done missed the boat on this one." Martha.

Of course he'd be lying to himself if he tried to say he hadn't thought of her at all since her leaving. Many of his fantasies included her and her kids. And was Longwill right? Should he have? Could it have worked out for them? In the back of his mind he hardly separated her from the dreams of his ranch, yet now as a hired evictor would she have been sympathetic to that dream? But it was too late now. She was gone and married to another dreamer whose dream she helped complete.

When it was time to leave for Colfax County, the newlyweds and Clay took John with them, who couldn't wait to leave Clifton. He looked forward to staying with Clay at his new ranch. If all worked out, Clay even promised him a partnership in the endeavor, and both looked forward to running a small cattle company at the very least. At the boat landing his father wrapped his long muscular arm about Clay's shoulders with a clasp and said, "And you take good care of that leg, son, hear me? Mind now, and get it looked at now and then by a doctor."

Touched, his son answered, "It'll be just fine, dad, really. But I'll surely do that."

He had asked Coleman not to mention his self-shot foot, only the broken leg. A half-truth was better than none.

Returning to Cimarron they claimed their horses and wagon they had left with friends, and where they spent the night. Following a steak and egg breakfast the quartet was on the road by seven for Coleman's ranch, a twenty-mile trip. Clay and John rode a pair of mounts while the newlyweds took the buckboard drawn by a pair of mules. Before noon several hours later, as they approached Coleman's turnoff to his ranch, roughly ten miles farther, Clay pulled up a moment and said, "Lou, me and John will leave you here and go on over to my place. Maybe I'll be able to find out the particulars by now."

"Well, all right, Clay. But don't be shy if you have to have a place to stay tonight, hear?"

"Thanks. We'll most likely see you tomorrow, though. Good luck again, you two."

It was another twenty miles before they approached his fence line and he smiled with pride to see it had been wired in. Following the dirt trail he came to a gate which he unhooked from horseback. Entering and re-latching it, he moved on between a scattering of cattle followed by John. To the north several hundred yards from the river he saw with satisfaction the stone house had been finished. The barn, too. In the yard two men were loading items in a wagon, seeming about to make a departure. One of the men looked up. "Mister Allison?"

"Yes, sir," replied Clay.

"We're just leaving. Hope everything is satisfactory for you. The crew fenced in your section and finished the house and barn. Just one big room for the house, but weather-tight and dry."

"Looks good and solid, thank you. Barn's nice, too."

"And yesterday we brought in them fifty cows for you. We'll be moseying along now, Mister Allison. If there's anything else you might need, just talk to Doc Longwill."

"Thanks, gents," saluted Allison as the two wagoned off.

"Well, John, this is it."

"Looks wonderful, Clay. And, wow, a river in your own front yard!" he laughed. "Just look at that," he admired.

Dismounting, Clay commented, "Let's put these nags in the barn. Hope they left some feed like I asked them to."

There was, feed and hay both, and Clay couldn't help but think that this was real service. Unsaddling the horses, they left them and entered the house. It was one large room they stood in, a fireplace at one end, but vacant of furniture.

"Like it, John?"

"Certainly do. Big enough."

"We can partition off a few rooms as time allows. Shouldn't be much trouble."

"And look at that view of the river from this window, Clay. Beautiful spot."

"May have to get me a rocker to sit before this window and pinch myself every day."

"Them cows included with this place?" asked John.

"Sure was. Part of the deal I made for the whole section. And at their expense they fixed up this stone house, rebuilt the barn and fenced it in, Nice, huh?"

"Really is, Clay, really is," returned John in warm envy. "How'd you swing a deal like this, anyway?"

"Let's take a walk, John. Tell you about it. I want to explain things."

They strolled towards the river bank where the grass thinned out. Several cows lazily shuffled along the water's edge in the warm June afternoon sun, swatting away pesky flies with their tails. It was a countryfied, bucolic scene right out of a book, thought Clay. Pastoral as all hell.

"It's like this, John. It's a jungle out there, and I don't aim to be one of the ones to get swallowed up, hear?"

"What do you mean?"

"Let me clarify. To put it briefly as I can, some fifty years ago a couple of men got a grant of land from the Mexican Governor in Santa Fe. A few years later a man named Maxwell married the daughter of one of the grantees, and after years of buying and inheriting, he came to own the whole grant. He moved on it with his wife and kids which is now Cimarron and built that big old mansion there, which is slowly rotting away.

"Anyways, while he owned it he claimed more acreage than was given, but no one knew or seemed to care then, and a bunch of people, mostly Mexicans, settled on the place here and there over the years, and he'd charge them rent in exchange for cattle, crops, or whatever, money being scarcer than honesty.

"Shortly after the Rebellion was over gold was discovered on 'his' land, and the stampede of people it brought showed him he was no longer the self-proclaimed feudal lord of the country. So he sold out quickly in eighteen hundred and seventy. The group who took over, a cobble of financiers, politicians, lawyers and assorted thieves, who believed—or maybe they didn't—Maxwell's overblown tale of owning nearly two million acres. Either way, the bandits salivated at what a green future it would give them, so eventually surveyed it out to solidify Maxwell's dream-claim of over one million, seven-hundred thousand acres. Legally, according to Spanish and Mexican law, it was originally more like ninety-seven thousand acres. The legal size is one of the sore points of the court fights going on now. They then began rent collections on the miners, squatters, settlers, and all homesteaders of every shape and form, and forced evictions of those who refused to pay. It was as bright as kicking a bee hive.

"On the other side of the mountains in the capitol is a group called the 'Santa Fe Ring' who are the power behind the grant, and they intend to keep it and develop it every way they can. Fighting them on this side of the mountains is a handful here in Cimarron called the 'Colfax Ring' who want to keep it for themselves, since it's in their county. And of course neither side give a damn about the original settlers, being two sides of the same coin. They only plot and manipulate on how they can get their grip on this piece of real estate.

"That trickles down to me, John, and my little ranch here. The Santa Fe Ring presented me with an offer I would be a fool to refuse. All I got to do is raid the countryside and convince the hard-nosed squatters to unsquat. They hired me as a sort of enforcer, an evictor. The chief unsquatter. For my services the Santa Feers in a year or so will give me their blessings in the form of a deed to all this. All this explaining has got me a little tired, for I'm not ordinarily this windy as you know, but what do you think?"

"Clay, I believe you have here a choice piece of land worth fighting for, and I'd be pleased to help you keep it."

The next day the brothers rode out to the Lacy-Coleman pastures and retrieved Clay's hundred cows. The two herdsmen were busy with a cattle dealer, which was fine with Clay, for he didn't relish expounding, explaining or rationalizing his Ring agreement to either man, and what he knew would be a sore point with both. Having a quick cup of coffee with Saluda, they gathered and drove off the herd.

Before too long Clay collected a hardcore handful of cronies whom he led on raids into the countryside and terrifying "hurrahs" on the town. Chickens and geese especially, for some reason, became targets of choice, and many times after the dust of the town settled behind them, avian dinners became a local repast. Before the first week was out the Santa Fe Ring was pleased to see some profit in their Clay-investment, for a handful of Mexican farmers had quietly moved off.

The Allison ranch became a sort of headquarters, or at least meeting place, for Clay and his followers, where drinking, gambling and barbeques were held at the drop of a hat. Dragging a fiddler or two out to his ranch, or a talent with a harmonica, a semblance of music rent the air far into the night while some of the men danced up a storm, a handkerchief tied to the arm of the one who played the female role. The drunken din disturbed no one for they were over twenty miles from town, with only the coyotes, rabbits or prairie dogs to issue complaint, and they knew better.

As time went on Clay's drinking increased, for there was a numbness he liked about it without even acknowledging it. Although he felt it gave his instincts a sharper edge, it gave his already bold behavior a touch of dark insanity, somewhat like a madman with a sense of wry humor. At one time he was in a hotel bar having a rollicking time with several cronies when he drew his gun and shot into the ceiling, one, two, three times. Soon his friends drew their six-shooters in imitation and blasted away heavenward, everyone roaring with laughter, hearing the sounds of boots scraping and thumping from the upper room as the occupants made for the stove to stand upon in order to evade the incoming bullets.

Late one night in Cimarron as he was exiting Lambert's saloon inebriated, he saw William Morley, one of the editors of the *Cimarron News*

& Press, and Justice of the Peace Trauer. With fire in his eyes he grabbed each by an arm and roughly towed them down to the bank of the Cimarron River, only a few hundred feet away. On the way he spied an axe behind a darkened cabin, so thrust it into Morley's hand. At the river he instructed Morley to chop down a tree, and for Trauer to play his Jew's harp, which he always had with him.

"Chop, goddamn you, Morley," spat Allison. "You Yankee scum!"

Morley had served in the army also, but as a Yankee, and worse yet, was with Sherman's troops as they burned, looted and plundered their way through Georgia and the Carolinas. Naturally, he was the lowest of animals in Allison's eyes. Clay had also been directed to give the editor a hard time by the Santa Feers, he being not only in sympathy with the Colfax contingent, but guilty of writing anti-Santa Fe Ring editorials in the *Press*. Morley, terrified of Allison, always made certain he was in hiding whenever he and his groupies paid Cimarron a rousing visit, but this night he was unexpectedly ambushed so made the best he could of bad karma. Although Trauer merely had the rotten luck of being with Morley that night, he had the good sense to obey Allison's barleycorned instructions to the letter and played his heart out. Clay, becoming bored after conducting his woodchopper's ball for two hours, rudely straight-armed Morley into the icy waters of the Cimarron with a curse, then left.

Soaked in sweat, John looked up from chopping firewood on a late afternoon to see Clay riding at a walk toward him. He had been gone since the day before, mainly having to settle a few small matters in Cimarron. It got so he could read his older brother's mood in an instant, even at a distance; from the manner in which he walked or sat a horse, his expression, his body language, the unspoken aura he communicated. John could pick up the unspoken subtleties in him the way an animal could sense a change in the weather. He saw in Clay this time a buoyant, self-satisfied posture with a pleasant countenance. He also appeared sober. John rested the double-bladed axe head on a log and cupped his hands atop the upraised handle as Clay approached. "Howdy, big brother," John welcomed with a grin.

"Howdy yourself, young 'un," Clay smiled in return. "That's a healthy pile of firewood you got stacked up there. Trying to set a record?"

"Well, I recollect having to cut wood when it was below zero a few times back home, so thought I would rescue myself from that agony this winter."

"Good man," laughed Clay. "And smart."

"You seem in a perky mood this late in the day," observed John with a chuckle. "Kick somebody's ass in town?"

"Better than that. I done settled rancher Ernest's hash."

"You mean Fine Ernest?"

"The very same."

John was a little puzzled, and although knowing Clay and Fine were like oil and water, hoped their settled differences didn't take a drastic turn. "Well, I hope Ernest is still walking about."

"That he is, though his feelings may be a bit bedraggled."

"And how is that?" queried John as Clay dismounted and took the axe.

"You recall farmer Coe and friends complaining about Fine's cows breaking down their fences and trampling their crops?"

"Oh, sure. When Coe finally shot some rock salt up a few of Fine's cow's asses to make his point. Then Fine got the law on them, right?"

"Right," he replied as he hewed away at a log. "But the court kept delaying their hearing, so I talked to a judge today, explaining the delays were unfair to the farmers, having several times to leave working their fields and wasting their time for a hearing that never takes place. He saw my point and instantly set a firm date. I was on my way out of town when I fortunately met some of the Coes and told them the news. They were pleased, of course, as was I."

"Hell, Clay. That was a real fine gesture, if you will excuse the pun."

"Excuse accepted," he laughed. "Then of a sudden, who should be prancing by on his lovely roan? None other than Fine Ernest himself. So I gets down from my filly and hails him, and he too unglues himself from the saddle and joins me aground. But of course he had a doubtful smile and was a tad nervous, seeing the Coes, wondering what was what."

"Oh, oh," groaned John. "Sounds like he was in a fine embarrassment."

"You betcha," he answered, chuckling and chopping. "I explained to Mister Ernest my visit to the judge and the solid date he set for the hearing, then drew my trusty Colt. Grabbing him gently by the shirt I slowly twirled him about as I lightly tapped his hat brim with my gun barrel, informing him firmly that he would be one smart hombre not to hassle my farmer friends any longer. That if he did, he'd best not allow the sun to set on his ass in this county a minute longer."

"Didn't he claim to have ridden with Quantrill during the Rebellion?"

"If he did," snorted Clay, "it was as a horse holder."

"And so what did Ernest have to say about his dervish-dance?"

"Nothing. He was speechless. But I suspected he comprehended my meaning clearly, for he turned awfully pale and just rode off quick as he could, like he had a sudden and important engagement elsewhere."

"So what's the cattle association you belong to going to say about all that, since Ernest is an officer?"

Some months previous Clay had been invited to join a local cattle-man's organization as head of the rules committee. Normally having a disparaging attitude toward what he called "cow clubs" in general, he went in with them anyway, knowing it was only a surface gesture by the Colfaxers, they hoping to placate his ego and draw him into their bosom away from the Santa Fe Ring.

"Forgot to tell you, John. As Fine was trotting off I told him to let the fellers of the cow club know that I had resigned then and there. Christ, it was all a joke to me anyway. The Colfaxers and Santa Feers all wear the same coats, hats and britches, and there's no way if you got them herded together in a corral you could tell them apart. Both sides are nothing more than maggots feeding on the same varmint. Besides, riding for the Santa Feers is like riding for the Colfaxers, both wanting the same thing at the expense of the squatters and small settlers. Damn, I should be collecting double pay."

"Guess you're right there. I really have to laugh at the picture of Ernest being spun about while tapped about the head with a gun barrel. Love'd to have witnessed that."

"Well, he did piss me off treating them farmers thataway."

"Boy," nodded John humorously. "Our daddy would hardly believe you defending farmers from cattlemen. I think it would confuse him mightily."

"Oh, hell, John. I hate farming, not farmers. I have no love for it, but I have less love for a pompous ass like Ernest pushing them about. They work hard as hell, and ol' Fine galled me no end."

"Amen to that."

"And just what in hell am I doing here, chopping up this wood for you?"

"I was about to thank you greatly for it."

"Well, take this thankful axe and continue on, boy."

"Damn, I was afraid you'd come to your senses."

"Have you et' yet?"

"Naw. But this ungodly labor has famished me most unmercifully."

"You just chop on then. I'll go and fry us up some steaks and potatoes. Least I can do for a hard working fella out here all day wearing out an axe."

"By golly, now you're talking my language. You ain't a bad slave-driver after all, massa!"

Laughing, Clay led his horse to the barn.

Clay was in Cimarron for a few days and decided to have dinner at Lambert's hotel. Entering the dining room early in the evening of a Saturday, a half dozen tables were already taken, and it looked like the beginning of a busy night. A Spanish guitarist wandered slowly through the room strumming soft melodies. Against a far wall he spotted Doctor Longwell reading a paper over his customary cheroot.

"Would you like some company, Doc?"

"Clay," he smiled as he looked up. "You're a welcome sight. Have dinner with me, unless you've eaten?"

"Not yet, but I'm looking forward to one of Lambert's tasty T-bones."

"Good, join me. I'll buy."

"Surely will, thank you."

"By the way, heard the latest?"

"Don't think so. What is it?"

"To begin with, your 'friend' Morley's mother-in-law authored a letter outlining the corrupt practices of Catron and the Santa Fe Ring in their pursuance of the bogus Maxwell Land Grant."

"Good heavens, can such things be?" laughed Allison wryly.

"Not only that, she addressed it to an old friend of much clout, Attorney General Alfonso Taft in Washington, D.C."

"Hmmm, this is getting interesting."

"Yes," Longwill agreed, grinning. "But upon being told of the deed, daughter Mrs. Morley panicked, feeling her husband William had all the trouble he can handle as it is, so instantly marched off to the post office and retrieved the missive from the open cardboard box on the table, explaining it was mailed by mistake."

"Sounds like a little legal problem on the horizon."

"Right. When postmaster McCullough got wind of her act of illegal retrieval, he instantly marched over to the Morley domicile in a smoking snit where he accused her of tampering with the mails and announced his intention of pressing charges."

Their dinner arrived and with it a bottle of French burgundy Longwill had ordered.

"This is getting interesting, Doc. Please continue."

"May we first have a taste of a bit of French grape? I thirst."

"Good grief, most definitely. And let me join you. Pour on, waiter."

The waiter poured, then left.

"To Baccus," toasted Longwill.

"To Venus," joined Allison."

As they ate, Longwill continued. "The next day Mrs. Morley's husband cornered McCullough and read him the riot act."

"McCullough better look out. I think Mister Morley could do him a lot of physical damage."

"It gets a might stickier. Seems McCullough shot off a letter to Catron in Santa Fe describing the big crime, and asked for an indictment. Catron complied, and the warrant was given to a U.S. Marshal to deliver."

"You must be joking."

"But the marshal was called out of town and can't serve the papers until he gets back."

"Good thing," retorted Clay edgily. "This is going too far."

"Then Mrs. Morley, who is expecting her first child, went on a trip back east to visit relatives and won't be back herself for a few months."

"Catron, huh?"

"Well, silly as it all sounds," chuckled Longwill, "she did break the law, taking that letter."

"You speaking as a lawyer," cut Allison icily, "or as a human being?"

Longwill braced in his chair, a piece of steak on his fork half-way to his mouth, suddenly realizing whom he was talking to. This was not the jovial Allison he normally bantered with over an occasional afternoon toddy. This was the other Allison, whom he now understood had been drinking all day, the darker twin who was threateningly emerging before his very eyes.

"Ahem, as a lawyer, of course," he quickly attempted mollifying him. "But I certainly agree that she should not be treated like a common criminal."

"You can bet your boots she won't. Mister postmaster should know better, and understand the difference between a silly mistake and a bank robbery. And that turd Catron too. Anything I can't tolerate is the bullying of women. I'm going to have to quick find McCullough and define a few things for him."

"Now, now, Clay. Don't be rash. I'm certain things will work themselves out in due time."

"Yes, they will, mister lawyer," came Clay's rasp. "I'm going to see that they do."

Longwill sat rigid, the uneaten meat still before him on his fork, not daring to say another word. He looked into Clay's eyes which had grown darker as he spoke. They were now like a pair of long black tunnels he felt he could walk into. He imagined his echoing footsteps in the ebony halls, and grew more nervous. He was slowly drifting toward panic, and had the feeling of slipping into a bottomless hole in the earth.

"Do me a favor, Doc," whispered Allison evenly. His voice was known to fade gradually as he became more inebriated, lending it a strong menacing quality.

"Yes, yes," came Longwill's overly quick reply. "Of course, anything." Finally chewing his long impaled piece of steak, he washed it down with a goblet of wine in several swift gulps, then refilled his glass.

"You get word pronto to Catron and inform him that if Mrs. Morley is sent to trial, not a juror will leave the courtroom alive. Got it?"

"Yes, yes, I'll certainly let him know."

"Thanks for the dinner, Doc," stood Clay. "But don't ever talk to me like a lawyer again."

Allison walked out of the dining room as Longwill remained frozen in his chair, grateful to be alive. Watching Allison move away he looked to him like a great limping cat, and suddenly felt the need for some tranquilizing liquid. He grasped his goblet of wine and emptied it again.

Clay left his host and entered the barroom. He wanted a few more drinks to help make the long ride home more tolerable. As he walked into the saloon he saw McCullough talking to a companion and the bartender, and thought, "This must be my lucky night." He looked over the patrons, a couple dozen men drinking, smoking, chewing, gabbing, playing pool. Usual Saturday night bunch. He maneuvered between the tables to the packed bar to stand behind McCullough who was preoccupied telling a blue story. As the men laughed at the punch line, they noticed Allison behind them and stopped. McCullough blanched, somehow sensing he was in trouble.

"Good evening, mister postmaster," greeted Allison with a toothy grin.

"Why, uh, h-hello, Clay."

Stepping between McCullough and his friend, Allison spoke to the barman. "Bring us a quart of your best rye and three water glasses. Mister postmaster here is in a celebratory mood."

After delivering the bottle and glasses the bartender strategically scurried to the far end of his station. Clay half-filled the three vessels, but saw too late that McCullough's drinking partner had abandoned the premises.

"Drink up, mister postman," ordered Allison as he raised his glass. "It's Saturday night."

McCullough obeyed, and tears welled in his eyes as the alcohol seared his throat.

"Whatsamatter, postman," asked Clay with a light laugh. "Liquor too hot?"

"K-k-kinda," he stammered. "Just not too used to drinking so much in one g-g-gulp."

Picking up the third glass, Clay continued. "Seems your buddy done left. So I don't think he'd mind me using this to help put out that fire in your throat." He then very slowly emptied the drink over McCullough's head. The rye ran down his face, neck and shirt as he stood riveted to the floor, not daring to move. "Cooler now, postman?"

McCullough wiped his eyes feeling them burn slightly from the alcohol.

"I said, are you cooler now?"

"Yes, yes," he smiled crookedly, readily accepting it all as a bizarre segment of Allison's twisted sense of humor.

"Good. Then let us have another sip." This time he filled the glasses to the brim. "Drink up, postmaster. This'll really help put out that fire." More fearful not to accept the invitation than to walk into a den of lions, the postmaster grit his will and chugged at the glass. But half-empty was as far as he could go. His throat locked and his stomach bunched up, forcing him to return the glass to the bar, eyes wet with copious tears which still stung from his rye-shower.

"Wheee-whooo!" exclaimed McCullough.

Allison set his empty glass on the bar, refilling it. "Whatsamatter, postman? Turn into a postboy? You still got half a drink left, and I don't think it's very neighborly of you at all."

"B-but, Clay," he gasped, trying to catch his breath. "I'm more of a social drinker, and not too much heavy on liquor."

"What? You claiming I'm unsocial? What in hell's wrong with you, boy? Don't you recognize a social drinker? Empty that glass, pronto."

Word passed through the barroom of what was taking place, and it gradually grew cemetery quiet. Several made bets that the postman would leave feet-first and dead before the night was out.

McCullough gripped the glass in a shaky fist and chugged it down, coughing, choking and gasping his guts out.

"Good man, postmaster." smiled Clay as he refilled his victim's vessel. "Now listen real good," he went on in a low gelid tone. "You leave Mrs. Morley be. Got that? The only thing I want to hear of her being served is get-well cards and Christmas greetings. Understood?"

McCullough shook visibly as an aspen in a hurricane. "Yes, C-C-Clay. I understand."

"She ever come to any kind of trial, not one damn juror will leave the place alive. Including you. Savvy?"

"Yes, yes, I surely do."

To emphasize his instructions Allison drew his Colt and pressed it between McCullough's eyes, cocking and uncocking it several times.

"Oh, good lord!" wailed the postman as he watched the bullet-loaded cylinder rotate inches from his face. A strong rank odor rose from the floor around his feet, accompanied by a growing puddle of water. "P-p-please, Clay! Don't!"

Reholstering his weapon, Allison emptied his glass. He then took the bottle of rye and up-ended the remains over the postman's head, letting it run in a slow fountain until it was empty.

"Goodnight, postmaster," farewelled Allison in polite quietness as he limped across the room and out the door to his horse.

The smoldering atmosphere on the grant reflected a primer from Darwin's survival of the fittest, and there were so many sharks in the Colfax County aquarium it was difficult to tell who was feeding on whom. Of course the largest of the species was the Santa Fe Ring with their army of politicians, attorneys and financial cohorts, seconded by their pugnacious little brother, the Colfax Ring. The rest nibbled where they could in a fierce competitive battle to outlast or outlive their neighbors, betrayal notwithstanding. It was a sad and brutal time, sad because the primal motivation for survival permeated individual action on several levels, and brutal because human deportment often echoed early man's behavior on the African savannah. For instance, while some squatters sold out to the company and went their way, others settled up then hired themselves out as grant "deputies" to oust the more stubborn, thus giving a handful a chance to settle old scores.

Clay Allison, as a combatant, had both the talent and the psychological edge over many of the settlers and squatters. First, he was a war veteran who had seen, experienced and participated in violence for years at its rawest level, where killing merely meant eliminating an immediate threat. Second, he had the ability to take instant action to do whatever was necessary to secure an aim or purpose with whatever degree he felt it demanded. There were other veterans in the area for certain, but Allison was a man who had a short fuse when it came to push and shove, and carried it a cut above mere survival. During a personal encounter he looked upon his six-gun as an implement, a tool with which he made his indelible point. And he was an expert at "getting the drop."

Too, while he cared little about the historical or broader ramifications of the grant drama, and mainly looked upon the squatter as nothing more than a pack of freeloaders, most of the early squatters historically happened to be Mexican, or Mexican Spanish. They had hoped that their squatter's rights would be recognized by the new government. Clay, as a man of the South, was raised in and influenced by a slavocratic, white supremacist culture, and hardly associated them with individual rights. Tragically, many Southern immigrants came west toting their baggage of intolerance with them, conveniently transferring their raciest disdain to the Mexican as well as the Native Indian. Not that they were alone, for they were joined by many whites of every strata of the social spectrum north and south, hoards who were proud members of the burgeoning army of Manifest Destiny who continued spreading westward in a deluge.

"Well," sighed Longwill at Lambert's bar over his snifter of brandy, seated across the table from the Allison brothers. "Election time is just down the road."

"Yeah," agreed Clay. "Time for all pols to do their fancy two-step."

"You're running for Probate Judge, aren't you?" asked John.

"Yes. And Mills for the Legislature."

"You two shouldn't have much trouble," came John's response.

Doctor Longwill, always curious about human behavior and appearances, couldn't help but admire the pair's healthy athletic handsomeness as he hoisted his glass for a sip. Both topped six feet and emitted the aura of supreme confidence. Young John hero-worshipped his senior sibling to the point where he imitated his walk, gestures and speech pattern. He had also grown a goatee to match Clay's, and in a dimly lit room the two could uncannily pass for twins. The doctor thought it was admirable how taken John was over Clay's fearsome reputation, and how he gloried to bask in the elder's reflection. But he also wondered at the healthiness of a man who practically lost his own persona in the cloning process of the surrender of self. And of Clay seemingly encouraging the Trilby-shift. John was becoming a younger Clay. What went on there? It was interestingly odd. No, oddly interesting. No, interesting and odd. No, odd but interesting. Longwill shook his head at his rambling musings mixed with brandy. Or was he soaking his ponderings in the snifter? Ah, but too, he ruminated, trying to focus his mind, John's transmogrification was not only depressing, but downright dangerous.

"It's true enough, John," agreed Longwill, forcing himself away from his splintered intellections. "I have to agree that we will win. And I want you both to know we appreciate you helping us getting out the vote." He wanted to say more but his tongue was getting thick and his brain muddy. And in his growing inebriation he knew his complementing them was an empty gesture, almost an insult, for it was a given that it was just another "payment" they had to make on their future ranch, the obligation of a faithful, but indentured, servant. "What I meant was," and the doctor's words trailed off into embarrassed oblivion, making him wish he had shut his mouth in the first place. It would not do to rile the two Clay's. One was vile enough.

"No problemo, Doc," smiled Clay at Longwill's creeping cloudiness.

"Uh, by the way, Clay," Longwill labored. "I heard thish morning that Mishus Morley's indictment hash been quashed because of a forecasted dire weather condition."

"That's one way of putting it," laughed Clay.

"Yes, a typhoon warning," emphasized the guffawing doctor with his finger thrust in the air. "McCullough put in a quick plea to Catron about the prognostication and begged him to drop the indictment, and he wisely did so."

"See? I told you all I had to do was define a few things for him and he would be bright enough to follow instructions. It sort of makes me once again respect the limited intelligence of postmasters."

Only a few hours after the trio left the bar for their separate retreats, a fracas occurred during a Monte game at around ten that evening in the gaming room of Lambert's Hotel. Francisco Griego, often referred to as "Pancho," a gambler who was also handy with a gun, was dealing at his usual table when a pair of soldiers turned into a couple of bad losers. At a signal they rudely shoved Pancho aside, grabbed a fistful of money, then ran for the door. At that moment two freshly arrived infantrymen were coming through the entrance from the barroom and were rudely brushed aside by the absconding duo. As the dealer regained his footing and balance he drew his knife and gun and turned on the newly arrived men in error who were further shocked by the violent welcome they were given. One was stabbed while another was shot in the leg by the enraged Griego. A third Private, an innocent observer, Benjamin Sheehan, fled for safety into the street but was brought down in the middle of the road by a well-placed shot by the gambler, and killed. The three were members of the Sixth Cavalry stationed at nearby Fort Union, as undoubtedly were the previous two. The next day a warrant was issued for the now fugitive Pancho for, "unlawfully and with malice aforethought shoot with a pistol loaded with powder and ball, Benjamin Sheehan."

Before long Cipriano Lara, a respected and influential individual of the Mexican community, and close friend of the family, was contacted to help extricate the dealer from his difficulty. To do so, Lara had to make a trip to Santa Fe where he made an appointment with U.S. Attorney Thomas Catron and Attorney General William Breeden. Listening to his problem the two pals were all ears and exclaimed they would be only too glad to assist him in his, and Griego's, most dire dilemma. The Ring men refreshed Lara's memory of the upcoming elections and explained that everything would be returned to normal if he and Greigo would help hustle the Mexican vote for the Colfax County Santa Fe Ringers running for office, namely, Longwill for Probate Judge, Mills for the Legislature, and Stephen Elkins, Catron's ex-law partner, for Congress. "It is merely a case of one hand washing the other," the smugly smiling Catron pedantically lectured through clouds of cigar smoke. Feeling like a fettered sacrificial goat, Democrat Lara agreed to the Republicans' proposition, and his deal with the devil was made lighter for his conscience by the thought that he had saved a family friend from prosecution. But it was a bitter pill to swallow, for he was deeply embarrassed to have had to grovel and bargain with such notoriously unprincipled bandits, hat-in-hand. Hand washing? He felt he needed a bath. Why, he wondered, were gringos so predatory and calculating? Why do they need to assert themselves so, stepping on anybody who gets in their way, like Huns arrantly ravaging the countryside? Yet he knew it would be wrong to be so narrow and prejudiced toward them, labeling their behavior as a hallmark of the white man. He married a gringa years ago in Santa Fe and had many gringo friends, blacks too for that matter, and they were far from the low perros he just had to deal with. Like common dogs they were. But why were most of the men in power here deceitful gringos? Well, he did know a few Mexican politicians who were filled with chicanery, so it certainly wasn't a racial trait. Was it merely a case of individuals with an overwhelming need for power and control? Do they in turn seek similar souls to ally themselves with, until they become a gathering of men with sympathetic aims, a coterie of vultures to systematically prey on others? He recalled the odious Mills back in eighteen hundred and seventy-three and his salivating comments at winning his first election for Legislature. "I can pass any law I want to in spite of anybody that is not here, or most anybody who might come here. I have got in with the big side with a little sharp figuring." Talk about dogs! And that drunken bully Allison with his collection of raciest, raiding Tejanos. Worse than perros. Puta perros! Chingaderos! Ay, what's the use? Fucking gringos, he seethed. He then shook his head and shrugged his shoulders and returned to Cimarron.

In a short time Griego surrendered to Sheriff Turner in Cimarron and was taken before J.P. Simpson. Following a brief and private consultation with Mills and Longwill, the dealer was released within the hour on a thousand dollar bond, with instructions to appear at the next term of court in August. When court reconvened then, Lara was appointed interpreter, Griego's case was presented to the grand jury, and then satisfactorily discharged. Griego was now a free man.

The Reverend Thomas F. Tolby was a perpetual thorn in the leathered hides of the Santa Fe Ring from the time he arrived in Cimarron two and one half years before. From Morocco, Indiana, he had been assigned to Colfax County as a circuit rider by the Methodist Episcopal Church. Thirty-one at the time, he was accompanied by his wife Mary and their two small children. His route took him from the new county seat of Cimarron to the now gold mining village of Elizabethtown, the ex-county seat, a distance of thirty miles. Described as, "a noble preacher for one his age, but having a hard field," he soon became a popular and respected man with much of the citizenry. He also had a strong sense of justice, and was a man who not only sermonized on ethical and principled conduct, but lived it daily.

Unfortunately, during his residency his belief system alienated him from certain men of power connected with the Santa Fe Ring side of the grant dispute. He never missed a chance to verbally flog their dishonesty, theft and avarice. In his crusade for justice he also unswervingly felt that the maltreated Ute and Apache tribes, grudgingly tolerated by both the grant company and the settlers, were the rightful owners of the land and insisted that the county be returned to them as a vast reservation. Although an unpopular notion, it was already earlier suggested by Kit Carson and a few others that the U.S. Government purchase the Maxwell Grant for them, for it would save much money in the final analysis, making them self-supporting. Tolby had of late taken over several pieces of property along the Vermejo River to lay the groundwork for his own proposed tribal colony. Although the natives were removed a few years earlier from a reservation near Taos and shifted to the edge of Cimarron, it was an inadequate patch of ground, and the rations doled out to the tribes was of lean sustenance. And to round out his enemies, the crusading parson denounced the outlaw gangs that infested Cimarron and its environs, vowing to do what he could to disband them.

During the first week in September, Tolby had an inflammatory rant on the streets of Cimarron with the presiding judge of the fall session, Rufus Palen. The judge was no stranger to the parson, for they had encountered each other a few times before. Palen, a Santa Fe Ring man, in their latest confrontation, chewed out the reverend for criticizing the court. Tolby then castigated the judge for his seemingly overly-sympathetic treatment of Pancho Griego. The padre further announced that he would air his views in a national newspaper where two hundred thousand readers would read of his corrupt practices. Articles had already appeared occasionally in the *New York Sun* to the chagrin of the Santa Feers, which raked Elkins, Catron and others over the well known coals, and it was believed Tolby had authored them. As an additional splash of acid during their meeting, the parson threw in the name of Florencio Donoghue, a Ring man and postal contractor of Cimarron, and business partner of Griego, against whom he said he had enough evidence of mail fraud to send to prison. The two parted bitterly with threats on both sides.

Days later, as the reverend was riding on the outskirts of town, he heard an argument between two men coming from a copse of trees and shrubbery. Walking his horse toward the shouts he saw it was Griego exchanging curses with a gringo. As he sat his mount he watched in horror as Pancho pulled a gun and shot the man. Holstering his weapon the tall Mexican turned and paled at the sight of the witness. "I will see that you are prosecuted for this!" shouted Tolby as he quickly and wisely turned and galloped away. The distressed shooter stood frozen and helpless. Griego squeezed his fists in furious self-rage at his carelessness, at his not looking about before killing this fool. He wondered if he should follow the heathen bible-thumper and put him away? No, too late.

Tolby too was enraged, but at the scene he had just witnessed, a cold-blooded murder. It was a reflection of the continuous bloodshed and flaunting of the law which had become so common in the region. But also, he was elated, happy that he would see Griego brought to justice, and maybe hanged. As soon as he returned from Elizabethtown Sunday where he was scheduled to hold services, he would press for his indictment. Yes! His crusading heart beat in joy to at last be able to personally strike a blow for the law-abiding community!

The day following, on Friday the eleventh, the final day of court, a routine warrant was issued for Griego to appear again, this time to the charge of keeping a gaming table. The dead-end kid was back.

On Monday morning of September fourteen Elizabethtown dawned with a slight chill, but with the promise of a clear day of pale, if not warm, sunniness. Parson Tolby had held services the day before, Sunday, then spent the night. Now he prepared for his horseback return to Cimarron. He bagged some sandwiches and a piece of cake given him by one of the parishioners. Saying his thank yous and goodbyes, he mounted his horse and headed south. Five miles later he took a left fork eastward. Within minutes he passed through the hamlet of Pascoe, population one hundred thirty-five. Named after resident dairyman Henry Pascoe, the majority of residents were gold miners working for the Aztec Quartz Mill at Mt. Baldy east of Elizabethtown. After about three miles he began ascending a steep, gradual rise. Upon its summit he paused a moment and dismounted to stretch his legs. He had an unhampered, panoramic view of the far-reaching landscape. He could see for miles the north and south stretches of the Moreno Valley. To the west sat the tumbling range of the Sangre de Cristo Mountains, beyond which sat Taos, thirty-two miles to the southwest.

After a few minutes Tolby remounted and continued his ride, descending slowly on the winding road which would lead him into the ruggedly beautiful Cimarron Canyon. The dirt trail had recently been improved and widened for stagecoaches, and followed the swift but shallow and narrow Cimarron River. The original trail had crossed and recrossed the stream thirty-three times in fifteen miles. Following his winding ride through the verdant scenery of the thickly forested stretch, he would exit the canyon onto a flat pastureland twelve miles short of Cimarron. During his journey he found himself somewhat excited at the thought of bringing Griego to justice. Soon as he returned to Cimarron he would call on the sheriff and start legal procedures. Yes.

At the bottom of his descent he was thrust into the edge of the green paradise on the floor of the canyon. As he crossed the first wooden bridge of the many he would take over the river, he saw a perfect grassy spot where he could rest a bit and have lunch. Dismounting in the small glade, he let his horse graze as he sat with his back to a tree and unfolded a sandwich. The last sound he heard was the crack of a rifle shot coming from somewhere to his front. The bullet thumped into his chest and slammed him against the tree trunk with such force it took away his breath, and life.

Later in the day cowboys beating the brush for strays found the crumpled Tolby against a tree with a bullet in his chest. Robbery was not seen as the motive for his personal effects were left untouched. His horse, calmly munching, was tied to a tree six-hundred yards from the corpse. His saddle lay nine-hundred yards in another direction. The killer may have led the mount deeper into the woods for better concealment, possibly less chance for early discovery, then decided to take the saddle as booty. But being either an easily identifiable item or finally too bulky to bother with, the shooter changed his mind and tossed it to the ground as he left the scene. The parson's discoverers draped him across his horse and brought him into Cimarron.

On the following day court had been adjourned four days. Also on that day Pancho was arrested on the gaming charge, then released on a two-hundred dollar bond secured by Lara and Donoghue. Upon acceptance of bond, and since court had terminated its session for the year, Griego was ordered to appear at the next term in eighteen hundred and seventy-six. It was also election day, and the three Ring men easily won their slots.

Four days later a dispatch from Cimarron appeared in the *Daily New Mexican* in reference to the Tolby killing, stating that, "It is thought that the murderer is a white man and paid for the job."

The Cimarron Masonic Lodge, of which Tolby was a Second-Degree member, immediately offered a five-hundred dollar reward. On September eighteen he was interred in the town cemetery with Masonic honors. A little more than three weeks later Governor Samuel Beach Axtell issued a proclamation of an additional five-hundred dollars "for the apprehension and conviction of person or persons who committed or instigated the cruel deed." But as time went on nothing came of the monetary enticements.

For six weeks no new evidence or suspects arose to give answer to the killing, only the undercurrent of suspicion that the Santa Fe Ring had the parson quieted for his constant carping against them, and especially for the revealing newspaper articles in the *Sun*. So of course the anti-Santa Feers were more prone to create and enshroud them with dark rumors of a conspiracy. But who was the triggerman? Was he still among them, one of the handful of neer' do wells ready for a quick buck? Or was he an imported assassin who came and went like a slippery miasmic ghost, and was now elsewhere, perhaps in another state, continuing his work? Several rumors floated about, even an outrageous one that Tolby had been the target of a jealous husband. So for over a month local citizens wondered who it was the *Daily New Mexican* of Santa Fe described as, "a white man paid for the job."

Because of his rough reputation Clay Allison's name was often brought up in whispers here and there. His killings were recalled, his drunken antics, his meanness when under the influence. For over five years he was the one man no one dared cross or have a cross word with. But his friends defended him, knowing it was not his method to ambush a man in the woods, or shoot a man from ambush. He was a confrontationalist, and proud of it. Look at Colbert, shot in the head from the front, a fair duel if there ever was one. Of course there were no witnesses, and where was Colbert's sidekick, Cooper? Some said his body was found a week or two later in the hills behind the Clifton House and buried there. And Kennedy's execution was a volitional group affair. Nothing unusual there. Hell, everybody knew Kennedy was as guilty as sin, and he even had a fair trial before a second voluntary jury took over and sent him to hell. Well, yes, but what about Clay working as a hired hand for the Santa Feers? Don't that mean something? What if…?

"I'm telling you John, and you too, Doc," snarled Clay over a bottle at Lambert's. "If I personally hear anyone claim I shot Tolby, I'll kill his ass quicker than lightening!"

"Clay," emphasized Longwill. "There is absolutely no way you are responsible for the death of Tolby. And there is no way the Ring is, either. Believe me, they would not be so stupid. That killing was a local affair. But damn if anyone can figure out why."

"That's no comfort to me either way, Doc. I'm so suspect most people avoid me, whether I'm drunk or sober." Clay suddenly roared in laughter at his last words, realizing the drollness in them. John and Longwill joined him.

"Hell," sighed Longwill. "Glad you haven't lost your sense of humor, anyway. Listen, I understand Parson McMains has been scouring the countryside playing the grim avenger, trying to dig out who could have done this. Maybe you should get in touch with him and see if he's come up with anything."

"McMains? Yeah, you're right, he has. Don't know him too well, although I've been to a few of his anti-grant meetings for curiosity. Think I'll look him up."

"Be careful though," cautioned Longwill. "He's a little fiery-headed and apt to go off the deep end. Whatever he might come up with, try and make certain it isn't just a suspicious mind working. He's in a fury over Tolby's killing, and I don't blame him, but he would love to connect it to the Ring, whom I know had nothing to do with it."

"Hell, I trust your judgment, Doc, regardless of the Ring coat you wear. But then I've been wearing the same coat too, much as I'd never admit it to anyone else but you and John. You just keep in touch and let me know if anything new comes up, and I'll do the same on this end, all right?"

"Yes sir, you got that right."

Following Tolby's slaying his pastor friend Oscar P. McMains took up the anti-grant cudgel and ran with it. The thirty-four-year-old preacher had come down from Colorado six months earlier to serve as Tolby's assistant. Born in Ohio, he worked nine ministries in ten years in south-central Colorado before being sent to Cimarron. To boost his income he worked as a part-time printer for the *Cimarron News & Press* having learned the trade in his mid-teens. Soon he became so absorbed in the Maxwell Land Grant fight it eclipsed his ministerial duties to the point where he was relieved of his religious assignments. Yet he maintained his role as a some-time minister, performing marriages, baptismals and occasional services.

Roughly six weeks after Tolby's shooting, McMains picked up rumors of a pair of suspects, the cousins Manuel Cardenas and Cruz Vega. Digging into their past, he found they had been orphaned young and raised by the Griegos. As boys they earned the reputation of incorrigible delinquents, and if anything was amiss in Cimarron the two were immediately sought. Both had served six months in the New Mexico Mounted Infantry during the Civil War and fought at the Battle of Valverde in the southern part of the state. While Vega appeared the less inclined toward violence, Cardenas proved the opposite. In eighteen hundred and sixty-three, shortly after his discharge, Cardenas killed a man in Taos and was sentenced to three years hard labor for murder in the fifth degree.

Probing further, the clergyman heard that Cardenas was in Taos at the time of the discovery of Tolby's body, and was said to have announced a little too prematurely that, "a Protestant heretic had been killed." He also found that on the day of the murder, postal contractor Florencio Donoghue hired Vega to deliver the mail to Elizabethtown, and sometime later Cardenas joined him on the trail. Vega was reportedly a short ride behind Tolby on both their return to Cimarron, and if so, he had to have seen or heard something.

With this information McMains was ecstatic, feeling he was finally onto something. Now he had to somehow arrange the questioning of the two men. He approached a merchant-friend, Isaiah Rinehart, but he was not interested, feeling a little uncomfortable at McMains' methodology. Frustrated, the parson cast about in his head for someone he could trust, someone also with the desire to get to the bottom of the crime, someone who was not interested in only paying lip-service to justice. Slightly depressed, he walked his horse along a trail on the outskirts of town, wondering what to do. As he looked up he saw Clay and John Allison riding toward him. Providence! he thought.

"Mister Allison," he hailed with a smile.

"Reverend McMains, I presume," greeted Clay.

"That it is. And I assume this is your brother, John?"

"Yes. We all have not been formally introduced, but here we are. Hope you're well?"

"Better, now that I've seen you. We must talk, Mister Allison. Please."

"Call me Clay. All this mistering gets me nervous."

"As you wish, sir. I suppose you are on your way to your ranch?"

"Yes, we are."

"Then allow me to join you, and we will talk along the way. That is, if I am not intruding?"

"No, please join us. Be a pleasure. If you haven't had dinner, join us for that too. I'm sure we can rustle up an extra steak or two."

"Thank you, Clay. You are more than kind."

As they rode toward the coming evening McMains revealed all he had discovered of the cousins' background, movements and suspicians. "There is no concrete proof of their guilt, Clay, but I propose they be taken up quietly and questioned as to their movements, and what they may know of the sad and tragic affair."

"Damn," elated Clay. "I believe you done hit the nail on the head, parson. Back then somewhere, somehow, I smelled a fucking beaner in the woodpile! Damn if I didn't! Excuse my language, sir, but I'm afraid my excitement at such good news has carried me away."

"Quite all right, Clay, quite all right. And so, are you with me on the idea of questioning the two?"

"Yessiree, by God! Just try and stop me. I'm with you a thousand percent, and then some!"

"Good. Get a few of your men together and I'll set it up. Come into town this Saturday night. I'll meet you at the Ponil bridge on the main road at midnight and we'll take it from there. If anything happens, like any change in plans, I'll send word."

With that the three ate a hearty meal of steak, sweet potatoes and tortillas, rounded off with at least a gallon of coffee.

Allison's eagerness toward McMains' plan to "interview" the suspects centered around his desire to clear up the circulating stories of his being the possible shooter. He also of course would be the last to admit or accept that he had not helped matters any by his own nurturing of his reputation for raw violence, thus opening the way for detractors to target him. He now felt a great burden lift from his shoulders, sensing that a confession was just around the corner.

He didn't know the two suspects, but had seen Donoghue in Cimarron now and then. As for Griego, he had seen him only once, and that was about a month previous in a cantina in what the Anglos called "Mexican Town," a small barrio across the Cimarron River from Lambert's hotel. It was a settlement of adobes which held a grocery store, several bars and a whore house. There, many a cowboy would party it up on weekends, including the Allisons. A few times before, during one of his visits, is when he saw Griego, late at night in one of the bars. The music was played by a trio of Mexicans, a guitar, violin and a base viol, as Mexicans and gringos mixed it up on the dance floor. As he was dancing with Tina Menchaca, his woman of choice whenever he visited, he noticed a well-dressed Mexican smoking a cigarro looking his way, and they caught each other's eyes several times. He was sitting with five or six men at a table drinking, eating and laughing. "Tina, who's that Mexican dude dressed in black looking this way?"

"Ahhh, that is Francisco Griego, es muy bonito hombre."

"Bonito, eh? Hope he isn't foolish enough to be measuring me up for a notch."

"Jesu, Maria! You men and your stupid machismo flexing! Mexicans and gringos alike, both like children in the playground playing king of the hill. Don't any of you grow up?"

"Whoa, take it easy," he grinned. "I'm not looking for his scalp."

"Then why make such a challenging remark?"

Tina was from Mexico City and had some education. But the family fell on hard times and she took to the fields for work with the peons. Quitting that laborious direction she did house keeping and cleaning for the upper classes in town. Tired of being treated as a social inferior by whom she felt were no better than she, she drifted north with many others looking for a better life. A year later she was in Santa Fe where she hoped that the late great gringo encroachment into the southwest would offer better economic opportunities. But she found both cultures held the female as little more than a household drudge, an attitude archaic and stifling to her. She found a few old friends from Mexico City, a cousin even, and they lived together, pooling and sharing their earnings in order to survive. One, then two, of her female friends finally went to work for a madam.

"Tina," said her cousin. "You are such a pretty woman, why don't you come with us and work the streets for a while. Linda and I quit the house and went out on our own, and concentrating on the more well-to-do, are doing quite well."

Tina, twenty, was an exceptionally attractive woman. Light-complexioned and finer-featured because of being more Spanish-blooded than Mexican, she had shoulder length jet-black hair, large eyes of deep green, and a perfect set of ivories which lit up her face when she smiled.

"Oh, Soledad, I don't think so. All those damn dirty pigs out there you sometimes have to service would send me vomiting. I have nothing against what you and many women have to do to make a living, but it's not an appetizing road for me."

"But we take only the more well-off men. Even some of the Mexican merchants have become a few of our clientele. It's more like being their second wives, but without the housecleaning and cooking," she laughed.

A year earlier Tina had had her first man, her first love affair, and her first heartbreak, a scoundrel waggoneer from Arkansas who left her for another. Finding herself pregnant she aborted. Then more pissed than heartbroken she hunted him down with an ancient pistol in order to shoot him. One night she found him busily making the beast with two backs in a hotel room with his new beloved. Standing in the middle of the room she stared a moment, fascinated. Having never seen couples copulate before, she almost forgot what her intentions were. The woman could see her from beneath her pumping swain standing with the pistol and screamed again and again, but the Arkansan paid absolutely no attention to her alarums, he joyously believing she was caught up in the passion of his expertise thrusting. But something caused him to slow, then turn, perhaps some echoedsense of his embedded survival instinct. His eyes bugged at seeing the tiny, armed Tina, and he froze in mid-stroke. In seconds Tina quashed the desire to kill him and merely beat him a dozen times about the head and shoulders with the firearm, leaving him bleeding and unconscious on the floor and the woman frantically sobbing.

A week later she mulled over Soledad's suggestion and decided to give it a try. Her youth and subtle beauty brought her more customers than she cared to handle, and so she could pick and choose as she felt. But sadly, the trade quickly coarsened her, giving her a cold layer of cynicism. Most of her customers were gringos, some Mexicans and Spanish. She met Francisco Griego one night, and was enchanted by his good looks and glibness, and devil-may-care personality. But like so many of the others she bedded, he was married, and with so many of the others she looked to herself as their second wife, the one who could bring back a touch of brief romance and excitement that became lost with the years of boring monotony living with the same person.

But even whores in Santa Fe were not immune to economic pressure, and this time it came in the form of professional jealousy. The madams found their best customers lost to a half dozen independent interlopers. As a result several were beaten, while another was slain in a dark alley. Tina packed and left. She went to Taos, then to Cimarron from where her cousin had written her.

She met Griego once again, and he still paid well, as did Clay Allison and others in the more professional class. She was looking ahead, saving her earnings with the idea of renting a house with her cousin, somewhere away from the crowd for a more conducive atmosphere more in keeping with their select clientele. Then in ten years she would be gone, with money saved, to maybe San Francisco, and find a well-to-do husband while she still had what was left of her looks.

When Clay first met her he was drawn like a magnet. Not only was she exceptionally attractive, she was brainy and witty, and spoke excellent English with hardly an accent, and the accent seemed more European, maybe Italian. Perhaps it was because she had taught herself a smattering of Italian and French, and it affected her pronunciations in a feyish manner. Clay once made the mistake of speaking down to her, and never did so again, finding she was nobody's fool. "Just what is a pretty and smart light-skinned woman like you doing working in a, uh, place like this?"

"Ah, you mean I remind you of some of your white whores, senor redneck? First, I am a Mexican and proud of it. Second, I am light-complexioned because the copulating Spanish whoremonger Conquistadors left a lot of bastards behind while busily looting Mexico of its gold. And thirdly, women are not looked upon as much of an asset, except for cooking, cleaning and childbearing, hence our limited opportunities for an education to better ourselves in so many of the professions still dominated by your macho species. And so now, you tell me: what is a handsome, well-mannered, fairly successful cowman, although of limited education, doing here, drinking rotgut and paying for pussy when it appears obvious you certainly have the intelligence to find a decent woman to spend your life with?"

"Good grief," stunned Allison. "You're the second woman I've met with a brain that is both attractive and enchanting, as well as puzzling and a cipher. I don't know whether to turn you over my knee and spank you for mouthy insolence, or to kiss you and ask forgiveness for being a male."

"Well, mi bonito corazon," she smiled. "I think your last suggestion would be a wonderful dessert to my words. They are wasted on you anyway," she quipped as she slid off her chemise.

The soft glow of her perfectly flawless body shown in the dimly lit room like a smooth ivory statue. Clay never tired feasting his eyes upon her, wishing often they were together elsewhere, in a clime where no one knew her past, where maybe they... and then he would shake his head as if waking himself from a dream to join the world of reality which coldly equalized everything to a common denominator, even dreams.

McMains had three days to set things up, and while Cardenas was still holed up in Taos, he found that Vega was in town. He quickly got a hold of a farmer, William Lowe, and had it arranged for Vega to guard his cornfield over Saturday night against invented thieves. Lowe had hired him and Cardenas both over the years for occasional labor, so it wasn't anything unusual to make him suspicious of anything.

Early Sunday morning Vega was kicked awake next to the dying embers of his campfire. As he looked up he saw a ring of kerchief-masked cowboys variously armed staring down at him. Several were passing a bottle back and forth in a thirsty fashion. "Get up, you goddamn beaner!" ordered the tall one. "We want to have a word with you."

As he began to rise in panic, a half-dozen hands pulled him roughly to his feet. But before he was standing he was punched back to the ground where he was kicked, stomped and whipped with lariat ends. "Stop, stop! Por Dios, who are you? What ees eet you want?" Vega cried out.

"We want to know who shot parson Tolby! You or Cardenas?"

Frightened, howling in pain, he curled himself into a ball in order to make a smaller target, but it was no use. He was yanked to his feet again, beaten severely as a pair of men held his arms, then a noose tossed over his head while his wrists were tied behind him. Telegraph lines were lately being installed from Raton, and it was a convenience the questioners took advantage of. A rope was thrown over the arm of one of the poles and the bleeding Mexican was pulled upward off his toes and held as he gagged and choked. After a few moments Allison ordered, "Enough, Zenas. Drop him!" Down he was dropped, coughing and sputtering.

"Talk, goddamn it! Who shot him?"

Fearing to say anything, Vega held his silence, crying in pain and terror.

Zenas, haul 'em up!" Up he was elevated on his tip-toes and held. After ten or fifteen seconds, Clay called out, "All right, Zenas, drop 'em!" Down he fell in a trembling heap. Two or three of the inquisitionists stepped forward to kick and punch him again. Face lacerated badly, eyes mere slits from lumps on his face, he begged them to stop. "We'll stop when you answer our questions, greaser. Now talk, damn you!"

"Now, men," spoke McMains, horrified at the murderous turn of events. "Perhaps if we..."

"Shut up, Mac," replied Allison. "I'm in charge here. He don't talk, he's a dead man!"

"But, Clay, we must ascertain his responsibility first. He may be innocent!"

"For the last time, shut up, or get your ass outta here. Yank'em up, Zenas!"

Frightened, McMains slowly backed away from the group who were now wild men intent on blind vengeance, confession or not. Laughing and drinking, several stepped forward to use the half-suspended Vega as a punching bag. Sickened by what could hardly be discerned as a human face in the noose, the reverend turned and ran into the dark night, splashing across Ponil Creek, seeking safety in a nearby ranch house from what was now an out-of-control mob.

"Drop 'em, Zenas!" Down the teen-aged vigilante dropped him.

Vega lay quaking from head to foot, wheezing and whining for mercy.

"You want to go home where it's nice and warm and safe?" asked Allison.

"Si, si," sobbed the beaten body of Cruz Vega. "Por favor!"

"Then speak up. Tell us what happened. We already know most of it. We just need the details. Then you can go."

"Gracias, mucho gracias, senor," he sighed, trembling. "Eet was my cousin, Manuel Cardenas. He was waiting near the forst bridge een the trees for Tolby, who was just ahead of me earlier. I had galloped aroun' and ask heem, please not to do this, he was only a gringo priest, a good man, but he don' listen. He shoot heem then ride for Taos."

"Who put you up to this?"

After a small hesitation, Vega said, "Florencio Donoghue and Francisco Griego."

"I figured Griego was in this. But why, what in hell for?"

"A few days before he go to E-Town to preach he see Francisco shoot and kill some gringo, and he tol' heem, the padre said, he would tell the law and put heem in jail. Francisco was 'fraid for hees life, he already shoot some soldiers. And so he tol' Florencio, and Florencio hire me to run mail that day, and for Manuel to do the shooting. He mostly hire me instead of another so there would be no witness. Please, por favor, I feel so bad for padre Tolby, but Manuel would not listen."

"Thanks, Cruz. Boys, take him for a ride through the pasture for a while. I've heard enough."

"Gracias, senor, mucho gracias," effused Vega, thinking he were at last to be released.

Several men lashed a lariat around his booted feet and handed the end to a rider, who in turn looped it around his saddle horn. In a moment Vega was hauled through the brush and greasewood feet-first like a sack of grain behind a galloping horseman. His twisting and bouncing body hit dirt, rocks and stones which tore at him and his clothes, making a further tatter of both as he was towed back and forth across the field. The rider traded off with another, then another, as each took the rope-end for a turn through the brambles.

"That' s enough," called out Allison, "Let's get outta here!"

Vega lay on his back near the glowing ashes of the campfire. The back of his head was bloody from a large open break after bouncing off a dozen rocks, and he had breathed his last some time in the middle of the sport.

"Well, I'd say his mail-delivering days are over, boys," laughed Allison, up-ending and emptying a bottle. He then drew his Colt, cocked the hammer and squeezed off a round into the dead man's body.

About ten in the morning, Vega's battered corpse was discovered in the field, and an inquest was held on the spot. A tuft of hair ripped from his scalp was found next to him, and around his neck was a loop of rawhide. In the back of his skull was a large hole, likely sustained while being dragged over the stony terrain. A cud of chewing tobacco and an empty liquor bottle lay near the corpse. It was also noted he had been shot once in the chest.

Pancho Griego was informed as to the fate of his nephew and picked up the body in a wagon. Taking the cadaver to a blacksmith shop owned by Will and Henry Wilcox for a coffin, they cleaned up Vega the best they could.

On a chilly November Monday morning, Greigo and a handful of mourners transported the boxed remains to the cemetery for burial. Before they had a chance to drive their shovels into the dirt Clay and a handful of his followers rode up.

"What you got there, Mister Griego?" queried Allison

In quiet fury Griego looked at the dozen mounted men, all their Winchesters pointed skyward, the butt ends resting on taut thighs. "We are about to bury my nephew who was found in a field yesterday morning beaten and murdered."

"My, that is a sad state of affairs. But let me inform you that the parson-killer is not to be buried in this graveyard. Except over my dead body. He said Cardenas pulled the trigger, but as far as I'm concerned, he's just as guilty. Now move on out of here. Now."

Out-manned and outgunned, Pancho could also smell the booze floating in the air like a thick cloud. "Let us go muchachos."

The small group of Mexicans, some walking, some riding, turned and left the cemetery with the coffin-laden wagon in tow. After a few hundred yards they stopped and began to clear away the earth. Allison's group were upon them immediately.

"Another thing, Mister Griego. He's not to be buried within city limits. Savvy?"

In heated humiliation and raging frustration, he wished to cry out a string of curses as he drew his gun and took a few of these sanctimonious gringos with him. But no, to die like a useless fool would be an even greater insult. He would bide his time, and wait. He turned to his group and motioned them to leave with him. Just yards beyond the city limits they stopped again and cleared the earth with their shovels. As Allison and his men rode off, Griego said softly, "There will be a reckoning, my friends. Have patience."

By late that afternoon word had spread like a firestorm that Griego was gunning for Allison, and Clay, no stranger to war, looked forward to the confrontation. As he visited a saloon here and a saloon there, he was kept apprised of the hot rumors that came to him like bulletins from the frontlines. It was late in the afternoon when they finally met, and it was a surprise that a startled Allison thought would be his last. Alone, Clay was walking toward Lambert's just down the street from where he left his horse tied up at the rail an hour before, when he suddenly came face-to-face with his protagonist, Francisco Griego. With Pancho were a pair of his companeros, Florencio Donoghue and Jose Griego, a cousin. They were also armed for bear, with loaded six-guns and Winchesters, and this time it was his turn to be outgunned and outnumbered. Allison froze in mid-step, left hand raised palm up, right fist clutching the butt of his Colt. Never one to admit defeat, or even the possibility of being in a second-best situation, he calmly stared into Griego's eyes and said, "I know you're a damn good man with a gun, Pancho, but I also hear you are very fair, a man of honor. After all that's happened, don't you agree we should sit like intelligent men and discuss our differences over what has taken place, and why we are doing what we are doing?"

"I know what I intend to do," retorted Griego. Nodding his head. "Eliminate a gringo who has become a local pain in the ass."

"I'd be the first to admit I've been tough on a few people around here, but there isn't a one of them, if they could come back, wouldn't agree they deserved it."

"Like a band of drunken Tejanos beating a tied-up Mexican to death?"

"Put yourself in their place a minute. Suppose some gringo murdered some Mexican Penitente. Wouldn't you and a few of your amigos look into it, even a bit forcibly, to find out who did it?"

Griego stared at Allison in fascination and could not but help admire his coolness. He wanted to drop him in his tracks, and was ready to do so in a moment without a qualm, or scruple, as Allison undoubtedly knew. What made this man so fearless? Was he estupido, or did he truly have ice water flowing in his veins as many claimed? If he wasn't stupid, then he was the most dangerous man anyone could confront. His silly jabbering was a bunch of boniga, cow shit, a desire to buy time. Hell, as far as the three of us were concerned he was already living on borrowed time. With a quick pull of our triggers we could immediately terminate what few minutes we had loaned him. Yet here he was unbelievably blathering away as if he had all the time in the world, as if he were casually discussing the weather. Mucho huevos.

Allison had been calmly dropping words upon Griego who was half-listening, when the tall Mexican in black laughed and shook his head with, "Gringo, you have more balls than sense."

"Then, hell's bells, Pancho," grinned Clay. "Let's go have a drink or two at Lambert's and iron this out. On me. What do you say?"

"I must be the stupid one, gringo." With that Griego turned and handed his rifle to Jose, saying, "Here, take care of this. I might need it later." Griego and Allison then walked on to Lambert's and into the barroom.

It was vacant with only a pair of lanterns on the bar top giving off illumination. As they approached the bar Henry Lambert spoke up. "Greetings, gentlemen. Must be the Monday night blues, hardly any bar business at all. I'm busy cooking for the evening dinner crowd, but let me serve you before I leave. What'll it be?"

"Give us a bottle of your best rye, Henry, and two water glasses. Me and Pancho here have a hellova thirst, and might be a while drowning it out. Put it on my tab."

"You betcha," laughed Lambert. "You boys help yourself, see you later."

Having poured the glasses half-full, Clay raised his and toasted, "To your health," and downed it. "And yours," echoed Griego as he also emptied his.

Refilling the vessels, Allison looked over toward the wall at the pool table. "Say, hombre, are you any good at pool?"

"One of the ways I make my money, gringo," he smiled

"Damn, and I thought I was about to make an easy pile of dinero."

"Not this time, senor. You have more than met your match."

"Well, shit. I'm a good sport and don't mind losing to a man of skill. Let's go."

Griego turned and walked to the pool rack against the wall on the far side of the pool table. Selecting a cue from a few he hefted, he turned and said, "I'll even let you have the first break."

But what he saw when he turned was the end of the game, and his mouth gaped open at his colossal stupidity. Allison stood before him with a cocked Colt leveled at his chest. It was all over.

"I already took the break. Adios, bonito. Isn't that what Tina calls you? Bonito hombre? How about estupido bonito? Or estupido hombre? Either way, greaser, hang up your cue. You've scratched."

Three quick shots roared through the room as Francisco Griego was impacted against the wall and slid to the floor behind the pool table. Allison calmly finished his drink, corked the bottle and took it with him as he made a swift exit. It had been a busy Monday.

Not long after Lambert discovered Griego's body Tuesday mid-morning, the Mexican population, already infuriated over Vega's thrashing and shooting, heavily armed itself and moved about town in restless clusters. Near noon, as if in answer to his challenged actions and authority, Clay and a dozen of his cronies galloped into Cimarron creating general chaos and terror, racing through the streets and shooting at anything that moved. Chickens and geese again were the preferred menu for a handful of families for several days. Allison and a few of his followers entered the bar at the St. James, ordering bottles of liquid fire to feed their already fueled stomachs and heads. Before too long, John Dawson, an old cattle-driving crony of Allison's, loped into town and tied-up before the St. James. Breathless and eager, he was on a self-appointed mission of diplomacy, looking forward to calming the big man down and divert his small army out of town.

"Clay!" he howled in a friendly fashion at the bar. "How in the world are you? Ain't seen you in a coon's age."

Allison's beady red eyes took him in with a snarl. "Who in hell wants to know?"

"It's me, Clay, ol' John Dawson, your ol' trail-buddy from back in Texas."

"Well, hell if you aren't! Have a drink on me, boy," and he poured Dawson a heavy dose of firewater in a glass.

"Well, uh, don't you think you should kinda slow it down a mite? I mean, I—" and he stumbled over his words as he beheld Allison's crimson orbs squeezing in on his face with malice.

"John, better you should show your respect for our friendship as well as your life and drink up. Now don't give me another word of bullshit, or I'll bury you next to Griego."

"N-no, Clay, sure," and he swiftly drank up and hurried out before wasting another second of his precious life. Physically shaking as he leaped into the saddle and raced off, the picture of Allison drunk on blood and whiskey followed him for miles, and he realized what a fool's errand it was to attempt reasoning with him.

Two days later at three in the afternoon Allison returned to replay his performance with his Tejano Myrmidons to once again hold Cimarron at bay. This time he and several of his men paid a visit to the *News & Press* where they bullied the printer, Will Dawson. They shoved him about smacking his hands with a rifle muzzle, and threatened him by flourishing a knife in has face. Allen Wallace tried to intercede, but was pushed aside with warnings. That evening after their usual dosage of refreshments at Lambert's the revelers decamped.

The following night, like the proverbial copper coin, Clay thundered into town with his groupies for a return engagement, once more taking over Lambert's saloon. As the evening wore on the men grew louder and boisterous, like an out-of-control army of occupation. Someone broke out a fiddle, another a mouth organ, and everyone jumped and hopped about like an erratic bunch of beans on a hot stove to the off-key violin scraping and the dissonant high-pitched whine of the harmonica, calling it a hoedown. There was still a nice-sized blood stain on the floor before the pool rack where Francisco Griego spent his last night on earth.

"Hey, Clay," yelled Crockett. "This must be the spot where Pancho was! Looky everybody!"

Here and there a drunk would amble over to eye the sacred stain, a few emitting a whistle of appreciation and awe.

"Move the hell outta there," ordered Allison. "Push 'em back, John!" he yelled. Within a few moments he had his boots and pants off, then tied a red ribbon around his penis which he pulled out of his long johns. Howling and whooping like a Buntline Redskin, Allison hopped about on one foot then the other in a war dance of his own invention atop the bloodstain, and in between his whoops calling out, "Pancho, go! Pancho, go! Pancho go to unhappy hunting ground!" Everyone burst out in laughter at the sight of the bouncing Allison and his bobbing penis decorated with a red strip of fabric.

It wasn't too long after this colorful celebration that Manuel Cardenas crawled from his hole. For some strange, unfathomable reason, perhaps having inherited the unmitigated gene of a risk-taker, he returned to the cauldron. In Elizabethtown he was swiftly snatched up for a preliminary hearing concerning Tolby's death. The man who grilled him was Joseph Herberger, a psychotic-tempered saloon keeper who executed his own brand of personal justice. Back in eighteen hundred and sixty-eight he beat a Captain Keefer to death with a fireplace log over a liquor bill, and in eighteen hundred and eighty-seven he would shoot a rival bar owner to death because he drew more customers. His journey in life finally ended in a madhouse.

"So tell me, Mister Cardenas," asked Herberger, seated across from the suspect. "What do you know about the killing of parson Tolby?"

"Not too bery much, Meester 'erberger."

"Just call me Joe," the inquisitor smiled, as he drew a Colt from his waistband and cocked it slowly, the barrel pointed toward Cardenas. The familiar four clicks of the hammer being thumbed back echoed metallically and cold. Laying the revolver on its side, barrel still pointed at the Mexican, Herberger spoke softly and slowly, as if in confidence, yet with murderous inflection. "You tell me the truth and you won't get hurt. You might even walk out of here alive. What do you have to say?"

Cardenas' eyes rolled around as if looking for an exit, or a champion to rally to his side. But he could see nor find either. "Uhummm, Meester erberger...."

"Just call me Joe," he urged with a broad smile.

"Uh, Senor Joe. Hokay, eet was like thees. Florencio Donoghue an' Pancho Griego hire us. Cruz would follow behind Tolby then kill heem in the canyon. I was only there een case somebody, like a witness, have to be scare away. I was on the road going to meet Cruz when I hear one shot. My horse, he even jump at the noise. I ride a little and see Cruz on heese horse holding a rifle. I ask, "Muchacho, deed you get a bear or something?"

"No," he say. Then he laugh and say, "But I got a gringo, they always in season." I say, "Cruz, I don' think thees ees right, shooting a padre. He was a good man. Ees no right, amigo."

But he say, "No, Manuel, eet had to be. He was witness to Pancho killing a gringo and Tolby was going to report heem. So we have to save Pancho."

"Ahhh," grinned Herberger. "And I think I know who was behind Griego and Donoghue."

Cardenas was confused. "But, no, only they…"

"Keep quiet and listen to me. You want to leave this room alive? Or maybe strung up on that tree out there?" He motioned to the window with his thumb.

"No, no, no, I leesen. Por Dios!"

"The men behind Griego and Donoghue were Longwill and Mills. Comprende? That's the story you will tell the grand jury, understand? And that's the story that will save your life. All right?"

"Ohhh, I see. Of course, of course. I onnerstan' now. Si."

"Good. We're through now. We'll be taking you to Cimarron for the grand jury inquest down the road. But don't forget your story."

When the "new" information seeped into Cimarron that the Santa Fe Ring duo Longwill and Mills were the contractors behind the Tolby assassination, there was unsurprisingly a not-too minor seismic reaction. Doctor Longwill was alerted of the accusation by Judge E. F. Mezeck, and the two immediately sped in Mezeck's buckboard to the safety of Fort Union. Giving chase was Sheriff Pete Burleson with freshly appointed deputies Clay and John Allison who were hot to grab hold of him for a questioning session, but were a hair slow at nabbing him. Hearing of the couple's flight, the trio gave chase and were within sight of the bouncing wagon drawn by a pair of sweaty steeds being frantically whipped by Mezeck. It was nip and tuck the entire forty miles to the Fort, and closing in near the end as the two approached the fortress gates Clay let out a roar, "Damn you, Longwill!

Hold up there! We only want to talk to you!" But the good doctor exchanged what was left of his and Allison's friendship for survival, and rolled into the compound, sliding to a stop before the commander's office. Leaping to the ground they ran in and explained hysterically their life-and-death dilemma. At the door the pursuing trio were met by Captain Ellis informing them that the two men were in his custody as his wards seeking safety from a hostile environment.

"Now listen, Captain. I'm Sheriff Burleson from Cimarron and all we want to do is question Doctor Longwill a bit concerning a murder he may have had connections with."

"Sorry, Sheriff, I respect your authority, but at the moment they are in my custody since requesting military protection. They aren't going anywhere until legal proceedings are followed. I could not possibly under any circumstances release them to you."

The Allisons were in a fury, as was Burleson, for after all their wild chasing they had hit a brick wall.

"Goddamn you, Longwill!" shouted Clay through the closed door, giving it a booming kick. "You ever show your thankless ass in Colfax County again, it'll be for the last time!"

"Corporal of the guard!" called the captain. Several men appeared with rifles at-arms, and a few others were advancing behind them. "Escort these three men to the gate and see that they don't re-enter this compound again! Good day, gentlemen." He turned and entered his office and closed the door. Clay seethed at the wooden barrier, wanting to break it down and empty his gun into the doctor's head. Fortunately he was sober, so the soldiers and Longwill were safe.

Mills, less intimidated, angrily took a coach from Trinidad to Cimarron the day after Longwill's escape to Fort Union. In Cimarron he was rudely dragged off the vehicle by a heated mob with the intentions of swinging him from a tree. Miraculously rescued by a few of his cooler-headed friends, namely Frank Springer and Henry Lambert, he was placed in jail with Florencio Donoghue.

The November grand jury hearing in Cimarron was a long session, lasting until ten that night. The murder charge against Allison for the killing of Griego was dropped since there were no witnesses, and no one appeared for the prosecution. Testimony also demonstrated that Griego had made threats against Allison's life, so the shooting was ruled justifiable. As for the Cruz Vega caper, six men were indicted for murder, and eight for assault in a menacing manner. While John faced the assault charge, Clay was the only one charged with both. The men were instructed to appear at the next term of court in eighteen hundred and seventy-six. During the hearing Cardenas retracted his earlier statement made in Elizabethtown, labeling Longwill and Mills as the men behind Griego and Donoghue. He insisted that Joseph Herberger had coerced him into implicating the Ring men at gunpoint. Herberger claimed indignantly that there was no force used to get him to make the statement, that he went into the room alone and laid his pistol on the table and told Cardenas he would not be hurt. All he had to do was tell the truth. It was eventually revealed that Longwill and Mills had assured the inquisitionist a political plum during the last elections, but had reneged on their promise. The result was revenge and their names tacked onto Cardenas' confession. Mills was then released for lack of evidence, and since Longwill was still in Santa Fe, where he wisely remained for the rest of his medical career, no decision was made concerning him.

As Cardenas was being escorted under guard back to jail, shots rang out in the dark night and he fell to his death in a perforated state. Everybody scattered for safety, including the unknown sniper. With this last killing the Mexican community became enraged, feeling that the violent deaths of three of their own in such a lawless fashion was unjustified, murderers or not. It was Clay who became the target of their outburst, his raciest bulldozing having reached a saturation point with them. The situation was so critical, a pair of lawmen suggested he keep a low profile for a time.

"Damn," oathed Allison to the newly elected sheriff, Orson Chittenden, and his deputy, Burleson. "I don't see what them beaners are so excited about. You'd think I'd shot a bunch of angels or saints, for Christ's sake! And besides, most people know that loco saloon keeper Herberger nailed Cardenas, and not me. Not that I wouldn't have minded getting him myself."

"Hell, we know all that, Clay," explained Burleson. "But just for a little while do like we say until they cool down some."

The two lawmen were imploring Allison to lay low for a week or so at Chittenden's ranch, fearing that a sniper would be hunting his scalp before too long. Word was out that he was the target of choice. "It's you in particular they want, Clay," emphasized Chittenden. "And there's no sense in handing them a bullet to use."

"Ain't no way I'm running or hiding from any greaser mob, the hell with them!"

"Please, Clay, you'll be doing us as well as yourself a big favor. There's no sense in purposely antagonizing them people."

The debate continued for some time before Clay grudgingly acquiesced to their wishes. So for two weeks Allison took a vacation from Cimarron at the Chittenden home, twenty miles south of town.

Violence also took a brief and well-deserved vacation during the remaining seven weeks of eighteen hundred and seventy-five. But, not to be deterred from its acclimated thirst for the flowing red stuff, a little discord was being sewn for future strife. There was a falling out at the *Cimarron News & Press* over editorial policy. William Morley and Frank Springer, although remaining with the paper as inactive partners, resigned as editors and left printer Will Dawson in charge. Consequently, the formerly anti-Santa Fe Ring tone of the publication frittered away as Dawson, although altruistically announcing he would maintain an apolitical stance, firmly moved in a pro-Ring direction in several December editorials. This swiftly reignited the furnaces of the local anti-Ring folks, and things began heating up. The vicious harassing, knife threats and hand-beating Dawson had experienced the previous November when Allison and a few of his men paid the paper a visit had strongly influenced his taste for a longer life, so to ensure longevity he obligingly turned his coat. This was the discord which caused partners William Morley and Frank Springer to leave in a snit, and they left trying to figure out how to be rid of him, and with the sour insinuation that Dawson was now probably in the pay of the Santa Feers.

In December Chief Justice Rufus J. Palen passed over to the great beyond and Dawson vigorously stoked the furnace with a long and glowing extolment, describing the deceased as a paragon of virtue unsurpassed, adding to the hagiographic portrait the word "incorruptible." But of course Palen was not looked upon by the anti-grant citizens of Cimarron as anything more than a tool in the Santa Fe Ring's pocket, and the eulogy failed to win over the hearts of the people. They recalled explicitly that Palen and the Reverend Tolby had engaged in an angry and vociferous dispute on the streets of Cimarron just before the parson's death, and believed after that Tolby was a marked man. And to confirm their suspicions, hardly a week after their clash Tolby was murdered.

Next, in the December thirty-first issue, Dawson severely castigated the latest anonymous Santa Fe-postmarked letter which had been published in the *New York Sun*. The article was another slashing commentary on the Santa Fe Ring and its corrupt, exploitive practices concerning the Maxwell Grant. Defending the Ring, Dawson labeled it, "another of those lying, brutal letters," calling the writer "a coward, a disturber of the peace." The author was Morley, whom it was believed had co-authored the earlier letters with the late Reverend Tolby. A copy of the *Sun* article was circulated about town, then a letter signed by one hundred thirty-seven citizens was sent to Dawson requesting that he reprint the *Sun* piece in the *News & Press*, claiming that, in substance, it was true and that Dawson's critique regarding it was in the extreme. Among the one hundred thirty-seven signatures were McMains, Clay and John Allison, and Morley and Springer.

But Dawson ignored their request, thus igniting Allison's wrath once again. This time ironically it was for the editor's pro-Ring stance, for Allison had freshly broken with the Santa Fe bunch in favor of the Colfaxers. The reason for his shift was the Tolby murder, and his belief yet that it had been a Santa Fe Ring assignment. Clay desired now to put as much distance as possible between himself and the Ring, issuing them a divorce in the hopes of reshaping his image.

Earlier the following year, on January fourteenth, eighteen hundred and seventy-six, more fuel was heaped on the fire. Santa Fe Ring robot Governor Samuel B. Axtell signed a judiciary bill attaching Colfax County to Taos County. Although he claimed the aged ploy of maintaining law-and-order, many detected the odor of Santa Fe Ring interference and its desire to exert stronger political control over Colfax County. Axtel held such deep contempt for Colfax County, he seriously toyed with the idea of eliminating it altogether, affixing the western half to Taos County and renaming the other half. It wouldn't be too extreme to wonder whether he played with the idea of honorably naming the new half Axtell County, thus perpetuating and propelling his name far into the future for the sake of history and historians. Yet whatever his ego-dreams and grandiose fantasies, he would be remembered by the locals either way, for this now meant grand and petit juries of Taos County would have charge of all Colfax County cases. Also, to twist the knife, no Colfax citizen could serve on juries, plus they now had the added discomfort of traveling roughly sixty miles across the Sangre de Cristo Mountains to Taos to make court appearances. The people were naturally furious at being so ruthlessly manipulated.

But Dawson, in a moment of enlightenment, must have seen the unfairness of Axtell's proposed plan of attachment, or struck by a guilty conscience, for in mid-January of the new year eighteen hundred and seventy-six he wired the Governor, on a Sunday yet, pleading him not to sign the judiciary bill until he heard from the people of Colfax County. Alas, Dawson was too late, for the Gov. curtly wired back, "Bill signed." Shortly after this William Morley, W.C. Cunningham, a director of the Maxwell Grant Company, and Henry M. Porter, rancher/merchant/banker, also cabled Axtell in an effort to change his mind, but their efforts too were in vain.

As a result a handful of locals expressed their release of built-up frustration on a convenient target, the *News & Press* office. Near midnight on January nineteenth Allison and several of his men broke into the building. Using a charge of black powder, they destroyed the press and threw parts of it into the nearby Cimarron River. Clay then grabbed a stack of sheets printed on one side and roamed the streets of Cimarron and its bistros selling them with "Clay Allison's Extra" scrawled in red crayon across the unprinted side.

The next morning, as Allison strolled over to view his remodeling efforts, he saw none other than Mrs. Ada Morley, William's seven-months-pregnant wife, in quiet tears, examining the damaged interior.

"Are, are you Mrs. Morley?" he queried, embarrassed, removing his hat, knowing it was none other but.

"Yes," she retorted angrily. "And see what you've done! "

"I, I'm sorry," replied the big man, awkwardly rotating his hat in his sweaty hands.

"Are you in the habit of destroying another man's honest work?"

"N-n-no, maam. I'm sorry. Truly."

"Sorry? I should say you are. Look at it! Just look at it!" And her tears welled anew, but tears more of rage than sorrow.

Allison thrust a hand speedily into his jacket for his wallet. In moments he withdrew several hundred dollars and thrust them into her hands with, "Please, maam, take this. It should cover the damages, and if it isn't enough, don't hesitate to ask, or bill me for the balance."

She looked up speechless at the frazzled Allison, but thankful at his gracious gesture.

Returning his wallet, he said, somewhat lamely, "I don't fight women," replaced his hat, turned and trod away in his best Quixote-like manner. His vengeance had been directed toward Dawson, his editorials and the Santa Fe Ring, and for a change, was not aimed at Morley. Damn! he thought as he trudged off. Saving face can be embarrassing!

The growing chaotic situation in Cimarron had deteriorated to such a degree that Sheriff Orson K. Chittenden had lost all control. Allison and his men continued terrorizing the countryside and the town while the town itself sat like a keg of powder. Earlier, in November, a spate of killings and the town's riotous atmosphere gave the governor reason to put Cimarron under martial law, and troops from Fort Union marched in. Just prior to the destruction of the newspaper's printing press, the troops were withdrawn, peace seeming to have broken out. But it turned out to be the lull before the storm. On January twenty-first Chittenden wired Axtell, "It is impossible for me to enforce civil law." Axtell shot back with relish, "Will accept your resignation forwarded by mail." Chittenden, who had been in office barely four months and was unsympathetic toward the Santa Fe coterie, was removed a month later "for failure to file bond." Axtell gladly appointed Isaiah Rinehart, a pro-Santa Fe Ring man. And on February twenty-first, immediately following Rinehart's appointment, the governor got around to his thorn-in-the-side, turncoat Allison, and issued a reward for his arrest:

"Whereas it appears by affidavit duly filed before Hon. Henry L. Waldo, Chief Justice of the Territory, that said R.C. Allison is guilty of the crime of murder in killing Chas. Cooper on or about January nineteenth, eighteen hundred and seventy-four; and whereas said Allison is now at large and is reported to be a dangerous man; therefore, I thereby offer and promise a reward of five hundred dollars to any person who will arrest and bring before Judge Waldo, at Santa Fe, the said R.C. Allison."

Another man who made a special journey to Santa Fe was the chameleon of chameleons, the lawyer Charles Springer. He was sometimes wryly compared to the distant cousin of the Cro-Magnon by a handful of politicos because no one knew for certain what side he was on. But Charlie knew, so could care less of the identification. He was going to be on the winning side, wherever it was, and whenever it happened. The lawyer too, hoped to change Axtell's mind as to the attachment bill, but as did the others, he also failed. During Springer's brief visit with the governor, he was enlightened as to his venal side. Axtell repeatedly raged in bitterness toward Allison, that he especially intended to have him indicted and punished, and compelled to leave the country. Springer earlier heard of

Allison's resignation from the Santa Feers, but didn't realize how personally Axtell took it. During the governor's splenetic tirade Springer thought him short of a brick or two, and was glad to vacate the capitol for the unpredictable violence of Cimarron. When the five hundred dollar reward was announced for Allison's apprehension, Springer then knew Axtell intended to carry out his personal vendetta to the last syllable. But he did not realize at the time to what lengths he was willing to go in retaliation against anyone whom he felt stood in his way for any reason.

Governor Axtell's scheme for settling Colfax County's hash read more like the final scene of "Hamlet," but with gunplay replacing the swordplay. He enticed the District Attorney of New Mexico, Ben Stevens, to help carry out the plan, and Stevens went along with it. Cleverly, since certain leading Colfax County citizens had earlier wanted to meet with him concerning the county attachment, he used that as a pretext for a gubernatorial visit to set up a meeting with several named individuals. Among the men he named to meet his coach were Clay Allison, William Morley, Frank Springer and Henry Porter. The fulcrum of his plan hinged on the demand for Allison to immediately surrender his arms, a request he was certain to rebuff, and upon his refusal the military escort would execute them all indiscriminately. "Have your men placed to arrest Allison, and kill all the men who resist you," he instructed the D.A. via letter. The wished-for elimination of the named trouble-makers would be a boon for the Santa Feers, plus enhance their political position in Colfax County, at least in the governor' s head. But Stevens ultimately had not the stomach for such Roman methods, or perhaps he suffered from a shot of cowardly conscience, and although the army officers consented, the plan failed.

The military escort assigned the role as assassinators, thirty troopers of the Ninth Cavalry under Captain Francis Moore, left Fort Union on Friday, March fourteenth, eighteen hundred and seventy-six, and arrived in Cimarron that afternoon. They had been preceded by Stevens who, upon arrival, went through the theatrical motions of creating an atmosphere of belief in the pending visitation of the governor. Axtel was to arrive, Stevens insisted, the following day via stage, and he continuously emphasized that certain citizens, especially Clay Allison, should be on hand. But they were also to keep it quiet as Axtell wished to meet only those who had petitioned his presence. But somewhere along the way the plot was discovered, and as a result no one was on hand to meet the coach, which did not contain the governor anyway. Stevens, who was a friend of Morley's, took him into his confidence, and in turn Morley confided to the others of the dark and villainous deeds stemming from the state capitol.

Although frustrated in their initial attempt to corner Allison, Captain Moore didn't give up. A few days later, Moore, accompanied by Sheriff Rinehart, Lieutenant Cornish and thirty-five troopers, galloped out to the Allison ranch to take Clay into custody and bring him to Cimarron for questioning. Allison, already aware of their intent from the earlier failed set-up, wisely did not resist, although he was allowed his revolver and saddle rifle. That too was an obvious ploy, for how could they excuse the shooting of an unarmed man? But Clay played the docile and cooperative captive, further frustrating the armed guard. In the cell of the Cimarron hoosegow Clay sat on one of the bunks and played the waiting game. After over an hour no one questioned him and mostly ignored his presence, so Allison knew he had them. Soon the officers spoke to each other of leaving for a toddy at Lambert's saloon, then walked off. Allison stood in the open doorway and watched them depart, at the same time noticing a few cavalrymen in the yard ignoring him. "Well, now," he figured. "They must want my departure in the worst way, nothing working out for them." Before too many seconds he casually strode through the open jail door, across the yard, then through the open gate of the wall that surrounded the jail. He was completely ignored, even after he mounted his horse. He then cantered off toward his ranch, more pissed at the waste of his time for having been made to accompany his escort to town. They could have found their own way, he snorted. And Axtell must be crazier than a dozen hoot owls.

Hardly a week later the Grim Reaper, impatiently awaiting his cue in the wings, was finally summoned to help maintain Cimarron's sanguineous reputation, and again unsurprisingly in Lambert's saloon. This time, within seconds, the population was lightened by three.

"Mister Lambert," instructed Captain Moore, "our troops have been ordered to stay out of all saloons, so if any of them happen to stray in looking to buy any alcohol, by the drink or bottle, do not serve them. Tell them your bar is off-limits and send them on their way."

"You have got my word, Captain."

"They get smart-mouth or pushy, send for me immediately."

"Yes, sir."

But in some outfits there are a few who don't seem to get the word, and that evening three of such turned up hoping to quench a thirst.

"Sorry, fellows," said the bartender. "Your C.O. instructed us not to serve any of you. In fact, you ain't even supposed to be in here."

"We know, we know," replied one of the privates. "We don't mean to get you into any trouble. But if you would just pour some alcohol into our canteens, we'll jus' get on outta here."

"Naw, cain't do that, either. Cain't serve you a'tall."

The pleading and denying went back and forth to the consternation of not only the bartender, but the handful of patrons standing at the bar, especially Davey Crockett and Gus Heffron at a table. Henry Goodman was with them, another of the original herders of the Goodnight Trail.

"Goddamn it," oathed Gus, nudging Davey in the ribs with his elbow to egg him on. "Don't them nigger solgers know a 'no' when they hear one?"

"Pushy coons, ain't they?" Davey replied, actually not needing any encouragement for interfering. The three of them had been consuming liquid fire for nearly two hours, and the match was about to be lit.

"Hey, nigger!" called Crockett from their table near the center of the room. "Dint you hear what the barman said? He said 'NO,' so get yore black asses outta here, heah?" To emphasize his point he stood on rubbery legs and waved his cocked revolver.

"Now, damn it, Davey!" exclaimed Goodman. "Put away that gun and let them be!" "Hell no, Davey!" urged Gus. "Tame them black suckers!"

Goodman saw where this was headed and without hesitation left the saloon and the building, secreting himself across the street behind a pile of lumber, awaiting the outcome.

"Teach em some manners, Davey!" insisted Heffron. "Give 'em hell!"

Two of the cavalrymen headed for the exit, nervously eying the weaving Crockett waving his sidearm. When the pair reached the door Crockett opened fire and killed them in their tracks. He then turned toward the third man and shot him as he was clawing at the flap of his holster. Frank Springer happened to be one of the patrons imbibing at the bar when the shooting commenced. In record time he flew across the room, leaped over the two prone troopers, then sped out the door and down the street, galloping in a style that would make a marathoner proud.

Davey broke out in gut-breaking laughter as he watched the fleet-footed lawyer show off his footwork. "Jus' look at that white boy run! Hell, Gus, we oughta enter that dude in a footrace contest, if we can catch 'em!"

The next month in mid-April it was Allison's turn to answer to a murder charge in the Cruz Vega case. He and John and ten others, accompanied with Sheriff Rinehart, made the ride to Taos to answer individual indictments for "assault in a menacing manner" and "murder." Allison and six were charged with murder, and while Clay was the only one charged with both, John was facing assault. After a preliminary hearing, the group was instructed to appear at the next term of court the following year, eighteen hundred and seventy-seven.

A month following his Taos court appearance, Clay received a letter with no return address. It was in a plain white envelope and postmarked Santa Fe. Curious and intrigued, he opened it as he walked from the post office, wondering over its anonymity. It was a brief missive requesting a meeting for a friendly discussion regarding their "late" difficulties. He stopped in his tracks when he saw the signature: S.B. Axtell. The Governor gave his word of honor Allison would have no reason to fear legal or military interference, for there would be no cavalry escort nor any law officer to arrest or hinder him. He would be staging from Santa Fe to Trinidad, and if Allison was sympathetic for such a conference, he was to come alone and to confide in no one.

"Well, what do you think, John?" queried Clay.

"Hell, how could you trust the man after the bogus meeting he had already set up? Then next have the cavalry come on out here to haul you off to town. You know they wanted to kill you."

"Yeah, but only if I went for my gun. I outfoxed them and played possum. Threw them off their game."

John shook his head. "I think you were lucky, and you were loco to go with them anyway. All they had to do was bushwhack you and claim you drew first."

"True, but something told me they wanted to kill me honestly," he grinned.

"Honestly?"

"Sure. In town where they needed witnesses. Not out in the woods where I was outnumbered twenty to one. They thought after a bit I'd get antsy and hotheaded and shoot my way out of jail and town. That's why they let me keep my Colt and saddle gun. If I'd a kilt a dozen or so niggers, no skin off their nose. They figured to get me at any cost before it was over."

"So now you're going to meet Axtell and give him another chance."

"You bet."

"And what if he's got soldiers in the bushes somewhere along the line?"

"John, I just don't believe he will. I believe he wants to make a deal of some sort."

"A deal. You are plain loco. He only wants your scalp, pissed because you quit him."

"It's like poker, young 'un," he laughed. "Just because you lose a hand or two you don't quit. You ante-up and deal a new hand."

"Poker. And you're going alone?"

"Yep. That's the way he wants it. And being a man of honor, that's exactly what I'll do."

"I'd be glad to go along and ride shotgun."

"Naw. Stay put. If it turns out to be a trap and I get snookered, well, hell, no one lives forever. But to be honest, I don't believe I've used up my nine lives yet."

"That's a cat, big brother. You're a human being."

"Oh, c'mon, John. Where's your sporting blood? "

"Dying's no sport to me. Or letting some two-bit politician lead me by the hand to an executioner."

"Young man," smiled Clay. "You have no faith or trust in your fellow humans at all. You're more of a cynic than I am."

"Nope, just more cautious. I like my head right where it is, on my shoulders."

Was he being a fool, as John believed, suckered into a set-up, a trap, an ambush where the governor's face would be saved after his last clumsy failure to eradicate not only Allison but a handful of others who were a thorn in his side? No, he thought. Axtell may be cold-blooded, but he isn't completely stupid. Yet he did make a stupid mistake, he laughed. Maybe he isn't drinking the right brand of bourbon? He wondered if he shouldn't take along a quart of that tasty rye, and at least try to change his habit for the better? He hoped too, he could somehow save his ranch, for he grew to love the place and its beautiful location, and hated the thought of losing it. Sure, it was a part of the deal he made with the Ring, and it was a shoddy way to grab a hold of the dream he had when he first saw Texas, of owning his own spread and being his own man in the cow business, and now to see it possibly frittering away almost killed him, hurt him to the point that several times as he walked alone along the bank of the Canadian tears of frustration and depression wet his eyes. He was glad John or any of the men didn't see him in such a state, or they would have had a hell of a fight on their hands at their laughter. Most likely the burden would have been theirs to resolve and handle, and he knew they would have gotten the short end in any case.

With John seeing him off, Clay met the early morning stage to Vermejo from Cimarron for his curious appointment.

"Damn it, Clay. Sure you want to lone-ride this? Why don't you let me come along? You know what a risky stunt it is, going solo."

"John," smiled Clay. "Stop your long-faced worrying. I'll meet you here in two or three days. We'll have dinner at Lambert's and I'll tell you all about my little excursion."

With a farewell slap on John's shoulder, Clay stepped up and into the coach with a Colt on his hip and a Winchester in his hand. As it rocked off with a jolt he leaned out and waved goodbye, confident, unworried, and in a fatalistic mind-set.

It was a forty-mile journey up the Vermejo River to the village of Vermejo, which sat in the northeastern corner of Colfax County a few miles south of the Colorado border. The dirt lane hugging the river passed along the holdings of many of the cattle ranchers he knew, including Irwin Lacy, and farther northeast, Lou Coleman. He hardly saw either of the men over the past year for he kept his distance, knowing they would never approve of his alliance with the Ring. Recriminations would be sharp, and Clay felt sheepish at facing the two men he had great respect for, although disagreeing with them as to how to get ahead in life, namely the cattle business.

Allison's ride was uneventful and he arrived near eleven a.m., time enough for breakfast and several cups of coffee. Leaving the station restaurant he saw attorney William Lee walking toward him. "Good morning, Bill," he welcomed the lawyer with a grin and an extended hand. "You know I'm to meet the governor around twelve thirty or so at Rutherford's Mercantile store, and wonder if anything's been changed?"

"No, no, Clay. He should be pulling in pretty soon. He'll come by my house first, and when he does I'll send him over to you."

At a quarter to one Clay watched from Rutherford's doorway as Axtell rounded a corner and strode toward him. Grey-headed with a patrician air, he was in his early sixties. Healthy, handsome and smooth-featured, he was of medium height and weight, and Clay was surprised at not seeing a typically corpulent politician. Axtell flipped away a half-smoked cigarro and strode as if on a casual afternoon walk. One cool hombre, thought Clay. As the governor stepped into the building the two men, meeting for the first time, looked at one another with a quiet eye, neither critical nor accepting, but more like a pair of duelists measuring each for a casket.

"Well, Mister Allison. This is quite an honor."

"Yes it is," agreed Clay with a firm handshake and nod. "And about time, too," he added crisply, not about to let the pol one-up him.

"Let us board my coach and be on our way. Unless you have some pressing business here before we leave?"

"No, sir, let us move on."

One of the passengers clambered atop the vehicle in order for Allison to sit next to Axtell. Two other men sat across from them.

"These are two Pinkerton men, Mister Allison, and are merely assigned as guard-escorts, and have nothing to do with our social visitation."

"Howdy, gents," nodded Clay casually, as he adjusted his holster more to the front of his thigh and his rifle vertical and butt-first between his knees, then lit up a cheroot. The hefty men, clad in dark suits, homburgs and white linen dusters, sitting Buddha-like with hands folded in their laps, nodded in unison and smiled a mute greeting. As the coach lunged forward and settled into a lazy rocking motion, Clay turned to Axtell and asked, "I just need to know what kind of man are you to so interfere with my personal freedom? Namely for one, issuing warrant's on me for Cooper's and Vega's murders, both of which I feel are bogus charges."

"Then why don't you just surrender yourself on bail and stand trial like a man?"

"Hell, I'd have no objection to that, if I could be sure of a fair trial. But I'll never allow myself to submit to a trial in Taos by a bunch of greasers."

"You certainly have the right to apply for a change of venue to another county, if you so wish."

Ignoring the suggestion, Clay asked, "I assume you know District Attorney Stevens of Las Vegas?"

"Yes, I do. A fine man, although a little weak in the knees when it comes to making firm decisions."

"Decisions?" irked Clay. "You mean like warning Morley of an arranged ambuscade, and saving our lives?"

"Good heavens, Mister Allison!" exclaimed Axtell in wide-eyed indignity. "Do you take me for a common assassin?"

"No, not a common one, surely."

"Well, I thank you for the compliment. But you must believe me that someone along the line overstepped their authority."

"Like the handful of troopers that rode out to my ranch and took me back to the Cimarron hoosegow?"

"That too was some idiot's mistake," he shrugged in disinterest. "I have no idea why you were taken in. It had to have been the sheriff's personal doing."

"I think they intended to hold a session of target practicing, with me as the bull's eye."

"Whatever for?"

"To make up for the failed execution of the bunch of us meeting your coach the day before, and my leaving the Ring. They thought this time I'd get riled up and go for my gun, which is what they were waiting for. But I was as docile as a newly-laid egg, so they let me walk away."

"Mister Allison I am truly sorry for all the mix-up and confusion. The officer in charge of that detail will have a lot to answer for, believe me."

Clay stared into Axtell's eyes with the icy gaze of a killer, but held his inner rage with an iron grip. How could one even discuss the weather with such a lying, conniving varmint? He wished in the worst way to pistol-whip him about the head and shoulders, then fling his battered body from the coach like a sack of wormy wheat. But next of course he'd have to kill the twin toads across from him. Then the three outside. So what would he do after that? Run and hide the rest of his life, or until they caught him and shot him? What in hell did this excuse for a man want with him, anyway, except to flaunt his petty control?

"I was concernedly thinking, Mister Allison. Would you not reconsider your resignation? I am certain we could come to some form of agreement which would be more than satisfactory for the both of us."

There it is. His ranch. Hanging by a thread. His stomach churned.

"Can't do that, Governor."

"And why not?"

"Good grief, are you so uninformed? The Santa Fe Ring has been blamed for the killing of Tolby, and since I worked for the Ring, many look upon me as the shooter."

"Then in turn I must accuse you of being the uninformed one. That killing was a local affair. We had absolutely nothing to do with it. Some rumors point to the dead Griego as one of the men behind it. The other is believed to be Donoghue."

"Well, I've heard so many stories, it is a poser. But I really can't afford your kind offer of re-employment until the killer is caught."

Shaking his head in disappointment the governor went on. "You had caught one of them already, Cruz Vega. But in your passion for justice you killed him. Now that he is dead, what good is he? And, ah yes, what of Griego? Your wondrous display of marksmanship cost him his life, also. You are an efficient executioner, Mister Allison, but a bumbling detective."

Clay squirmed, knowing he was right.

"And then there was Cardenas, killed by a shot in the dark. Ironically, while his testimony cleared us of any involvement in the Tolby murder, we are still blamed for it."

"That was crazy Herberger who killed him."

"Regardless, of the four plotters and executioners, three are dead. And guess what? With three of the principals deceased, the fourth, Donoghue, hadn't a chance of conviction for lack of proof. He is now in Santa Fe prospering as an adobe contractor. He should send you a postcard of thanks."

"Maybe I should ride on down there and one dark night put a bullet in him," replied Allison sarcastically.

"Mister Allison," began Axtell.

"Why don't you just call me Clay? This 'mister' stuff is getting to me."

"Fine, Clay. Dispensing of all unnecessary formality is right down my alley. Call me Sam. And as I was about to say, I actually envy you mightily, if I may cast you a compliment."

Puffing on his smoke, Allison raised his eyebrows.

"Yes, I truly do." He reached inside his jacket and withdrew a metal case. "Cast out that piece of rope you are polluting the coach with and try one of these imports."

Allison tossed out his cheroot and took one of Axtell's offerings. Lighting up, he inhaled, then slowly blew smoke upward. "By God, this is heaven on earth. Now that you've spoiled me and upgraded my taste, what'll I do to afford it?" he laughed.

"Take the rest of these, Clay." The governor scooped up what was left in the case and handed them over. "I'll send you a box from Santa Fe soon as I return."

"Sam," smiled Allison. "I take back half the bad things I've said about you."

"As I began to say, Clay, I do envy you. It is your capacity to instantly resolve your differences, come hell or high water, that I admire. Something I wish I had the talent and nerve to do. I've never killed a man, and don't believe I ever could, although there are at least a dozen I inwardly express death wishes for."

"Now wait a minute, Sam. If you're trying to hire me to level out the population a bit, forget it. I'm a shootist, not an assassin. I only kill when someone is a threat to me."

"No, no," laughed Axtell. "I'm not out to hire you to clean up my back yard. I'll take care of them my way. I merely want to say I admire your quick and efficient manner of eradicating human obstacles. Of course

I dispense of my enemies or rivals via legal manipulation through economic or legal coercion. Yet your method is more permanent, and I must say, devoutly to be admired."

"Thank you, Sam. I am flattered."

"Out of curiosity, how many men have you put away?"

"Including politicians?"

"No," guffawed Axtell. "Only humanoids."

"Five, in Colfax County."

"Only five? Some credit you with a dozen."

"People enjoy spreading yarns at campfire tale-telling, but I don't refute them out of self defense. The higher the count, the less likely people will bother you."

"You were in the war, I understand."

"Yes, and I put away my share of Yankees there, many dozens, I imagine."

"I never served. Physical confrontation is just not my cup of tea. Honestly haven't the stomach or nerve for it. More of a milquetoast, actually."

"Nothing to killing a man, Sam. Especially if it's you or him. Then you do it like swatting a pesky fly."

"I understand you also have the rare gift of getting the drop on your assailants."

"Very true, and proud of the slippery trait. It took a while to develop, but I had to since I wasn't one of them fast-draw artists. Kind of like chess really, trying to figure out your opponent, setting him up, then going in for the kill. And of course one mistake is all you are allowed."

"Although tighter rules, I would say."

"Yessiree, no referee, coach or umpire."

"I enjoy hearing how you maneuvered Griego about. A real work of the master, Clay. Recalls to my mind the mongoose and the cobra. Marvelous game, and exceedingly clever. I'd be indebted to you forever if I could hear it firsthand from you, if I would not be imposing."

Allison couldn't figure out what all the palavering was about, all this unimportant—to him—bantering back and forth. What was he leading up to? It was like Axtell was using him for a small entertainment to break the monotony of a long, boring trip: his court jester. Well, what the hell, he'd play along and see whatever the outcome was. Maybe something good can come of this, even though he was through riding for the Santa Feers, guilty or not of their killing Tolby. Hell with them.

"Well," began Allison. "I kept hearing all day Pancho was gunning for me, but I was in town looking for him myself. I had tied up my horse at Lambert's where I had a toddy, enough to keep me loose but not bleary-eyed drunk. Nobody was in Lambert's bar, so as I was taking a stroll toward another saloon when all of a sudden I run smack into Pancho. He had two friends with him and all were armed with six-guns and rifles. I remember being really madder than hell at myself for being so careless at letting me be surprised that way."

Clay calculatingly lit another smoke enjoying the rapt attention of the three men who waited with bated breath for him to go on. Blowing smoke rings toward the roof, he continued.

"Florencio Donoghue and a teenaged Griego kin were the two with him. I recall thinking the eighteen-year-old was too young to die, for he didn't look like he belonged in such a nasty set-up, helping back up a pair of men who should have known better than to have dragged the kid along. I also knew they aimed to shoot first to regain their so-called honor, so I had to be cool and talk quick so as to delay their intent and throw them off guard. I knew if I could have them start talking and thinking, at least Pancho, I could buy myself some time in order to eventually outfox them."

"Amazing how fast the brain can work in a tense moment of danger," spoke the governor, "knowing survival depended on calculated action."

"Very true," agreed Clay, puffing on his cigarro. "So I said to Pancho, as I raised my left hand palm out and gripped the butt of my Colt with my right, 'You have me outnumbered and outgunned, Frank.'

"Then he said something like having a gringo to eliminate who was a pain in the ass to the Mexican community. In turn I implored, kind of groveling-like, 'I believe you are an intelligent man who would be willing to discuss our differences, are you not? You know the murder of Tolby in such an uncivilized way, the shooting of an unarmed man from ambush is something honorable gunmen such as you and I would never tolerate.' We jawed back-and-forth for a little time, and when he started talking, I knew I had him. And for some crazy reason I felt sorry for him, it was all so easy.

"So I says, 'Let's you and me go on over to Lambert's and have a talk. Drinks are on me.'

"He stared a moment, then handed his rifle to the kid and says, 'Take this, Jose. I might need it later.' And off we go to his funeral. Of course I didn't have the heart to tell him it was that. It was good that Lambert's bar was empty for it made things easier, no witnesses and no customers getting drilled accidentally. As we walk up to the bar Henry Lambert comes in from the kitchen where he's busy cooking up a storm for the eating crowd. 'What'll you have gents?' he asks. I says, 'Give us a bottle of your best rye and two water glasses. Me and Frank have a hellova thirst to drown. And put it on my tab, Henry.' 'No problem, Clay,' he says. 'I have to get back to the kitchen, so you fellas drink hearty.'

"As Henry leaves I pour a stout level into our glasses and turn to Pancho saying, 'Here's to our health, Frank, and a peaceable solution to our dire difficulties.' 'I'll drink to that, Allison.' He answers. And we did.

"Reloading our empty glasses I looks over at the pool table and ask kind of innocent-like, 'Hey, Frank, how about a game of pool? Think you're good enough to beat this ol' run-down cowboy?' 'Oh ho!' he laughs. 'Pool playing is one of my incomes, Allison. Let's go.'

"All right!" I says. But take it easy on me. I've got the lousiest eye for this game.'

"Pancho downs half his drink and walks to the cue-rack against the wall on the far side of the table. I empty my glass and walk toward him watching as he selects and weights several cues. I stand with the table between us and draw my gun from my holster and quietly cock it. After a bit he chooses a cue and turns with a happy smile on his face. When he sees the Colt pointed at him, the bottom fell out of his life. The smile was frozen on his face but it was like his eyes died before I even pulled the trigger. 'Sorry, Frank,' I informed him. 'But seems like you scratched.' Then I put three bullets into him and watch as he bumps his back against the cue-rack and slides to the floor half under the pool table. I reholster, go to the bar, cork the bottle, and take it with me as I swiftly vacate. End of chess game."

"Marvelous strategy, Clay. Truly marvelous."

"All in a day's work, Sam. Nothing to brag about."

"That is why we want you and need you, Clay. A rare talent such as yours is much appreciated and respected by us. And you can not only expect to receive ample rewards for your efforts on our behalf, but in time there will be a profitable position somewhere for you in our, ah, family. And soon the common employ of herding cattle will be but a distant memory for you."

It was now or never, thought Allison. He was nobody's puppet, tool or lackey. And sure as hell not the Ring's. At least he would be honest with himself. Oh, God, and most probably there goes the ranch.

"Sam, let me level with you here, whether you like it or not. First of all, I'm a herdsman, a cowman. Of a small order, you can be sure, but a cattleman nevertheless. It's what I want to do and what I love. I left Tennessee after the war for Texas and had no idea what I was going to do or where I was going to do it. When I got to the western plains that bordered the frontier and saw my first herds of hundreds and hundreds of cows, something hit me. Maybe it was in my bones and just had to find it, but I knew then my life was in cattle work. I hired on with a man named Dalton, and he gave me a lot of slack to learn, and I learned fast. So fast I quick became good enough to be his ram-rodder, his foreman. I drove his first herd over the Goodnight Trail with a group of other cowmen and their herds, and I never looked back. It's a good life and a rewarding one, and although it has its headaches and heartaches, I wouldn't trade it for the world.

"Secondly, driving across the Texas desert to New Mexico that first time I dreamed of one day owning my own ranch and herd. The dream excited me so much I imagined it was my cows I was herding over that trail, that I was taking my own cattle to market, and every mile we rode was like I was riding toward my dream. After bringing cows for other cattlemen back and forth from Texas to New Mexico I became impatient with my dream, wanting the reality of it all. I finally had a small herd, the first half of my dream, but was having a hard time finding space to put them in. The big ranchers were favored on the grant, and also I didn't have enough money. I could have gone to work for other ranchers, even thrown in with a few as a partner, but I didn't want that, I wanted to have something to call my own. I wanted to bring my dream to life, not work for someone else, helping carry someone else's water. So with half my dream I was stuck in a mud hole. Then Doc Longwill, one of your messenger boys, suggested I throw in with you people. In exchange I would be awarded the deed to a choice section on the Canadian River. I went to look it over. It was the most beautiful setting for a ranch I ever saw, and I instantly fell in love with it. I gave Longwill my 'yes' for the ranch, and made my pact with the devil. But now I'm done with the Ring and anything that smells of them. You are an unholy bunch, Sam, and have brought nothing but grief to anyone or anything that stands in your way. There is no honesty or decency in anything you people touch, from here all the way to Lincoln County. Nothing personal, Sam, but you people are like a pack of hyenas out of control."

"Ah, Clay, I never would have believed that you had a touch of the philosopher in you. I am very impressed. No, not impressed, but touched, touched at your feelings and sensitivity toward what is so important to you, the pursuance of your dream. But to label us devils and hyenas is an injustice, for we too have our dreams, dreams of wealth and never-ending control. Don't you see, Clay? It is a matter of personal perception, of what is important to you, then you pursue it to end of the world if you must, to the end of your life if need be. And you are right, a man without a dream is a half-man, and a man who doesn't dream is no man at all."

"But in your dream you leave an army of victims behind while twisting the law to suit your aims and purposes. It's a terrible injustice to civilized society that you do, a crime to humanity."

"Was your dream so unsoiled after you ran off a bunch of Mexican squatters to hold it?"

"At the time I didn't see the harm I was doing blinded by what I wanted. True, I never gave a damn about them beaners, and still don't, but now I see that they have a right to live in peace and make their own way through life without me or you stepping on them."

"Ah, from the common cowhand emerges the noble cowboy," replied the governor in icy sarcasm. "A touching portrait, Clay."

"I'm neither common nor noble, Sam. Only an aspiring human being with a tattered dream in my hands."

"You can still have that dream, Clay," returned Axtell saccharinely.

"No, Sam. Not now. The price is too high."

"So your answer is final? You've divorced us because of irreconcilable differences?"

"I'm afraid so, dear. Your heels are too round."

Axtell roared with laughter. "God bless you, Clay, for your sense of humor."

"Thought you'd like that," replied Allison, echoing him in laughter. The two detectives also joined in, shaking in their girth.

"Damn it, Clay. I hate losing your loyalty. But of course, as you have aptly described it, one's true loyalty is first to one's self. Stay on at the ranch for now, use it and enjoy it. You have a court case coming up soon, don't you?"

"Yep. Next year in Taos. Over the Vega mishap."

"Ah, yes. Well, use it a little after that, till the fall. Maybe something will turn up for you. Or, you may even change your mind, who knows?"

"Doubt that, Sam. But maybe I can get some financing somehow and buy the place."

"Perhaps so, Clay. We'll just let it rest until next fall and see what turns up. And if you do come up with any financing, just talk it over with the grant people in Cimarron. I'll put a good word in for you."

"Thank you, Sam. That I'll certainly do."

"And that's the way it went, John," smugly smiled Clay as he related his trip with Axtell. True to his word he and John were having a steak dinner at Lambert's hotel-restaurant, complete with a bottle of French burgundy, ala Doc Longwell.

"So he wasn't in a snit or pissed in any way for you quitting them yokels?"

"Nope. So now if I can come up with the money I can buy the place. He said it was fine with him, to just check in with the Maxwell people here when I can arrange the financing."

"I'm sorry, Clay, but I smell a skunk in the woodpile somewhere. It just don't make any sense to me at all."

"Ah, John, there you go again, peeing on my parade."

John paused over his T-bone with a worried gaze. "Those are terrible people you're dealing with, as you know, and I don't think they're going to let you off so easy. Especially Axtell. I've heard he's a cold-blooded, vengeful bastard. He's already tried to nail you with that phoney 'meet me at my stagecoach' bit in Cimarron."

"Yeah, I know, but I figure he's got all the use out of me he's going to get, so let it go at that. They'll probably rent some other gunman down the road to take my place. Just you watch."

"I'm not interested watching for him or his future gunman. I'm more interested in listening for the other boot to drop."

"I'm afraid you'll go deaf before you hear it, John. So just sit easy and enjoy the dinner. Let's have another bottle of that French vino in celebration of buying our ranch." Clay raised his glass in a toast, drained it, and ordered another bottle.

Not three months later one October night an event occurred which gave John an uneasy shudder, although Clay looked upon it as nothing more than a routine moment in the lives of men who lived by the gun. Local bad boys Davey Crockett and Gus Heffron finally got their earthly reckoning in Cimarron, with Crockett checking out feet-first.

Just the week before the two were on a drunken tear most of the day, harassing merchants, passersby and bartenders with curses, insults and drawn weapons. One afternoon Sheriff Rinehart made the mistake of trying diplomatically to rein them in, but they quickly turned on him and menacingly shoved a pair of shotguns into his face, predicting for him a brief term in office. Poking and pushing the barrels into his side and ample stomach for sport a while, they finally left with the laughing warning that he was alive only at their pleasure, and to leave them be.

That night it was the lawman's turn to settle things. With deputies Holbrook and McCullough, he lay in wait for the two in the dark behind an adobe wall at a crossroads where it was known the two would pass. They had not too long to wait, and as the desperados cantered out of the night about nine p.m. the sheriff yelled, "Stop where you are and get down from them horses! This is the law, and do it quick!"

They halted as ordered, but instead of dismounting sat peering at the trio. Crockett then spread out each of the wings of his vest with his hands and melodramatically instructed them to "Shoot and be damned!" The three lawmen explicitly followed Davey's orders and shot both men. Davey turned and galloped across the Cimarron Bridge to die there, and the slightly wounded Heffron was packed off to jail. A month later he escaped with a fellow prisoner, Bill Love, and was never seen in the area again, both heading for Durango, Colorado.

"That's a hellova way to go," spoke John as Clay passed on the news of the duo's deaths. "Shot off their horses like that. Kind of cold, and I don't know why, but it just gives me the creeps. The finality of an ambush, I guess. I suppose it reminds me too much of Axtell's earlier ambuscade plan for you."

"Hell, them two was long overdue way they kept pushing their luck. A gunman usually dies by the gun, John, and I don't think too many of them die in bed or of old age. But being only a shootist," he laughed, "I wouldn't know about that."

"I understand Crockett left a four-month-old baby by his Mexican girlfriend, Emilia. That's a hellova note."

"I agree. That's the saddest part of the whole affair. Hope she has family enough to help her raise the child."

Crockett leaving a child behind made Clay remember Martha Matthews and her two children. "You done missed the boat on this one, Clay," returned the words of Doc Longwill, and they had haunted him since. But it was too late to want and too late to wish, so all he could do was daydream occasionally and wonder how her new marriage was working out. He wished also he had gotten her address from Longwill so as to drop her a line now and then, in the hopes of—what? Her husband dying somehow and she left adrift once again for him to come to her rescue, and maybe marriage? Sometimes he embarrassed himself with his mental meanderings, thinking he was going loco. But a family in his mind was an extension of his ranch-dream, a woman to love and marry and give birth to the next generation of Allisons. A wife to live with and to share life with and to dream with, and to make those dreams possible. The Matthews came to him now and then like wisps of distant memory, soft, lovely reminisces of another world he somehow missed grasping and might never have the chance to grasp again. They brought home to him the needed, no not needed, but the indispensable extension of his dream, family.

So one afternoon he rode off toward Cimarron to seek out Tina Menchaca. She had left the house she worked in and with a girl friend rented a small place on the outskirts of town, hopefully catering to more selective clients. He had spent time with several of the women in the house she left, but they were dim coals to the fires of Tina. He missed her brightness and ready wit, biting as she could be, and too there was that strange wondrous romantic feeling he was embraced with when with her. The other women left him bored, dead, and sometimes mortifyingly impotent. He decided to seek her out.

Near dark he reined up at her house, dismounted, and stepped onto the porch. He wore his best clothes, black suit, hat and shined boots, and had neatly trimmed his Vandyke. He also held in his hands a cluster of mixed flowers, which left the florist flabbergasted at Allison's request. A light shown through the curtained window. Rapping tenderly, he waited nervously. The door opened and Tina stood before him, lovelier than ever. Removing his hat and extending the flowers, he said shyly, "I hope you like these, Tina. I wanted to get roses, but they seemed out of season."

Ignoring the bouquet, she sarcastically spat, "Well, la dee dah, aren't you the one."

Allison didn't quite know what to say, knew if he tried to pussy-foot around she would verbally assail him mercilessly. So he dove right in. "Tina, I honestly miss you. I know it sounds stupid coming from a galoot like me, but I wanted to talk seriously about something, so found where you were living."

"So now you are here."

"Yes, maam.

"You look like you're dressed for a wedding."

He wondered in panic if she had read his mind and blushed, slowly turning his hat brim in an anxious circle. "I-I...."

"Or maybe a funeral. Which is it, Clay?"

"Not a funeral, that's for certain."

"Oh. Did you come by to dip your wick?"

"Aw, please don't talk like that, Tina."

"But that's the business I'm in. What else would you be here for?"

From behind Tina emerged a tiny, red-headed woman in her early forties. Barely five-feet-two, her waist-length hair was thinly threaded with strands of white. "Muy malo," she whispered with bulging, fearful eyes upon seeing Allison. She whispered again looking upward at Tina who stood a head taller, "Es hombre muy malo."

"What's she calling me bad for?" asked Clay sardonically, hat and flowers still in his hands. "I don't even know her."

"She's Helen Winona, a sensitive. A spiritual who can pick up on people and read them."

"Christ, not another dime-a-dozen self-help bruha?"

"That's an insult, Clay. She's no phoney crystal-gazer, if that's what you mean."

"Sorry. No insult intended. Just that I never had much luck with fortune tellers."

"She's part Indian and from west Kansas. When she was a little girl the white man's army came across their small group and slaughtered them in the name of Manifest Destiny. She ran into the brush with a leg wound and was the only survivor. She was adopted by a tribe of wandering Wyandottes and eventually married into them. She was so filled with visions and omens that came true, they called her Princess. Her bright copper hair came from her Irish father, a wagoneer who died soon after she was born. Because of her rich-colored hair they called her 'Bountiful Light'."

"Bountiful Light. Pretty name. But why is she calling me bad?"

"You're not bad. You just carry bad vibrations."

"Vibrations?"

"Ugliness. Squeezed-in anger. Karma."

"Damn if I don't believe I got off at the wrong stage stop."

Bountiful Light, with tightly pursed lips, rolled her eyes upwards while fluttering her hands in the air like a heat-struck hen, chanting, moaning and swaying. She was barefoot and wore a short dress of soft suede. As she whirled dervish-like, Clay could see where the flesh near her right shin was scooped out from a bullet wound. The hem of her dress swirled umbrella-like in a wide circle about her waist, revealing curvaceous thighs and legs of porcelain, and a thick tuft of pubis.

"What's she doing now?" Allison dared ask.

"Protecting herself from your devilish aura."

"Does the Princess want any money for all this enlightened display?"

"Not a cent. But she accepts volunteer donations."

"Too bad. I learned in the army never to volunteer for anything."

"Malo! Malo!" cried out Bountiful Light, as if hearing Allison's denial against funding.

"Now I know I'm going to get it," responded Allison.

"Clay," asked Tina. "Just what in hell do you want here?"

"To be perfectly frank, I wanted to talk to you about coming to live with me at my ranch." He didn't mean it to come out so bluntly, but was glad to get it over with.

"You mean to make an honest woman out of me?"

"Uh, well, just short of marriage. But if things work out between us, who knows?"

"Oh, good heavens, I am so flattered! What in hell's wrong with you, cowboy? This is the most lame proposal I've ever been insulted with, except for the few who have run off without paying."

"Damn it, Tina, I may as well say it now. You are the prettiest, brightest and most capable woman I have ever known, and I can't get my mind off you. If you would come live with me for a time I would greatly appreciate it. It's a beautiful place out there, right on the Canadian, and only me and John live there. It could stand a woman's touch, and I would do right by you, I would." There, thought Allison, I've said it all in one mouthful and hope she takes the offer. "It would please me so much, it really would."

Tina and the Princess stood staring at Allison as if he were daft.

"Esta loco, too," uttered Bountiful Light from behind Tina. "Muy malo e muy loco."

"Clay, what makes you think I'd live with a crazy-assed drunk and killer like you?"

"You mean you'd rather spend your life spread-eagled for any man with the right price instead of setting up housekeeping with one man like a righteous woman?"

"Righteous? And what in hell makes you think you're so righteous? You self-absorbed redneck!"

"But it's a decent offer, Tina. Why can't you see your way to accept it?"

"Because I'd still be a whore, that's why. Except that I'd also be cooking and cleaning up after you with no raise in pay!"

"Damn, Tina, if I don't think you are as loony as that Kansas half-breed hopping around behind you there, jabbering spiritual gibberish!"

"Get to hell off my porch and away from here before someone sees you and thinks I've took to bedding down white trash!"

Allison could see all his efforts were going south, good intentions that he had. Why couldn't she see to reason? "Well, Tina, I'd best go. I didn't mean to upset you."

"Before you leave," she shot viciously, "let me commend you on the way you murdered Francisco Griego. Why didn't you just shoot him in the back and get it over with?"

"What do you mean? I'm no back-shooter! I hit him three times in the chest!"

"In the chest? You drew while his back was turned. How macho of you, how manly. And you go about bragging on it. Have you no shame? Have you no decency? Get the hell off my porch, and good Christ, please don't ever come back. Just sit your sad ass on your horse and get!"

"Malo! Malo!" chanted Bountiful Light, hopping and skipping around the room, her tiny bare feet slapping the wooden floor in a rhythm all her own. "Muy loco e Malo!"

"Damn if I don't believe you and that Kansas half-breed are both from the same loony bin!" In a fit of frustration and anger Allison threw the flowers on the porch and kicked them through the doorway into the room, his bountiful light of romance having turned into a dim candle. He yanked his hat over his head with a grumble, leaped into the saddle and galloped off, the shouts of "Malo!" echoing from the Princess. He could hardly wait to get to Lambert's saloon to clear his reeling head from his momentary lapse of temporary romantic insanity, and regain his emotional equilibrium.

Allison's time was soon spent in trying to figure out how and where to gather enough money to buy the ranch. He tried several banks in Raton and Trinidad, but the answers were the same, no deed, no loan. No collateral, no money. He needed the deed before they would lend on it, and he needed the money to get the deed. There were definite disadvantages at being a squatter, and he began to sympathize even more with the people he had run off. He finally went to the Maxwell Grant Company in Cimarron with hat in hand, but they were as cold-blooded as any banker. They wouldn't budge either. He wondered if Axtell put out the word to hamstring him for quitting the Ring. It made him more adamant than ever: damn if he'd rejoin them bandits! He'd figure out how to outfox them yet.

In early December a rancher and some-time acquaintance, Frank Fagaly of Las Animas, Colorado, got word to the Allisons he wanted to purchase some cattle. Could they run up maybe eighty head to him? It would be about a one hundred-mile drive northeast from the ranch, and a week before Christmas they gathered the cows and moved out. It was a chilly day with an icy breeze slicing across the plains to make it less comfortable, with vast patches of old snow spread on the ground here and there. But they welcomed the sale, hoping more like this one would ease them toward an accumulation of funding for the purchase of the ranch. But of course they weren't kidding themselves either, knowing it would take a lot more than a piddling sale or two like this. What did help though was the siphoning off from a vast herd owned by Colorado ranchers who ran the 101 brand, and conveniently grazed on the lower dry Cimarron, just north of Allison's place. To alter it into Clay's boxed-circle brand, it was easy to draw a line with a running iron across the top and bottom of the 101. This is what influenced Clay in the first place in the creation of his trade mark, and now it came in handy. It was called, Looking Ahead. But he realized too that he had to be careful and not get greedy, for hemp-justice was strong in the area.

Four days later at nightfall they finished pushing the cows into

Fagaly's pens on the edge of Las Animas. As the cattleman handed Clay a check he invited the two to join him for a drink at his saloon, the Olympic Dance Hall.

"Drinks on me, boys. You certainly don't intend on starting back tonight after that cold ride, do you?"

"Hell, no, Frank," replied Clay. "We were going to grab a meal somewhere, then a room for the night."

"Well, good. You two just go on to the Olympic and I'll join you shortly."

The weary Allisons trod to the hotel to reserve a room, then toward the saloon in the dusky afternoon leading their mounts. In not too long a time they were accosted by the town constable, Charles Faber.

"We got an ordinance against toting weapons within city limits, fellows."

"That right?" retorted Clay laconically and unimpressed.

"That's right. You the Allison boys who brung in them cattle?"

"Men, actually," shot Clay, slightly bristling. "And yes, we did."

"Now, I didn't mean anything personal, Mister Allison. But I'll have to take your guns, or you can go down to my office and check them in there. We'll give you a receipt to get them back."

"Tell you what," instructed Clay. "We're tired and near froze to death. Frank invited us to have a quick drink with him at his saloon, which is where we're heading. After that we plan to eat, then call it a day. Tomorrow we're getting out of here early and don't want to waste time looking for our guns, so we'd appreciate you forgetting about that ritual. How about it?"

"Mister Allison. Go right on, then. But I don't want to see either of you on the street armed. Got to go straight to the hotel from Fagaly's saloon, hear?"

"We hear, we hear," answered Clay, gritting his teeth with a wave of his hand as the two proceeded along their way.

After a half-dozen heavy belts dinner was forgotten by the brothers, the booze numbing their appetite for food. About a dozen patrons in various stages of drunkeness and jollification were hard at it this cold night, highly grateful to the alcoholic antifreeze which warmed them through and through. A fiddler, soberest of the bunch, struck up a series of tunes as several of the men took to the floor and danced clumsily together, trying to recall which foot went where. Clay in his enthusiasm leaped about and stomped on toes and feet, his laughter mixed with the pained shouts and curses of his targets. John tried his hand at stomping a foot or two, and missed a few to the heehaws of several who jibbed at his bourboned stumblings. In the middle of all this spirited display there appeared in the suddenly opened door none other than constable Faber and a pair of deputies. Faber lowered his shotgun, a double-barreled Greener he had borrowed earlier for the occasion. Someone yelled "LOOK OUT!" and a deafening roar blew through the room as John was caught in the side and chest with the shot. Clay, suddenly on call, pulled his Colt and sent a bullet across the room which killed Faber outright. Unfortunately, as the dead constable dropped in his tracks, his finger squeezed down on the second trigger and this load too caught John, this time in his leg. The smell of cordite hung heavy in the air as everyone stood frozen in time a moment, wondering what in hell all the shooting was for. Clay, with the roar of a wild animal, sped to the door for more satisfaction, and as the constable's panic-stricken deputies fled into the wintry darkness never to be seen again, he sent several shots after them to speed them on their way. Returning to John's semiconscious and shredded body writhing and groaning in pain, he saw the floor and his brother both a crimson mass of blood. Clay was beside himself with grief and horror. "John! Good God, John, please don't die! Please!" Clay frenziedly went to the dead lawman's body and dragged it next to John, shouting frantically, "John! Here's the son of a bitch who shot you! I killed him, John, I killed the bastard! Look! See him?!" The barman and several of the customers hastily made a pallet of boards and lay John upon it, then with Clay alongside they made their way down the street to the Vandiver House where the Allison's had their room. A doctor was summoned who mercifully rendered John fully unconscious then worked as best he could to stop the bleeding. Fortunately, none of his vital organs were hit, most of the damage being surface buckshot wounds. Soon Sheriff John Spiers showed up, placed the brothers under arrest, and, when the doctor did all he could, moved them to the new county jail as its first residents. Clay was lodged in a cell on the main floor, and John placed in an upstairs room set up as a hospital dorm.

At the next morning's inquest the Allisons were charged with premeditated murder, although Faber had fired first. The charges were based on the claim that the Allisons had set up an explosive situation with their overly enthusiastic reveling and foot-stomping. Nobody questioned at the time what it was Faber objected to, whether it was foot-stomping, out-of-synch dancing, or off-key fiddle playing.

Spending New Year's Day of eighteen hundred and seventy-seven in jail was a first for the Allison brothers, and Clay became unusually mollified and cooperative. It was in reaction to John's survival of his gunshot wounds. He was so grateful and relieved for his younger brother's pulling through that after it was over the stress seemed to have drained and tamed him somewhat. But it was the overwhelming guilt that nearly crushed him, feeling responsible for putting him in harm's way. It was this cross he carried, silently and wordless, the onerous burden of personal accountability. It also carried the festering desire for vengeance, to retaliate for the harm done to John, for he deeply believed the shots were meant for him, and that the sender was none other than Axtell. That John took the hit in the dimly lit room was because they resembled each other, for both were the same height and both wore Vandykes. Neither of them had met Faber before, and so Faber would be inclined to make the mistake, unfamiliar as he would be toward them. But now Faber was dead and the two deputies long gone, and if he were right in his assumption, Axtell was having another laugh at him for his talent at killing perpetrators of the crime, with the result of having no one to question. He could hear the governor's sarcastic laughter now, and the words, "Good shot, Clay. Thank you." As the suspicion silently ate at his guts he methodically planned Axtell's murder.

While under incarceration the brothers were treated with tolerance and consideration, many aware of the circumstances of their arrest, of a man defending himself after being shot at first. In frontier society the law was less complicated, not confused by law books and judicial hair-splitting. It was closer akin to the biblical eye-for-an-eye definition—you shoot at me, I shoot back, and may the better shot win. But as civilization moved westward across the plains toward the Pacific, infiltrating much of the cubby holes of the country, it gradually tamed the lawless land with courts, judges, lawyers and sheriffs, and many of the manly traditions fell by the wayside, from the "code duello" onward, to surrender itself to the robed ministrants of legal retribution.

In early January John was released from jail for better medical treatment in Trinidad. Clay remained where he was, and at a hearing on the eighth in Pueblo, Colorado, their attorney Thomas Macon won for them a reduced charge of manslaughter. Bail was set at ten thousand dollars. Near the end of the month John was well enough to travel, and the two brothers returned to their ranch. On February third they returned to Pueblo for another hearing, and John was released for lack of evidence. Returning to their ranch much relieved at John's release, they still had to hope for a similar finding for Clay. On March third, Clay signed over his ranch, hogs, cattle and horses to John for seven hundred dollars.

"John, in case they find against me, this will legally give you ownership to all the stock and the ranch. The money is just on paper, I got enough to last till I find some place to hide for a while. No way I'm going to sit in any cell for killing an ambushing idiot. Everybody in town knows I was in the right, so let's hope lawyer Macon convinces them. If not, I ride on out."

"Damn, Clay, I hate to see you run off like that, but I don't blame you. I'd do the same, was me."

"Well, I understand Macon is pretty good, so maybe me and my horse'll be saved a backbreaking gallop," he chuckled.

"Clay, I keep thinking about that bush-wacking in Fagaly's saloon, and damned if I don't think it was a set-up, y'know?"

"Who do you think would have pulled such a stunt, anyway?"

"Your friend, the governor."

"All right, John. You get an A plus for scrutinizing the inscrutable."

"The what?" John laughed.

"Just pulling your leg, John. But I been thinking the same thing. It has all his earmarks, doesn't it? I wonder if the cattle buy was just to get us up there so Faber and Fagaly could earn themselves a little money? I've a hankering to run up there some night and take Fagaly for a walk in the alley for a little conference. I don't know him well enough to call him more than a light acquaintance, and he never did show up for that drink, or even anytime later offer his condolences. So he might have been in on it."

"He had to have been if the buy was a part of it."

"True enough. Really tempted to go have a talk with him."

"Why don't we wait till your hearing? One thing at a time for now. Lay low in the weeds until I get better, too. Also in the meantime, we'd best watch our backs. I dread any more ambushes. They're no fun at all, let me tell you."

"We'll keep a few of the boys around here in case."

"And how's all this going to affect the ranch? I don't think you're ever going to be able to find any financing for it. Even if you had the cash, I bet they would balk at selling it, even hike the price to couple million."

"I guess I can kiss it goodbye, and I hate worse than hell to do that."

"Sorry, Clay. I know it meant so much to you, and all."

"Not your fault, John. And I'm sorry as hell you got shot up. I just know it was me Faber was after."

But Clay didn't have to take his "long ride" after all, for at the end of March the grand jury in Pueblo found a "no bill" on the charges, concluding he had acted in self-defense. He returned to Cimarron breathing easier.

The month following, in April, he and eleven men, including John, returned to court in Taos as ordered the previous year to answer for the

Cruz Vega murder and assault charges. Before the courthouse entrance their defending attorney Melvin Mills signaled Clay for them to take a walk. Together they meandered across the tree-filled plaza and sat on a bench beneath the shade.

"How's John getting along?" inquired Mills as he lit up a cigar.

"Better than expected, considering. Tell Axtell he's in fine health."

Ignoring the barb, Mills continued. "Please listen, Clay. I've been sent by the Santa Fe people to defend you boys. Here's the deal. The charges will be dropped on all of you if you and John quit the area before a year is up. You'll be fined a hundred dollars, a token fee which they'll pick up. They feel a year should give you more than enough time to settle your affairs here. But if this goes to trial, the five of you charged with murder will definitely go to jail, including you. This arrangement doesn't include McMains, who's not smart enough to stop his crusade against the grant. They'll just keep hamstringing him in the courts until he gets tired or dies."

"And if we don't leave what'll they do, set up another ambush?"

"Clay, I don't know anything about that. This is all I've been told to relay to you."

"By who? The Gov?"

Mills sat silently uncomfortable, fidgeting with his cigar.

"C'mon Mills. Stop squirming like an old woman and answer me like a man. Was it him?"

"Yes," he sighed self-consciously. "But he's not alone in this decision. A half-dozen held a meeting and figured this was best."

"A half-dozen. Was Catron one of them?"

"Please, Clay," he pleaded. "I'm only the messenger."

"I know, following orders like an obedient goat. Catron's so scared of me he's kept out of Colfax County two years. He knows his fat ass isn't bullet-proof. Was he one of them?"

"Yes," came Mills' laborious answer.

"Figures."

"This hearing can be the end of it Clay, with all of you going free. I'd honestly take it. What shall I tell them?"

Allison sat staring at the cluster of men before the courthouse. There was John, alive and healthy and joking with Thorp and Morrison. McMains seemed to be intensely discussing some point of law with Terhune and Davis. It was a bright, sunny afternoon, and an intermixing of Mexicans, Indians and Anglos strolled back-and-forth about their business. It was a peaceful scene with peaceful people on a peaceful day, while Allison sat torn and immersed in an inner war within himself. Leave New Mexico or die. Run with your tail tucked between your legs like a beaten dog, or stay and be shot in the dark down the road by some two-bit gunman renting himself out for a few dollars. If it were only him he'd stay and be damned, stay and take as many of them with him as he could. Hell, he wasn't afraid of a war with these scum. He could rustle up a small army and have a real shoot-out with these trashy land-bandits. In fact he'd love to start it right now and right here by shoving his forty-four into Mills' side and blow him off this bench. But, no, he had to keep his head. It was John he was concerned over. If anything more happened to him it would kill him. The guilt was nearly unbearable as it was, still seeing him writhing on the floor in a sea of blood. All my fault too, being shot-gunned by mistake for him. Yes, it was best and smart both to take the deal handed me before anything more happened to the kid. They're holding all the cards in this game as it is, that's for damn sure. Christ, I hate this. Like leaving a half-full plate.

"Yeah, Mills. I'll take the deal." He then rose depressed and bone-weary and limped across the plaza to John's side, wrapping an affectionate arm around his shoulders. "How you doing, sport?"

"Never better, big brother," he grinned widely. "Just peachy."

Returning to Cimarron ten of the group immediately made for Lambert's saloon for a celebration, while McMains went on home. While the men joyfully felt they had beaten the Ring with their dismissal, Clay was uncustomarily quiet, plus didn't drink much. John noticed and commented, "Clay, you all right? You seem countries off."

"Just pondering, John. Thinking about my next move."

"You mean ours, don't you?"

"Well, yes, of course. Look, I'm going on to the ranch, I'm bone tired after all this. You stay and enjoy yourself, but be careful, hear?"

Clay rode off into the early evening grateful everything played out where no one went to jail, John was healing well, and he could now make plans for them to move on. But they thinking they had whupped the Ring was a laugh. He was glad they had no idea of his second deal with them devils, and hoped they getting so big-headed of escaping prison time wouldn't cause them to make foolish moves in the future. But it was over far as he was concerned, and the hell with it. And the hell with McMains and his grant fight. Losing the ranch was a bitch, yet in a way in the back of his mind he had always sensed it was nothing but a carrot the Ring dangled in front of him. A part of him too was relieved it was all over and done with. It was like a chapter in his life closing and another opening up. He'd go back to the Panhandle where he heard there was yet a lot of grazing land. They would take a bunch of cows with them and resettle somewhere. Hell, it ain't the end of the world. But Christ, how he'd love to settle up with Axtell and Catron before he left!

Before too long, and fitting to his nature, Clay returned to Las Animas with the intent of having a personal conference with Frank Fagaly. He was also there to purchase a few cows this time, and thought it would be a perfect moment to kill two birds with one stone—or bullet, he mused. He made himself very visible around town as he inquired of everyone he met that he was hunting for Mister Fagaly. But it appears his quarry had left town not minutes before Allison's arrival for a vacation on the eastern horizon somewhere. Disgruntled, Clay lastly dropped in at the Olympic Dance Hall before leaving, for perhaps the third or fourth time that day, saying to the bartender, "Give me four quarts of your best rye, young man." Taking them, he informed the barman that his boss owed the bottles to him, "But if he wants to dispute my claim, tell him to ride on down to Cimarron and look me up to collect." With that he turned and left the saloon, forked his horse, and returned home with his pet hound, Rebel, and handful of cows.

Fagaly failed to dispute or correct Clay's claim, and the question of the quarts would remain moot. "A cheap price, I would say," he addressed his horse as he tipped one of the bottles skyward now and then on his return ride.

The first week in August Clay, John and a few of their cohorts were putting the finishing touches on a batch of 101 cows to run off to the Panhandle the following day, when they looked up in unison to see a lone horseman riding slowly toward them. Too far to make out who he was, several of the men grabbed their rifles and cranked a round in the chamber, thinking it might be some ranch hand from the 101 foolishly looking for "strays."

"Now hold on, boys," cautioned Clay. "Let's wait and see who he is. Might be just a visitor."

"He does look sort of familiar," spoke John, reaching for his own Winchester.

"Sure does," agreed Clay. "But I can't quite place him."

As the rider got closer the brothers pulled off their hats and let out a hearty howl.

"Good God almighty!" they both exclaimed. "It's brother Monroe! I'll be damned!"

Cantering up to the knot of men, Monroe announced with a wide grin, "Good to see you two yahoos! And I can't believe my eyes that I caught both of you actually working!"

After introductions all around, Clay asked, "How about joining us for a steak dinner with all the trimmings, Mister Monroe? We're just now done branding here and was set to eat up a storm."

"By golly," replied a famished Monroe, "thought you'd never ask. Haven't had a decent meal since feasting at ma's table back home."

"Well, young 'un," informed Clay. "You are about to partake in some of the finest beef this side of heaven. We call it, One-Oh-One."

"Good grief, what in the world is that?"

"A breed me and John and these men here produced by special

inbreeding," revealed Clay with a sly wink at the others. "The result is unbelievable. One-Oh-One is short for One-Oh-Wonderful Critter. Ain't nothing like it, boy."

The other five men nodded and smiled their approval, rubbed their bellies and chanted, "One-Oh-Wonderful is right!"

"I don't know a thing about cattle or the inbreeding of them," said Monroe. "But lead me to it, this I got to taste. What'd you cross this cow with, anyway?"

"Never you mind," came John. "We'll tell you all about it after we all stuff ourselves. So let's get with it!"

As they chowed down Monroe gave a sprinkling of family news and local Clifton gossip. "But I just got itchy-footed and wanted a change of scenery, not being a Grange officer any longer. Me and dad didn't get reelected, so it kind of left me at loose ends."

"You still teaching school?" asked John.

"Oh, yes. But got tired of that too, so I thought a little vacation was in order."

"Vacation here all you want and as long as you like," spoke Clay. "By the way, how'd you get here, anyway? Not all the way by horseback, by the local brand on your horse."

"About the same as you and Coleman. From Clifton I grabbed a steamer, then a couple of trains, then a stage down to Cimarron. There I bought a horse from a Tony Meloche. After telling him who I was, he only charged me twenty dollars for the horse and threw in the saddle. He also told me how to get here."

"Good old Tony. Got to thank him next time I see him."

"So now. How about that wonderful One-Oh-One critter we ate up? What kind of a breed is that? That is the most delicious cut of meat I've had in my life!"

"Well, John," sighed Clay. "Suppose you be the one to enlighten him."

"This is the recipe, Monroe," designated John, as he held up a branding iron. Following his descriptive account all the men laughed, including Monroe. He turned to Clay and John with, "I should have known I was getting my leg pulled. But good lord, if anybody gets wind of this don't you think there'll be hell to pay? Like the possibility of a necktie party?"

"Only if we get careless or greedy," answered Clay. "And actually a lot of the small ranchers play this game, siphoning off a few cows here and there from the big boys, especially the Maxwell grant herds. I agree it's principally wrong, but it's economically correct, for it's the price the big ranchers have to pay for playing king of the hill. A few times we were most fortunate in coming across 'lost' Maxwell cows with calves, so we gently led them here to their new domicile, then branded the young ones so they would feel right at home. Guess you could say we run a home for wayward beef, y'know?"

Before long Clay entered the ranks of cattle brokering, as well as drover, on several drives. One was to East St. Louis, Illinois, the others to Dodge City, Kansas. It was in East St. Louis that he had an adventure, or misadventure, coming away with a few bruises and lumps. From the stockyards there he made his way to the Green Tree Saloon. Having several drinks he inquired of the bartender, "I'm in search of a man by the name of Alexander Kessinger. Do you know of him?"

"I certainly do. What is your business with him?"

"I intend on giving him a good kick."

Taken aback, the barman stalled while a customer, who heard the comment, scurried off to inform Kessinger, who happened to be nearby. In a trice Kessinger appeared and addressed Allison. "Good afternoon, stranger. I hear you are seeking a man named Kessinger."

"Yes, I am."

"I understand you have some difficulty to settle with him."

"Yes, I certainly do. I want to meet him. He is said to pride himself on being a brave and good fighter. I want to see for myself, and when I meet him he will hear and feel me as I pummel him righteously."

"Well, I know Kessinger and he is not going to allow anyone to get the drop on him."

"I also understand he is handy with weapons. I am also a shootist."

As Clay made a move toward his pocket, all the while not realizing he was talking to his quarry, the latter, thinking Allison knew him and was going for his gun, hauled off and solidly punched him, sending him to the floor. As Clay tried to regain his feet, his opponent kicked him a few times in an effort to deny him his footing. Clay grabbed a missed kick and flung Kessinger into several tables. In moments the two men were busy swinging and punching each other in heated frenzy. Kessinger went down twice, but bounced back into the fray. As Kessinger was dropped to the floor for the third time, two of his friends joined the melee and began pounding Allison fore and aft. Soon the four men were grunting, groaning and cursing as they exchanged and absorbed knuckles and gouges from each other's fists. Bloody noses and a few closed eyes were in evidence amid overturned chairs and broken furniture. Before too long a half-dozen men inserted themselves within the pugilistic festivities and separated the combatants. Once everyone settled down, the house sprung for a few rounds of drinks, after which the gladiators reeled off into the late afternoon, a little worn and a bit weary, but hugely exuberant after their robust exercise.

Allison enjoyed his new work as a cattle broker, for it took him on the road meeting other ranchers and brokers of the cattle fraternity, and he got to share with a few of the hustler's questionable brands and hot bovines that came across their way, sometimes in small herds. He especially enjoyed lifting cows from the Maxwell pasture whenever possible, still in a funk over facing the future loss of his ranch and the grant not making any effort to make it any easier for him to purchase it. The hell with them, he figured. Tit for tat, and he'd get all the free tit he could while he could. It gave him a shot in the arm and made up for his inevitable move. A few of the other herds also were not overlooked, like his old favorite, the 101.

While it was not a high volume of cattle being shipped to the Panhandle, there was enough traffic that, as the Allisons moved some cows eastward, they would meet neighborhood herders returning who would salute with a wave and a wink, and a pocketful of cash. Even many of the gold miners were high-grading from the fields and mines, taking home a few samples here and there in their pockets or lunch pails. As their stash accumulated they would ship it off in boxes or trunks mixed with clothes or household items out of state to relatives. It was rip-off time against the grant, and the working stiffs had no qualms stealing from whom they viewed as the master thieves of the valley. Others, also not recognizing the grant's authority, chopped down acres of timber for use as they pleased, while others burned or destroyed grant buildings and property. Arson and vandalism became the final weapons of choice in a losing fight against bureaucratic corruption, aside from armed threats against surveyors and occasional shootings.

One of the strong anti-granters was the Andrew Jackson Young family of the Upper Vermejo, and good friend of the Allisons. Besides the Tolby murder, which drove a wedge between Clay and the Santa Feers, it was Andrew Young who influenced Clay to cease his association with the Santa Fe Ring. In time the Allison brothers ended up marrying the McCulloch sisters, Elizabeth and Dora, both of whom were living with the Youngs. From Missouri and orphaned while still children, the sisters had been shifted about several times until finally moving in with their two brothers at the Young's, Andrew being married to their aunt.

Andrew Young was a member of the Colfax County Alliance, a part social and quasi-anti-grant group, which held family get-togethers, dinners and dance parties, and where John Allison met and fell in love with Elizabeth, then nineteen, and whom he rechristened, "Kate."

"Well, John, Monroe," Clay announced one night over a toddy and barbeque in their back yard. "In a few days I plan a trip to the Mobeetie area in the Panhandle. I hear there's still a lot of open-grazing left out there, and I aim to grab a few sections for us. I'll take a handful of cows to pay for the trip."

Although Clay intended on keeping his end of the bargain with the

Santa Feers by moving off the grant, he still kept to himself the agreement in order save face. He told no one, especially his brothers. "Hell, no one's going to win against them vultures," he justified. "Not the settlers or the squatters, much as many would have a legitimate foot in the courthouse door if they could find an honest lawyer. But Colfax County doesn't recognize squatters' rights or homesteaders' rights, so McMains can rant and holler all he wants. Both Rings recognize only one right, and that's the right of what they want. That's why I'm leaving."

The Santa Fe Ring was relieved Clay was finally vacating the premises. He was more than they cared to handle as a hired hand, too unpredictable, and had a drinking problem which made him a walking time-bomb. He was a good man with a gun, but unreliable where a cooler head was needed, and they wanted someone more amendable toward following orders. The Ring's investment demanded a more tractable and thinking combatant, not an explosive bulldozer, and most assuredly not a loose canon.

The day before his start for the Panhandle, Clay was in Schwenk's Saloon, across from Lambert's, quenching his thirst. He didn't intend on over-doing it because of his forthcoming trip, but the thought of being forced into leaving the area by his former employers ate at him, and it made him testy and edgy. It wasn't long before he ran off the last four customers with his cutting remarks, and was about to leave himself, to the great relief of the bartender, when deputy Mace Bowman walked in, an ex-drinking compadre.

The two had been one-time cronies for a very brief moment in time a few years before, when he also had ridden with Allison's men on a few night raids against the squatters. In fact, Mace was one of the masked cowboys who whipped the confession out of Cruz Vega, then dragged him through the field behind his horse. His alias "Mason" was all that was left on the Taos court records, and he was never brought in for a hearing, no one "knowing" who Mason was.

The commonality of both being Southerners (Bowman was from Kentucky), both being white supremacists (Bowman's father and relatives were slave owners), and both having served in the Confederate cavalry (Bowman in the Eleventh Texas), drew the two together immediately, and they joined forces in attempting to drink the local taverns dry. But following the Vega killing Bowman withdrew from Allison and his men and began to take stock of himself as a lawman. From then on he took his badge seriously, to the point of becoming a fervent anti-granter which gave serious concern for a time to the Colfax and Santa Fe Rings. Later, his organized settler's group cut the fences and built structures on the illegally wired pastures of a defunct land grant the Red River Cattle Company contended was not public domain, but theirs through purchase. Later, when the courts found it to be a specious claim, the company was forced to remove themselves.

Bowman also had a talent which was envied by Allison, and who constantly pled for his tutoring: how he drew so fast with his six-gun. The two often held contests and paced off to draw on each other in various saloons before nervous customers who usually made for posts, ducked behind partitions, or often fled out the door. But Allison forever came out second best. So he finally surrendered to the fact that it was a God-given talent beyond his capabilities, and continued honing his expertise in "getting the drop" on whatever opponents he came across. And now, when Bowman appeared at the bar, it was not with an air of comradery that Allison viewed him.

"Well, well, deputy. If you ain't a sight for sore eyes."

"Set us up a pair of bourbons, barkeep," requested Bowman.

"I already got one, lawman." Bowman's badge brought rancid, hostile memories of Constable Faber, and of John lying in a puddle of blood.

"Suit yourself."

"How's business, Deputy?"

"Booming, cowboy. Just plain booming."

"Your bailiwick still up in Otero?"

"Yes, it is."

"Pretty wild little village, that."

"It's wild everywhere, but we certainly have our share of bad boys."

"Like Port Stockton?"

"Yep. Guess he wins the prize for being the meanest."

"Heard you and Pete Burleson run him out of the county."

"The state, actually. Amazing how his hearing improved with a loaded forty-five pressed between his eyes. Made tracks so fast, didn't hear him leave. Gone to Durango to join his brother, Ike."

Clay emptied his glass, refilled it, then slid the bottle of rye toward Bowman. "Help yourself, Mace."

"Don't mind if I do, thank you." Bowman poured himself a full load in his double shot glass. Sliding the quart back he asked, "I understand you plan to move off to the Panhandle?"

"That's right. Going out tomorrow to shop around for some acreage."

"Selling your ranch here?"

Allison bristled at the not-so subtle barb, Bowman obviously aware of Allison's deal with the Ring. It brought back his feelings of frustration and rage at the Ring and Axtell, for their practically ripping the ranch from his grip, and for killing his dream of becoming a successful herder. Bowman, he felt, was laughing at him, twisting the knife.

"You in the market to buy, Deputy?" Clay queried sarcastically.

"Naw. Not much for cattle, cowboy. I'm a horseman myself, and will keep my small stable business."

"I don't like your smugness."

"Really, now?"

"That's right."

"Maybe you're just being over-sensitive?" With that, Bowman took his elbows off the bar and turned to face Allison. With his right thumb he casually flicked the thong-loop from the hammer of his Colt. Clay watched, feigning boredom, then stood to face the lawman, his ice-blue eyes boring into Bowman's brown orbs.

With a mocking smile the deputy said, "I don't think you should try to draw until you take that thong off your hammer, killer."

After a long, quiet moment, Allison slowly slipped the leather cord from his holstered six-gun. Both waited in silence. The barman quickly scooted to the end of the bar, ready to hit the floor.

Bowman said icily, "Have at it, cowboy,"

Allison had the greatest urge to grasp the handle of his revolver and bring it up shooting, knowing he'd probably take two or three shots in the chest before having a chance of firing one. It was a death-wish at most and he knew it, drunk as he was. But he wasn't quite stupid-drunk enough to try it, realizing he didn't have a chance.

"Hell," he snorted. "No use in both of us dying," giving words to his often-claimed boast that he would have to be shot in the head and instantly killed or his opponent would die with him.

"I also believe a permanent change in location would do wonders for your health," suggested Bowman.

Allison, still staring at the deputy, carefully re-thonged his hammer, emptied his glass, then walked out of Schwenk's into the afternoon sun for the ride to his ranch, and the next day to Texas.

While in Texas he heard that one of his herders had been killed by Dodge City lawmen, and as a result Allison made an angered visit to the Kansas town.

It seems earlier in the year, on an early July morning, after spending the afternoon and night bar-hopping, four inebriated young cowboys decided to call it quits after a bellyful of booze. About two a.m. they went to the marshal's office, claimed their sidearms, then took to their horses. As they were galloping down Front Street, twenty-three-year-old George Hoy in a farewell salute of enthusiasm riskily punctured the dark sky with three or four rounds from his Colt. Wyatt Earp and Jim Masterson ran out on the street in time to see the riders making for the toll bridge across the Arkansas River and cut loose on them. Three of them made it across while Hoy, bringing up the rear, was hit at the edge of the crossing and fell from his horse, his arm broken in two places. He died some three weeks later in August of complications.

Many of the Texas cattlemen and herders had been complaining of the policemen's rampant passion for "buffaloing" unarmed cowboys, and that many were robbed, shot, and pistol-whipped indiscriminately. Wyatt Earp was an expert at the buffaloing method, and it was his favorite style of apprehension and fine-collecting, using the barrel of his gun as a club. But of course the Texans felt they were being especially targeted where it bordered on abuse of authority, and felt there were too many bullies wearing a badge.

In the first weeks of September Clay journeyed to Dodge with several friends, and upon his arrival he collected a handful more, until he had a small army of twenty-five, mainly Texans. Armed with Winchesters and Colts, they let it be known they were "lawman hunting." Chalk Beeson, city councilman and part-owner of the Long Branch Saloon, and cattleman Dick McNulty, quickly took it upon themselves to try and diffuse the situation by approaching Allison and reasoning with him. But Clay was in too heated a frame of mind to back down from his intention of bringing a fight to whatever lawmen he could find. The stories he had heard were legion of the abuse they perpetually heaped upon the herders in general, and Texans in particular. And he especially wanted Earp's scalp.

"Tell you what, Clay," spoke McNulty. "Let's you and me check out all these bars along Front Street here for policemen. When we find one we'll have a talk about what your complaint is and see what can be settled civilly. What say?"

"All right, Dick. Let's go."

Up one side of the street and then down the other they went, but not a badge-wearer could be found. Out on the street before his men once again, McNulty and Beeson once again discussed the situation coolly and calmly to where Allison finally agreed to their request of surrendering their firearms, that they would be in no danger, and which would be returned to them upon their departing town. Having seen the logic of their argument, Clay and a few of the men did so, while a handful turned and rode out of town, with, "You need us, Clay, just send word, hear?"

Allison wanted to look about one more time for Wyatt before taking his own leave, and strolled alone to the Long Branch where it was known Earp was a dealer. Sure enough, across the room Clay spotted Wyatt seated in the slightly higher lookout's chair overseeing a Faro game. Strolling through the scattered crowd Allison moved to Earp's right to keep an eye on his gunhand.

"Earp," he addressed, looking slightly upward. "Don't move or step down. I just want a few words with you before I leave town."

"Are you Clay Allison?"

"None other."

"Go ahead. I'm listening."

"I don't want to hear of another of my men being buffaloed or pistol-whipped by you or any of your men, understand? I don't know what your problem is, but if a pair of you can't overtake an unarmed drunk, then find another job."

"Hell, Mister Allison, you know when a man has a snoot-full he's not only a load of dynamite, but an unpredictable package."

"Like that poor bastard Guadalupe Flores, an unarmed drunk who was deliberately beaten on the head two different times in a row by some policeman? I wonder if that wasn't your handywork?"

"I don't know anything about that, Allison," Earp answered as his face reddened.

"Of course you wouldn't, you two-bit pimp. Just remember this, Earp. If I have to come back to look you up again, kiss your sorry ass good-bye." Clay then turned and walked out, claimed his firearms, and returned to Texas.

Perhaps twenty miles north of Mobeetie was Fort Elliot, a cantonment created to protect settlers from occasional raids by wandering tribes. Allison and a handful of ranchers were in the company of a group of soldiers as volunteers one October afternoon when word came that warriors had surrounded an isolated cabin and were threatening to kill the occupants, a farmer and his wife. The lieutenant in charge of the troops refused to attack, fearing it was a set-up for an ambush.

Allison turned to the officer and asked, "Let me take your twenty-five men and get this over with, Lieutenant."

"No, no! This is a military unit under my command, and no civilian is authorized to lead them anywhere!"

"Good gravy, you jackass!" roared Clay undiplomatically. "How in hell did you Yankee scum win the war with yellow-bellied turds like you leading the troops?"

"Mister Allison, you are out of order! Another such outburst and I will have to take legal measures!" A few of the soldiers snickered and rolled their eyes in embarrassment.

"Why you sniveling piss-ant! Take them bars on your shoulders and shove them up next to your courage!"

With that Clay turned to the civilians around him and asked for volunteers to follow him. Fourteen answered without hesitation and galloped off with a rebel yell behind Allison, who was already on his way a half-dozen lengths ahead, his pistol drawn and blazing. It was a brief but hot engagement, and the furious determination of the charging men unnerved the raiders where they broke off and fled. One of the ranchers was killed and Allison's mount took a slight bullet wound, but the rescued farmer and his wife were effusive with thanks and appreciation. Clay led the men back to the settlements with the body of the dead man draped across his saddle, and as they passed the officer mounted before his men, Allison led the ranchers in a series of hen cackles. Humiliated, the red-faced lieutenant sat mute.

In mid-December Clay returned to Colfax County to attend John and Kate's marriage celebration held at the Andrew Young home. John was twenty-four and Kate twenty. Her sister Dora, sixteen at the time, was looked upon with some favor by Clay, then thirty-seven, and although no plans or pledges of betrothment were made, there were unspoken thoughts of a probable second marriage in the future.

Clay may have been the local hero of the macho set, but it didn't appear to have helped his love life any. Back in the mid-eighteen seventies he had been eyeing one of the attractive Bishop sisters, Josephine. But he was cut short when her mother greeted him at the door one day and chased him away with a broom. Swatting him about the shoulders and back as he stumbled off, she shouted angrily that she wanted someone more substantial for a son-in-law than an expert with fists, gun or knife. Josephine did very well for herself in marrying Frank Springer in October eighteen hundred and seventy-six. Then there was pretty Carrie Gale. Again Clay lost. She wed Marion Littrell in September eighteen hundred and seventy-four. Littrell was range foreman of both the Maxwell Grant and the Red River Cattle Companies, future four-time sheriff, and a friend of Allison's. Earlier he had been anti-grant, but seeing where the grass was greener, eventually made the necessary readjustment. He was also another fast-draw artist who bested Clay in a series of "duels," and their last contest was over Carrie's little hand on a flat bridge over an arroyo below the village of Dawson. Accompanied by a handful of cowboys everybody placed bets on who would win both the duel and Carrie's hand, and to Clay's chagrin no one bet on him except himself.

"Well, hell with you spoilsports," mock-admonished Allison. "I love being the underdog, and just watch my smoke!"

Everybody laughed good-naturedly and stood back to watch the action. "One, two, three, DRAW!" called out the monitor, and every time while Clay was still clearing his holster Littrell had his firearm leveled at Allison's mid-section and clicked off an empty cylinder. After a dozen times, Clay threw in the towel with, "Aw, hell, Marion, you can have her. I'm not ready to get hitched just yet, anyway."

But at John and Kate's marriage celebration he could not but help feel envy at the beaming couple, obviously happy, radiant and in love. He not only thought back on Josephine Bishop and Carrie Gale, but on Martha Matthews and those two wonderful children of hers. And of course he wryly recalled Tina Menchaca and her refusal to set up housekeeping with him. It was no little bruise to his ego that even a prostitute didn't care to have him. Shaking his head silently to himself he enviously looked upon John and his bride laughing in the crowded room. Here he was pushing forty, and not even a hooker to show for it! But he grinned too, recalling Tina's room mate, Princess Bountiful Light, skipping and dancing about like a loco-weeded chicken, yelling, "Malo! Malo!" Christ, he chuckled, recalling those flashing bare thighs and bottom. Maybe he should send for her!

"Hey, Clay," asked John as he walked over to him from across the room. "What's so funny? What you cackling to yourself over, anyway?"

"What?" he asked, as if wakened from a trance. "Oh, hell, John, nothing in particular. Just how happy I am for you and your better half, there. You two make a good looking couple, and I wish you both the best of everything."

"Why, thank you, big brother. But don't you fret none," he winked. "I know Dora's sweet on you. I got an idea before a year or two I'll be dancing at your wedding!"

Returning to the Panhandle with Monroe and a small herd of cattle, the brothers satisfied legalities on several sections along Gageby Creek northwest of Mobeetie, and began laying the foundation and framework for future living quarters.

The Panhandle at the time was a lure for free range graziers, being largely unsettled, and the last refuge in the state for open range. The mostly unorganized twenty-six counties which made up the roughly twenty-two thousand square-mile region held a population of only one thousand six-hundred seven in eighteen hundred and eighty. Hence it began to draw herders as the eastern portions of the state filled with a migration more sympathetic to farming. The June eighteen hundred and eighty census of nine-hundred and four square mile Hemphill County, population one hundred forty-nine, places Clay Allison living with the J.C. Hoggetts. Next door were the Colemans. Yet unorganized, Hemphill also claimed the only teacher and geologist in the entire Panhandle.

Wheeler County to the south, where the Allisons eventually settled, measured nine-hundred fourteen square miles, and was the largest in headcount, five-hundred and twelve. This included the two-hundred ninety-six military personal of Fort Elliot on Sweetwater Creek, northwest of Mobeetie. The rolling plains of Wheeler County, organized in eighteen hundred and seventy-nine, began taking on the atmosphere of a thriving town with three saloons, three hotels, two doctors, one J.P., a postmaster, a gambler and three lawyers. The law was represented by a sheriff, a constable and a pair of deputies. One of the deputies, John W. Poe, would a year later be serving under Sheriff Patrick F. Garrett in Lincoln County, New Mexico, while on the hunt for Billy the Kid, and be in on the kill.

On March twenty-fifth, eighteen hundred and eighty Clay registered ACE as his brand in Wheeler County, and in May attracted notice again. He was one of twenty-two men who refused to pay taxes. Having enjoyed free grass and open grazing for years, the herders naturally resented such intrusion to their liberties. Yet, whatever their feelings, it was a clue that the world of free pasturing was nearing its end, and the introduction of barbed wire in the area by the large cattle companies the following year helped hasten the termination of unrestricted grazing. Pressure was put on the small ranchers, and some found themselves fenced in, and others fenced out, by the miles of wiring, sometimes with no access or easement to their property. It bore the uncomfortable echoes of the Maxwell Land Grant again, and Clay began feeling history repeating itself, and as if he were its foil.

On January seventeenth, eighteen hundred and eighty-one Lou Coleman and Clay Allison were summoned for jury duty at Wheeler County's third district court. It was also noted locally that "three of the Allison brothers moved in on the Gageby."

One of the top trail bosses of the time, Sim Holstein, lived a few miles north of the Allisons at Wolfe Creek, running the Cross Bar Seven. Also, a pair of young cowboys of the Mobeetie area would recall years later how they knew Clay as a quiet, unassuming individual, with no element of the desperado about him at all. To them he was a magnificent appearing man, over six feet, with keen, clear, blue eyes, well dressed and with the absolute qualities of a gentleman, polite in the extreme. It must be said that Clay in his sober and civil moments was as kind and sociable as a lamb, thoughtful of others in every way. But of course the two young eulogists were fortunately spared Allison's barroom antics when his brain became a raisin floating in rotgut, and also were not in the vicinity while he was earning his late title, Wolf of the Washita.

When Clay had earlier made his personal reconnaissance to the area with Monroe, he saw nothing but endless possibilities, especially after he was fortunate in picking up and holding a pair of sections along Gageby Creek in northern Wheeler County. He and Monroe picked out a spot where they spent a week laying out the foundation and beginning structure of a cabin. Both were quite pleased at the plans they shared for their future cattle business. Clay particularly envisioned the shards of his old dream come together again, like the fabled Phoenix rising from its ashes, and there was no stopping him now. This was truly it! He would have the last laugh on the Ring after all! And his old man.

Some afternoons as they walked along the bank of the narrow and smoothly flowing Gageby Creek, Clay would quietly thrill at his luck in finding and attaining such an Edenic splendor.

"Isn't this just plain beautiful, Monroe?"

"Yep, sure is. All the water we need, ample grazing, a scattering strand of woods here and there. Like a park, Clay. A wild little park."

"I can hardly wait to get John and Kate out here. I know they'll love it. And Lou and Saluda, too. Lou's been itching to leave Colfax County and the grant hassle, so this area's still open for him if he wants."

"He'll want," grinned Monroe. "I'm certain Saluda will see to that."

"Think the folks would like this place?"

"Folks?"

"Dad. And Mom. If they could see it?"

"Well, sure," replied Monroe, slightly taken aback, Clay never having much to say of their parents. "Why not?"

"Aw, just curious."

In his new exuberance Clay sent Monroe back to New Mexico to relay his enthusiasm and rosette picture of endless opportunities. It influenced Lou Coleman to finally sell out to his partner Irwin Lacy, who soon after moved his herds to Colorado where he found a new partner, George Thompson. Both Lacy and Coleman had for some time entertained the idea of getting out of Colfax County. Now both did so, going their separate directions. As for Clay joining the Ring as their man Friday, both his former employers were disgusted with him, feeling principally that it was a scoundrel's cowardly opportunity for gain. But too, since they were not affected, they ignored the angst Allison caused among the homesteaders and squatters.

Lou Coleman, with Saluda and their two offspring, found a section on the Washita River ten miles north of the Allisons, and he continued running a herd of cows. Shortly after, John arrived with Kate and year-old Esther, registering 101 as his brand, Clay's earlier one of New Mexico.

One afternoon Texas Ranger Captain George Arrington was in Mobeetie with a handful of his men. Clay and Monroe happened to be present, slightly loaded, having left a bar.

"Well, hell's bells, Monroe. There's ol' 'Cap' Arrington. Looks more like Santa Claus with that belly-long beard, don't he?" he chuckled. The Captain and Clay had met a few times the last couple of days, and although he heard Arrington was a hell-on-wheels enforcement officer, he felt Cap took himself a tad too seriously. Clay urged them closer to the small group, and soon stood just within the knot of men, right behind Cap.

Appearances aside, the ranger did have the reputation of being absolutely fearless, and with an extremely short temper to match. He was at the time engrossed in a warm debate with a local politico, the two having differences over regional legal authority.

"Watch me pull a stunt on Cap," whispered Clay to his brother. "I'm going to get his gun."

"Oh, God, Clay!" pleaded Monroe. "Please don't do it!"

"Shhh. Just stand and don't move. It'll be a cinch."

If Monroe could have moved he would have made instant tracks. But he was frozen in fear at what disastrous results they might be facing when Clay grabbed Cap's forty-four. He'd heard of the ranger's raging temper and wanted no part of it. Now all he could do was stand and sweat.

As Clay stealthily eased to Arrington's right side, the fingers of his left hand carefully and slowly slipped the cord off the Captain's holstered Colt. This done, Allison waited a few moments before proceeding to make certain the ranger had not sensed or suspected anything unusual was taking place. Satisfactorily seeing he was still verbally belaboring his point of legality, Clay continued. Ever so gingerly he raised the sidearm from its scabbard, creeping two, three, four inches upward, when Arrington paused in his rant and without turning said icily, "Put that gun back where it belongs, Allison, and re-thong the hammer. You got about ten seconds, or you're a dead son of a bitch." He then continued his arguing as if nothing had occurred. Clay, uncustomarily shaken, quickly whispered, "I, I'm sorry, Captain," and hurriedly reinserted the gun, re-thonged it, then swiftly sidled away from the crowd with a relief-sighing Monroe in tow.

"Good God, Clay! I almost had a heart attack! Next time you try a stunt like that, give me five minutes warning so I can quick leave town!"

"Aw, hell," shrugged Clay. "How in hell was I to know he has no sense of humor!"

Monroe never admonished Clay for his heavy drinking, for how could he, being an habitual imbiber himself. But he knew that Clay should try to abstain from alcohol altogether because of the dire effect it had upon him. It was the unpredictable results he feared, and although not often, it occurred enough times to warrant him not even wanting to be in his company when in a local saloon tipping a few. Monroe was mainly a solitary drinker, quietly sitting at a corner table or standing alone at the far corner of a bar, letting the booze slowly hammer him until he could barely climb into his saddle and return to the ranch. John was the lightest drinker of all three, and at times Clay would rag him mercilessly for having but three or four drinks, which he slowly sipped, before leaving for home. Yet Clay would pointedly apologize to him upon his departure with, " Just joshing, little brother. I only wish I had the good sense to quit and couple-up with a sweet woman and make my life worthwhile."

"You will, big brother," John would smile with a wave of his hand. "You will."

It was Dora all three brothers had in mind, without speaking of her. She was past eighteen now, and as much as Clay was taken by her he wasn't sure of her true feelings toward him. And being extra-ordinarily shy around women, aside from the ladies of the night, he was too insecure to make the proper move to let her know of his interest in her, regardless of both brother's urging.

"John's right, Clay," spoke Monroe. "You should make a move in a domestic direction, and before too long. What're you now, thirty-eight?"

"Thirty-nine last September. But good grief," he grinned. "I had no idea you came all the way from Clifton to preach to me of the virtues of sobriety and marital joy. So tell me, Tennessee padre, where's the lady you're going to hang up your bottle for?"

"Ah, Clay," he grinned. "You know there is no preacher in me. It's just that John and I feel a feminine presence in your life would be just the tonic for you, to concentrate on the more positive aspects of your life, to keep you away from many of your rowdier activities. As to the lady I would set my bottle aside for, I'm afraid she has come and gone long ago."

"Well, unless I misremember, about the time I left Clifton for Texas there was a hot rumor galloping about the countryside that you were thick with some local damsel."

"Yes, very true. But she's long gone, and back there somewhere in the past. Never worked out." He stared distantly across the saloon toward the door as if seeking escape, brooding over a distant face, ignoring Clay's commentary in what he felt was an intrusion into a personal memory he desired to keep interred. Somewhere in Monroe's earlier years there was an unrequited love theme he never spoke of, and to be reminded of it now made him feel uncomfortable, emotionally unwieldy.

"John and I," Monroe went on, "wish you would pay a little more attention to Dora. She's quite taken by you, you know."

"I know of no such thing," bristled Clay.

"But she is. She talks constantly of you to her sister, and Kate in turn passes her words and feelings on to John."

America Medora "Dora" McCulloch, Kate's younger sister by four years, had a crush on Clay since first seeing him at sixteen. His unholy and terrifying reputation to her held no fear or revulsion, for in her romantic mind she saw him as dashing and flamboyant. She mooned away her hours and days over him in a series of daydreams and teenaged swooning, tirelessly expressing her secret obsession of him to Kate. At Kate and John's wedding Dora couldn't keep her eyes from Clay, admiring him from across the room, her eyes glistening and her heart aching as she fixed her gaze upon him laughing, cavorting and dancing with most of the women all night, praying he would ask her for a dance, just one, but her wishes were all in vain. She caught his glance now and then but he would look away quickly, as if caught in forbidden thoughts, thoughts Dora also unspokenly shared. To her John was the handsomest of men, but Clay was more than merely handsome, he was excitingly gallant and touched her imagination to the core, fed and ravished her fantasies.

And so for years she would confess her love for him to Kate, and knew she would pass the news on to John, whom she hoped would in turn finally relay to Clay, her imagined beloved, like a telegram from her soul to his heart. Monroe was soon brought into the trio's confidence, and they became a quartet of conspirators surreptitiously plotting bringing the two together, honestly and sincerely believing that all Clay needed was the love of a good woman.

"I almost asked her for a dance at John's wedding party," confessed Clay. "But damn if I wasn't scared as a whore in church. She looked so pretty too, standing all alone across the room. But she was only sixteen and I thought she'd shy away because of my hellish ways."

"From what John told me, she was dying for you to ask."

"That so? Embarrassing what opportunities I've missed." He though fleetingly of Martha Matthews, wondering still.

"I think next time you visit John and Kate you should break the ice and speak a bit to Dora. We all know she likes you. She really does, Clay. Don't just stand on the pier and miss this boat. Get aboard, big brother."

Slightly taken aback at Monroe's words which echoed Longwill's years before, Clay could only agree. "Ah, ummm, guess you're right. Thanks Monroe. Hell, let's go have a drink on it."

"All right," he concurred unenthusiastically. "I got time for a quick one. Got some chores I been putting off for too long, and I got to go."

"Ah, another day won't matter," asserted Clay.

"These jobs will," insisted Monroe as they entered a saloon, within which he hastily downed a double-shot and left unregrettedly, with proper apology, of course.

It wasn't too long before the serpent of Clay's Eden rose its head on the horizon with the establishment of larger cattle ranches. Some, reflecting Colfax County, were fronted by absentee landlords, the monied class of noblemen from England, Scotland and Ireland, plus financiers from Chicago, Boston and New York. Add to that, the liberal use of the newfangled invention called "bobbed wire" put the final quietus on open-range grazing, neatly tucking up the larger ranches of the Panhandle. And to gain political control of local, county and state offices, the Panhandle Cattle Association (originally organized to combat out-of-control rustling, since Arrington' s handful of Texas Rangers were helpless to cope with the rampant virus in the vast Panhandle), cleverly chose loyal employees to run for office, with of course the result of a bovine oligarchy. Although there was some justification for the smaller ranchers balking at the somewhat feudalistic atmosphere permeating the vast cow country, Clay took it more personally and writhed at the invisible bonds, and imagined himself as the target. Added with all the above, Clay's heavy imbibing and outrageous antics while under the influence was beginning to wear thin with several people in the Allison camp. John's wife Kate was just waiting to explode, but until now had shown her antipathy only before her husband. Yet John knew, and was nervous over it, that she was but a fraction away from confronting his older brother. It was like a second Rebellion brewing, and Christ, he was the Yankee caught in the middle.

"John, I know you think highly of Clay, but I am sick of him coming around smelling like a liquor factory. When he picks up little Esther and sets her on his lap I could die, he stinking of rotgut and breathing it in her face. And he grabs Bertha, not two months old, dancing about with her in his arms. What if he stumbles and falls with her one of these times?"

"Honey, he means no harm, he loves the kids, wants some himself. And we don't have any liquor in the house, like you wanted. There is no drinking here, and you know I hardly touch the stuff. Only when I get with Clay and Monroe now and then."

"I know, I know, but can't he come in here sober for a change, or at least not stinking of it? I abhor the children being exposed to him that way. It isn't right, and it isn't healthy."

"Aw, they're too young to be influenced in any way by his drinking, honey. He's just crazy about visiting with the kids, is all."

"Well," she returned in exasperation, "you tell him to keep the hell away from here while drinking and stinking hear? If I have to tell him I'll burn both his ears clear off his head!"

"All right, I will, I promise, I promise."

"And I'm so sick of his constant belly-aching about the Maxwell Grant, the Panhandle Cattle Association, the barbed wire and the lack of open free range. Can't he get it through his thick head that times are changing? He either changes with it, or gets on his horse and gets out!"

It suddenly dawned on John that Kate was at her wits end and was distraught at what she perceived was a threat to their home turf. It was her way of letting him know that what she cherished was being imperiled, their home, and especially what she held sacred, their marriage. He set his paper down on the kitchen table and rose to go to her as she stood staring out the window, slid his arms around her from behind, and drew her to him. "Kate, sweetheart, I love you more than anything in the world, and nothing or anyone is going to make me feel any different or any less."

She turned, hugging him. "Oh, John, I know that. And thank you for those words, I love hearing them. And I love you so much it would kill me if anything went wrong between us."

"Don't you ever worry about anything, Kate. You're closer to me than my right arm. You're always in my heart no matter where I am. I don't want you to ever think that Clay's roistering about is any threat to us, or our happiness."

"Thank you, John. Maybe I do fear too much his influence on you. But I get so terrified when you're off with him, that you might get shot again, killed or hurt bad. I'm truly in a panic sometimes, alone here, waiting for your return. Not feeling safe until you walk through the door."

"Oh no, Kate, please. Our times out are as tame as can be. You fret needlessly, really."

"And I keep recalling that ugly nickname of his, Wolf of the Washita. Good lord, how can he be so proud of that? Or proud that people merely fear him? I honestly can't comprehend a grown man acting that way."

"I'll talk to him, honey. I will. And let him know it's not good for the kids to see him liquored-up that way. He'll understand, you'll see."

But with Lou Coleman and Saluda, the boot was on the other foot. It was Saluda who strongly defended her brother Clay, and sometimes rabidly if Lou weren't careful. Lou was now completely disenchanted with what he called Clay's bullheaded aggressiveness. In fact, the year previous in Cimarron, before Coleman sold out to Lacy and moved to the Panhandle, he and Clay had a verbal set-to which burned up the atmosphere for miles around.

Allison at the time made a quick side-trip to Cimarron during a cattle brokering job to urge Lou and Saluda into coming out "where there were pastures aplenty and opportunities unbound." Actually, Saluda, who adored Clay equally as much as Kate found him intolerable, had been ready to move for many months, but Lou was a more practical man who liked to see what he was leaping into before he made any kind of jump. Much as he was getting fed up with the Maxwell Grant troubles, he was disappointedly looked upon as merely dragging his feet by Saluda and Clay, and Lou was irked by the two not respecting his caution. Saluda of course didn't help matters any by continually putting pressure on him to get out of Colfax County.

As Allison arrived and trotted up to the Coleman house that day, Lou was just exiting his doorway. Clay dismounted and hailed him with a hearty, "Lou, you ol' dog! How you been?"

Coleman was in no mood to welcome Clay with a smile or happy hail of the hand, having ironically finished a heated dispute with Saluda a few moments before over their moving. He also let her know what he believed, that he felt her brother's claim was a lame assessment of the true picture of the Panhandle from what he could gather.

"Lou, I thought sure you'd be packed by now and on the way to Texas! What's the holdup?"

That's all Coleman needed. "What in hell you mean, holdup? Hell, can't no one leave a man in peace? Your sister has been carping the past year about getting outta here, and I got a good mind to send her packing so's I can get a vacation from all her jabbering!"

After that comment everything went to hell.

"Don't you talk of Saluda that way! You got a beef with me, spit it out to my face but leave her be, hear?"

"Damn rights, I hear! But I'm sick of her trying to make up my mind for me. Sure, I'd like to get the hell away from here, but ain't no way I want to jump from a frying pan into a fire, by God!"

"There ain't no fire over there, damn it! It ain't no garden of Eden for certain, but it's a hellova lots more green than what's left of Colfax County!"

"Speaking of Colfax County, I think you hiring out to the Ring didn't help the situation any. In fact, a lotta people feel you helped dirty the pond!"

"Oh, really? Well, my running off them small time settlers and greasers helped you big ranchers with more available space to grab up!"

"Goddamn it, you're a liar as far as me and Lacy is concerned! None was on the land we bought from the grant, not even a redskin! And you know that for a fact!

Saluda then made her appearance to throw in her two cents worth, and on Clay's side.

"Don't you dare call my brother a liar, Louis Coleman! I will have none of that!"

On and on it went, like a runaway team of Borax mules all out of control; Lou labeling Clay an unprincipled blackguard for his work with the Ring, Clay thinking seriously of making Saluda a widow, and Saluda threatening to whip Lou herself if he dared call her brother a liar again. After several dozens of rounds of verbal fisticuffs, which took up the better part of an hour, exhaustion mercifully set in. It was more a convenient therapeutic session for all three, of expending pent-up personal frustrations that mounted inwardly with time, and all appeared to have unloaded what each needed. Drained, they stood back a moment to gather their bruised egos with slight embarrassment, mumbling apologies and hells and hecks, and before too long they were at the kitchen table conversing as if they had briefly hit a bump in the road, but were now back on course, laughing and talking about Texas.

Returning to Texas, Clay for once gave serious thought to Monroe and John's prodding him toward Dora. And his pushing forty made him realize he may not have too many sunrises left if he kept on with his hell-raising and carousing. What concerned him more was that the edge of his personality was taking on a bitterness bordering on cynicism. He was waking up grouchy, often cloudy with a chip on his shoulder. Gone was his devil-may-care humor and zaniness toward life in general. He felt down in the mouth, a loss of direction, and found himself every day looking forward to a disagreement where he could settle somebody's hash just for the hell of it. Everything around him was becoming grey and meaningless.

One morning he rose, bathed, trimmed his facial hair, shined his boots, put on his best black broadcloth suit and pearl grey Stetson, and rode out to John and Kate's. Not as nervous as he thought he would be, he found himself humming a country ditty, something about a man who fancied a new-found love. John was chopping firewood as he reined up.

"John, you're making me plain sick with your domestic choring."

"Clay! This is a surprise. Ain't seen you for near two weeks."

"This being such a pleasant January Sunday afternoon, thought I'd drop by for a social call."

"Well, you're certainly dressed for something special. Big shin-dig somewhere?"

"Ah, ahem," faltered Clay, as he confidentially added, "Kind of thought I'd visit with Dora, you know? If she won't mind?"

"Why you big galoot," grinned John. "From what I hear and know, she'll welcome you with bells on. Get down and come on in."

Clay followed John through the doorway as John spoke to Kate just inside, with a wink, "Clay's come by for a visitation, hon. Got some of that delicious cinnamon apple pie left he likes? I imagine he has a sweet tooth for a wedge or two, don't you, big brother?"

"Uh, oh, of course. Certainly do. Would much appreciate it, Kate."

Kate smelled a subtly perfumed Clay in their midst, and was nearly bowled over at the lack of a scent of bourbon. "Heaven's yes, Clay!" she sang. "There certainly is enough for you to take one with you. Baked a half-dozen this morning."

As the three stood in clumsy silence a moment, John whispered to Kate, "Clay has come for a social with Dora, if she's so disposed."

"Oh!" elated Kate. "Of course. Come with me, Clay. She's in the front room, reading."

Hat in hand and suddenly nervous, Clay followed her like a submissive proselyte being led to his confessor.

"Dora," addressed Kate to her sister who was sitting in a lounge chair by a window engrossed in a copy of *Ivanhoe*. "Clay has dropped by for a visit and would like your company for a spell. Would you mind?"

Looking up from her preoccupied pastime with a combined mixture of bewilderment, surprise and joy, Dora rose quickly with a happy smile. Kate turned and left.

"Clay!" she breathed ecstatically. "This is a wonderful surprise!"

Mute and tongue-tied, Clay stood like a wooden Indian wishing he had a cigar.

"I, uh, it was such a nice break in the weather, thought I'd come by for a spell. Especially since I hadn't seen John and Kate in half a month."

"Please sit, Clay. So glad to see you. It's been at least two months, for us, I think."

"Yes, maam, seems so."

"Heavens, you don't have to 'maam' me. You know you can call me Dora, as always."

Allison blushed as he twirled his Stetson in both hands before him, self-angered at his hemming and hawing clumsiness. Such a bad beginning for good intentions bode ill for him, and he wished he could gracefully flee. Kate suddenly appeared in the room with a tray of pie wedges and coffee and saved his life from further mollification.

"Clay, Dora, here is some fresh pie and coffee. If you want more just help yourselves, or call." With that she removed the steaming items from the tray onto a table between them. "Clay, you sit now," she instructed. "And don't be shy with your appetite, hear?"

"No, maam," he grinned, glad for her timely presence. As Clay sat, she took his hat from his hand.

"I'll just hang this by the kitchen door. Now you two enjoy yourselves and don't mind us none. John and I have to go out to the barn a bit and tend a maimed horse, but pay us no mind."

She then left, and the last sound they heard was the kitchen door closing.

"Have you read this?" asked Dora, motioning to the book she held.

"Afraid not. But heard it's quite a rousing tale."

"Yes, it is: knights and maidens and romance."

"The staff of life, I'd say."

"And I agree."

Clay took a sip of his coffee, then forked a cut from his pie. "Kate turns out a cinnamon that can't be beat. Hmmm, just divine!" he praised as he swallowed and smacked his lips.

"She's finally given me her recipe and let me bake one. Do you like it?"

"You mean you baked this one?" he inquired with surprise.

"Surely did."

"You done fooled me. I thought this was Kate's."

"Well, seems I got the recipe right after all."

"You certainly did. And I'll have a second slice if it is permissible, Miss Dora," he grinned.

"You surely can, Mister Allison," she laughed as she exited to the kitchen and returned with her plate of pie. She served another wedge to Clay and refilled their coffees.

"Yessiree," elated Allison as he scooped up a fork of pie. "You will undoubtedly make some man a fine wife."

"Now, Mister Allison," she retorted in a light and saucy manner. "Just whatever could you mean?"

Reddening, Clay realized what he had flippantly said and slightly choked on a piece of crust. "I-I, I meant it as a friendly compliment, Dora. You sure are a fine baker. Really."

"I will forever cherish the compliment," she returned with a smile.

This wasn't going well at all, he thought, astonished at Dora's purposeful stance and untypical show of feminine independence. Yet he found it refreshing and pleasing that she spoke to him on an equal level, and not appear obsequious before a male, as many women were wont to do. This was the first time they had spoken more than a few words, and he found her enticing. He had always found her attractive and was drawn to her since first seeing her years ago, and now in her company he felt his brain turn to jelly and his knees to squash.

"Do you miss Colfax County?" she asked.

"Yes, I do," he found himself answering honestly, although hating what it had become.

"I felt it was such a lovely place to live, despite all their troubles."

Troubles, he thought, still blaming the Ring for the loss of his ranch.

"I was so sorry to hear of your losing your ranch. I understand it was a beautiful setting, on the river and all."

"Yes, it was. A truly magnificent location." He found it surprisingly natural to talk of it with her, as if it were an old nostalgic memory, not a bitter recollection. Like letting go of old anger. That, and she was so easy to talk to.

"Did you always want to be a cattleman?"

"No," he answered, recalling his first sight of the plains of west Texas years ago. "What happened was, after the war everything was such a mess with Yankee carpetbaggers, the White Man's Bureau and Reconstruction infesting the whole South like locusts, I had to leave. And farming was not an attraction for me at all, which was a dark disappointment to my father. Everybody seemed to be headed west anyway, so I thought I'd give it a try."

"It must have been a wonderful adventure for you to ride off into the west like a knight, not knowing what to expect."

"I don't know about adventurous knights," he laughed lightly, "but it was exciting as all get-out."

"Please go on," she pleaded, placing another wedge on his plate and refilling their cups. "I want to hear it all. Please."

He found in her audience what he had long hungered for, someone he could speak to of his deep aspirations and aims, the old dreams which seemed to be dying on the vine and turning him angry at everything around him, souring all he touched. He looked at her with a new set of eyes, visually drank in this lovely young woman whom he knew was drawn to him, and of course he to her, and luxuriated in the thought that it may not be too late after all, not too late to hope, to build, to remold his life into something substantial.

"When I stopped riding I was on the western edge of Texas, where civilization ended and the Indian country began. I never saw anything so vast, open and beautiful in all my life. It was as if I were at the end of the world and I was free do whatever I wanted, to create my own destiny with my own two hands. It's crazy, but I felt like a modern conquistador. It was a powerful feeling, Dora. The memory of it still moves me. After finding work with a local cattleman, I knew before the day was up what I wanted more than anything on earth: my own herd and ranch."

"Oh, Clay! I know you can do it. Don't let losing your New Mexico ranch disappoint you. You have a good start here already. Everybody speaks of what a fine cattleman you are. I've heard them, and know it's all true!"

Clay sat across from Dora, fork in hand, staring into her deep brown eyes, wishing he could see into their future, what was there for them. Her zealous belief in him amazed and pleased him. It was like an electric bolt to his dying enthusiasm, a resuscitation of his wavering spirit which was waning day by day, the resurrection of his old hopes and dreams of not only the possibilities of his imagined herd and ranch, but in himself. He lay his utensil next to his empty plate and rose to his feet, knowing what he intended to do, and what he wanted to do since rising that morning. Standing on a pair of unsteady pins, feeling less secure than he ever was in a duel to the death, he spoke with difficulty, in an almost inaudible rasp.

"Dora?"

"Yes?" Her heart sank, thinking he was taking his leave.

"Would you consider, umm, m-m-marrying me?"

Stunned and startled at once, she replied in a happy voice, "Yes! Oh, yes, Clay! I most certainly would!"

She instantly left her chair and went around the table to be received by his embrace, both of them sinking into the sweet enfoldment of love, cooing and sighing as they pressed themselves into the welcome warmth of each other's acceptance.

"Oh, Clay, I love you so much!"

"And I you, Dora! And I you!"

The following month on February fifteenth Clay and Dora were united in matrimony by Justice of the Peace George Smith at the Mobeetie Court House. Since John's abode was a bit roomier, a party and pot-luck celebration was held there for the couple. Clay had over-hastily sworn off alcohol to Dora prior to their marriage, but since this was a special event she gave him temporary dispensation. By mid-afternoon he was quite oiled and in a very happy state when Dora reminded him he had promised earlier to have a wedding picture taken at the local studio.

"Oh, lordy, honey. I plumb forgot."

"Well, why don't we just quick ride in the wagon to Mobeetie right now. It's but a few miles, and nobody will mind.".

"Ah, sweetheart, I don't know. I'm so drunk and having such a good time, can't we wait until tomorrow?"

"Please, Clay." Dora had a feeling Clay would be completely 'indisposed' and in no shape for a portrait-shoot the next day. "You promised. And it would be so special to have it done on our wedding day, don't you agree?"

Trying to focus his eyes and attention both at the same time on this new dilemma was more of a chore than he could believe, and he stood a moment trying to figure out how he could stay.

"Please, Clay. It would mean so much to me. I'll even drive."

He agreed and off they went, with Dora at the reins. She got her wedding picture, which pleased her highly, but Clay never cared for it much, showing him at his worse, half drunk, bleary-eyed, weary and aged beyond his years. "I look like something the cat done drug in," he would grumble upon viewing it. He was also in uncomfortable pain, for his leg and foot was beginning to give him trouble, trouble he made no mention of at the time, and kept to himself for a spell.

In April the newlyweds took a honeymoon stage-trek to New Mexico. Actually it was also a sort of combined business trip, for Clay was more firmly coming to the decision of moving from the Panhandle. They journeyed to Las Vegas, eighty miles south of Raton. They spent a week at the Hot Springs Hotel in Montezuma, five miles north of Las Vegas, relaxing and enjoying themselves as just another pair of tourists. Clay found the hot water of the springs soothing to his leg and foot, and wished he could stay there forever.

"Dora, honey, these waters have the most wonderful effect on my leg and foot. Wherever we settle, I hope we can find springs like these for me to soak in. It's truly a miracle."

"Oh, Clay, I'm so glad we've found something to give you some relief from all that pain and bother. I know it must be unbearable at times."

He had finally told her of the broken leg when he slipped on a piece of ice alighting from his horse one winter, and how he later put a slug into his foot. Of the latter he admitted, "It was such a stupid thing for me to do in the first place, avenging myself on a Yankee general like that."

Tolerant and unjudgmental as a woman in love is prone to be, she laughed gently at his antics, saying, "Thankfully it didn't turn out worse, sweetheart, much as you suffer now. In time I'm sure the pain to your injuries will fade, or perhaps we can find a doctor who can somehow alleviate them."

The thought of her unconditional love sometimes filmed his eyes when he was alone and dwelt on her endless concern and unselfishness toward him. Her patience and optimism also to him were of alien nature, being for so long in the company of men from his time in the army and his cattle years, harsh men who sought and demanded immediate results for any and every wish or slight, no matter how trivial, and could be brutally inhumane in accomplishing their ends. She was so gentle and trusting, even to the point of allowing him his drinking to hold back the throbbing agonies which at times were deep and hot, as a poker being shoved into his leg. He was glad it took away the sore discomfort, that he didn't have to drink too much to kill it. But he knew it was getting worse, and didn't dare tell her of his fear that something more was wrong, that relief by imbibing a ration of alcohol to make the aching subside would one day end. She deserved more in life than his pain, and he absorbed his guilt quietly, and hoped with her that possibly one day he would fully heal.

In Las Vegas he bought a wagon and a pair of horses for transportation, and in an interview with a reporter who knew of him let it be known that he and his wife were on a honeymoon vacation. He said they might head south to Fort Sumner, and there may settle down.

Allison dropped into the Las Vegas bank to visit with an old Cimarron acquaintance, Miguel Otero, who was assistant cashier and manager. From a fairly established family, educated, and having a knowledgeable economic outlook about the state, Allison plumbed him for information.

"Miguel, I'm looking to move from the Panhandle because of all that barbed wire fencing and loss of open range. What do you think of the Seven Rivers region?"

"Well, Clay," spoke Otero. "Times are changing. Most important of all, free and open range grazing is closing up here like in the Panhandle. It's becoming a thing of the past all over. The big ranchers are buying up and fencing in their land, making it tough on the small, independent outfits to make a go of it."

"You're telling me," replied Allison grimly. "I got pushed off twice and it wasn't any fun. First by the Maxwell people, and then by them ground-eating maggots of the Panhandle. I think grazing should be open to all cattle, bar none, and fencing outlawed."

"I honestly understand the downside of the question, Clay. But look at it this way," proposed Otero, knowing Allison's Santa Fe Ring history, and wishing to be as tactful as possible. "If you picked up say, five thousand acres, and had a herd of cattle, just enough for your size of pasture, wouldn't it be range-smart to fence it in for your own use, especially since you paid good money for it? If you let hundreds of other cows have free run of it, where would that leave you? Don't you feel you would have to protect your own investment?"

Allison hated to admit to Otero, let alone himself, that the logic of his argument left little room for debate. But it was not the obvious logic he was crosswise with, it was that he'd have to admit that the big ranchers he had had an eternal beef with were right. And to take it a step further, and more painfully, that he was wrong, and if he were wrong, he was his own worse enemy. It was a conundrum of the first order.

"So free grazing is near out in New Mexico, too," commented Allison almost wistfully.

"Pretty much. But you can buy acreage yet, and at a pretty good price. Especially if you have the cash. Then you can fence it in for your own use. Or even lease."

"Lease?"

"Yes. In fact, it's a good option with less overhead, depending on one's situation. Lease whatever size pasture you can afford, buy some stock, fatten them up for a year or two, then ship them out to market. Rent more pasture, repeat the process, and in time one can come out ahead of the game. I feel that would be a more profitable way to go, especially for a small herder. Of course that certainly depends on where and how much the herder can cut corners."

"That doesn't sound too bad, Miguel. Where's a good area to cast about for land leasing?"

"As you know, Lincoln County has had a lot of trouble the past few years, and the Seven Rivers area you are thinking of too was effected economically. Many ranchers are hard-up money-wise right now, and you probably could strike a pretty good deal with some of them for what you might like."

Allison, as a fairly successful cattle broker the past few years, had already heard of Lincoln County and its problems, and its potentially profitable opportunities due to its miserable and prolonged "war," and was glad to hear from a reliable source of its potential. He knew also that the good old Santa Fe Ring, ala Catron and Axtell, had had their fingers in a piece of

Lincoln County's pie. Maggots, he thought. They're everywhere.

"Thanks ever so much, Miguel. I'll drop on down there and look around. Any names you can give me which would be any help to me there?"

"In fact, yes. In Roswell is a man who is tops in the cattle and real estate business. He would be the man to start with, and who could in turn recommend others."

"Who would that be?"

"Frank Wilburn," revealed Otero with a nod and a wink.

Allison's memory suddenly shot back years before to Cimarron and Lambert's saloon in the St. James Hotel. Wilburn was the man who owed Clay's old bosses Lacy and Coleman money, and Clay in turn was appointed by them to collect. Recalling it now, how he shoved his forty-five practically up Frank's nose at the bar, threatening him with his life, embarrassed him deeply. He reddened. Frank was merely short of cash at the time and repaid Allison's employers before the week was out.

"Wilburn's in Roswell?" asked Clay somewhat sheepishly.

"He certainly is, and doing well. Like I say, he's one of the top men in the profession, and a straight shooter. Personality-wise he puts off people off here and there, but I say, so what? If it's results you want, go to the top. Right?"

"You bet," came Allison's not too enthusiastic reply. God, it really is a small world!

Otero already knew of Allison's "difficulty" with Wilburn, but diplomatically made no mention of it, merely passing on information the herder sought. Otero also recalled Clay's perforating the ceiling of the St. James Hotel bar one night with his sidearm, and being in the room above the saloon. He and two men were forced to swiftly test their agility by all three leaping atop a potbelly stove and clinging together to avoid the incoming ammunition.

"Well, thanks again, Miguel. Uh, I guess I'll look him up soon as I hit Roswell."

"Good luck, Clay. And don't be a stranger. Drop in any time you're in town."

Returning to his hotel, Clay talked it over with Dora that he would like to make a quick trip to Roswell to check out the availability of pasture land. Would she like to make the journey? "Of course!" she answered without hesitation, enjoying the traveling about.

"All right. Here's what we'll do. See if you agree with it. Instead of taking a stage from here, which would be a two hundred mile ride, we'll grab a train south for more comfort. We'll get off down the line at Socorro where we'll then stage to Roswell, around a hundred fifty miles. That'll be a shorter time aboard a bouncing crate and not as unbearable. There we'll grab a hotel room, and the next day I'll scout about for a man Otero told me of, who will be able to refer me to others if he can't help me. Two, maybe three days will give me the time I need to find what I want, then we'll come back by train from Socorro to visit the Youngs for a bit. How's all that sound?"

"Let's not waste all this time talking," she laughed. "Let's go!"

He returned her laugh and took her into his arms for an embrace. "You're a rare wonder, you are!" he elated. "Fun, and a joy to be with!"

The following day, after boarding his rig and horses, Clay and Dora were on a southbound train for Socorro.

Their car was hardly half-crowded and they each sat by a window, she facing forward, he aft. Dora had never traveled by train before, and Clay enjoyed watching her face as she excitedly viewed the incoming landscape along the Rio Grande. Much of it was sparse and sere, some of it broken up by trees and vegetation, sometimes with isolated villages and scattered herds of cattle.

"Oh, Clay! You're so lucky to have traveled so much! Don't you just love it?"

Allison's joy of seeing new places was quite jaded by now, but not wanting to spoil her enjoyment of new pleasure replied, "Yes, I do. New places, new people, new experiences. It's like turning a page in a novel, wondering what will happen next,"

"So aptly put, Clay. And so true!"

The miles clacked away beneath them, and the weather was perfect. Windless and sunny with a vast, cloudless turquoise sky spread above them from horizon to horizon. His foot began its familiar soft throbbing intermittently accompanied by hot poker-jabs. From within his coat he drew a flat pint-sized bottle and took a long pull, then recapped it to set it on his lap. His foot hadn't bothered him for three, four days, and he thought at last maybe the problem was fading away. But no such luck. It was a false alarm as all the times before. The longest free time from his agony had been a week, and it was heaven. It angered him that he was locked into the liquor habit because of his injury, and in turn despised it that he was coerced into doing something against his will. He wanted always to make his own decisions, right or wrong, to drink or not to drink when he felt like it, and not have to react automatically like a slave to his impairment whenever it called out for succor. He was mostly afraid of alienating Dora with the smell of booze on him. He had promised to hold back on his drinking and was pleasantly surprised that he didn't miss it as much as he thought he would. It actually felt good to be sober for so long a time, and have no hangovers. But as the throbbing started and worsened he had to lean on the medicinal value of redeye, an irony that was not lost on him. It was that or morphine, or even laudanum, but he drew the line. Booze was cheaper, and he felt he had at least some control, being more familiar with alcohol.

"Foot bothering you, hon?" asked Dora.

"Yes. A bit. I was hoping it was finally going away."

"It's all right, love. Take what you must."

"Thank you, Dora. Thank you."

The miles kept clacking away rhythmically with the metallic beat of the iron wheels and the throbbing of his limb: clack, throb, clack, throb, clack, throb, clack. A second long pull of rye helped him a bit.

To save Dora from public embarrassment when they traveled together, he took an old medicine bottle, poured out the contents, and refilled it with rye. Although not a common occurrence, it was a common enough event to witness people taking a drink from a prescription bottle for personal relief, sometimes using a tablespoon for dosage. Two years previous in Dodge he stopped at a small knot of people listening to a medicine man praising over miraculous cures of his commercial wares, a secret formula from the Middle East. The pint-sized bottle bore a bright yellow ribbon around it and a red, white and blue label. Across the label were crimson letters in Barnum print, "Dr. Shrub's Spiritual Equalizer." It guaranteed the moral balancing of the spirit and the de-galling of the gall bladder. Allison bought a sample from the sideshow huckster as a joke, a bogus cure from a bogus doctor.

He took a third long drink and slipped the pint back into his jacket.

"Feeling better, dear?" inquired Dora.

"Yes, thank you. The rye does help."

Smiling, she asked jocundly, "I wonder if the original contents would have had any positive effects on you?"

"No, no," he chuckled lightly. "It was all a sham. I have no idea who the slippery doctor was, but I suspect the charlatan would have been more successful as a politician."

As they rose from their seats in Socorro to leave the car, Allison spotted a seated elderly female upending a pint container of Shrub's. Their eyes caught as he slowly passed, limping slightly. Clay reached into his pocket to briefly reveal to her his own sample, then reinserted it. "Good health, my dear," he nodded with a confidential whisper and a wink, knowing from her glazed eyes she too was not imbibing the doctor's formula.

Blushing, she smiled and returned his nod with a thank you. The young man next to her, obviously her son and caretaker, spoke in a slightly defensive tone, as if caught in a crime, "Has Doctor Shrub's medicinal prescription helped you any, my good sir?"

"Miraculously, young man, truly!" endorsed Allison. "Two years ago I could barely remove myself from bed. Now look at me! Limping, yes.

A bit of pain, yes. But sir, observe me now, nearly recovered and hale as ever! It also cured my piles, ingrown toenails and crotch rash, by heavens!" He smiled down at the stunned, wide-eyed lady and waved his ivory-headed walking stick in the air flamboyantly, adding as he left, "Keep the faith, my dear! Keep the faith!" And off he went to join Dora on the station platform who was doubled up in laughter.

After a dusty, rocking ride across a mainly desert plain, they arrived in Roswell two days later ready for a dinner, bath and a good night's sleep. Following breakfast Clay gave Dora a sum of money for whatever shopping she may like to do, saying, "I'll try to get back to the hotel by two or three, or at least somewhere along there to let you know how things are going. If things go well, maybe we can be on our way back tomorrow for a visit with the Young's. The day after at the latest."

"Take your time, Clay. Don't rush your business on account of me. I'll just play tourist and maybe shop a little. Then return to the hotel." He gave her a light buss and she departed.

Roswell was a bustling and growing community founded back in eighteen hundred and sixty-nine by Frank Wilburn's brother Aaron and Van Smith, a professional gambler, naming the town after Smith's father, Roswell. Allison had no idea how he would be received, and wished now he had been a bit more tactful when he played debt collector on Frank some ten years before. But the man did have an outrageous sense of humor, so Clay banked on that plus his being a successful businessman savvy enough to want to make a buck where he could. Of course he couldn't ask for a better contact, according to Otero. So he mentally grit his teeth and prepared for whatever may or may not occur.

He had but to trod six blocks before he found the address he sought, and was glad his leg was behaving itself this day, with only a little soreness to remind him why he was slightly limping. A large-paned window announced in bold red letters, "Real Estate and Cattle Investments. Frank Wilburn, Esq." With a deep breath and his walking stick in his right hand, he turned the knob and entered. It was a roomy interior with three desks.

Eight people busily shuffled paper or conversed with a couple of prospects. Two were sitting at desks, one of them a young woman. None noticed him at first, so intent on their business at hand they were, and as Allison silently sought each face, he recognized Frank Wilburn handing some papers with verbal instructions to the seated woman. One of the men looked toward Allison and walked over with his hand outstretched.

"Good morning. I'm Fred Colton. May I help you?"

Removing his hat and shaking his hand, Clay answered, "Yes. I'm Robert Allison and looking for some pasture to lease."

"Well, Mister Allison. You've certainly come to the right place."

Wilburn was so intent in his own conversation he didn't hear Clay speak his name, but when Colton repeated the man's name he looked up.

"Allison?" he spoke. "Clay Allison? Good lord, is it really you?"

"It certainly is, Mister Wilburn," he grinned self-consciously. "And I'm here on business."

"Good grief, Clay," he stared in feinted shock. "I do hope you aren't collecting for Coleman and Lacy again!"

"No, no, Frank!" laughed Allison. "Nothing like that!"

"That's a great relief," joining with Clay in laughter. "God, it's good to see you. How in the world have you been?"

"Better now, seeing you don't begrudge me my earlier rude behavior."

"Ah, yes. That was certainly a blood-rushing experience for me, I must admit. But let us not dwell on the past, my friend. What is it we can help you with today?"

"I'm in the market for some pastureland, Frank. Something to rent"

"Clay, let's go next door to the café. I can use a sandwich and coffee. Join me as we discuss whatever it is you need."

The years and business had been lucrative for Frank, observed Clay, he having gained at least ten or fifteen pounds of flesh. He was well-dressed and appeared to be wearing the best that frontier Roswell had to offer in haberdashery. He also seemed less pompous, less full of himself as he remembered him. What the hell, he can't be all bad not holding a grudge, thought Allison, and he positively liked him for that.

After spending half an hour or so recalling old acquaintances, Allison explained briefly his intentions. "I'd like to lease enough grazing land for maybe fifteen-hundred cows. Keep them a year or so, fatten them up, then ship them to market. Meantime I'll have to head back to Texas to tidy up a few things before settling down hereabouts, leaving it in somebody's hands."

"Clay, you've come at the right time. Otero's right. A lot of ranchers around here are in a bad way. That stupid damned war that went on for two, three years, and is finally ended, depressed the region. Anyway, leasing pasture is a good way to go for what you want. Less investment involved, more profit. But that too depends on circumstances and unknown equations. Still, if you'd like there's a few good ranches you can get for a song."

"No. At this time just set me up with some grazing land cheap as you can."

""Here." Wilburn pulled out an envelope and rough-sketched several pastures available and their locations south and west. "Dirt cheap, Clay. It's sad, but the way things are. Someone's misery is another's gain. One of the basic laws in real estate. I can get any of these places for you whenever you say, and probably cheaper with a little sweet-talk when they see the cash. In fact with a little arm-twisting, I might even get them to pay you to get it off their hands!"

"By God," smiled Clay, shaking his head. "Seems like Otero's right. I came to the right man after all!"

Forty-five minutes later Wilburn and Allison came to a satisfactory solution. "What I'll do, Clay, is go ahead and close the deal on that one pasture for you. It's the best, since it's fenced. Then I'll pick up five hundred head of cattle for it and hire a couple of cowpokes to baby-sit the herd until you get back. I'll of course keep an eye on the place, too. How long do you think you'll be gone?"

"I'm thinking hopefully only six months. It'll probably take me a couple trips for me to tie things up. But whatever, I want you to add to the stock as time goes by up to say fifteen-hundred. Let's go on down to the bank so I can cash my draft and leave some money for you. I'm thinking a thousand for starters will tide you over some."

"That'll be more than enough for now. And you can be sure every penny will be accounted for."

"Frank, to be honest, I'd like you to be my financial advisor, if you would. Any friend of Otero's is a friend of mine." Allison added with a grin, "Whether you like it or not."

"Why, thank you, Clay. I'm honored."

"We'll keep in touch by mail, and let me know of any changes or difficulties that may arise. As you need money, let me know. I also have an account with Otero."

At the bank Clay gave Wilburn a check for one thousand dollars, and left two thousand in an account he opened with Wilburn. "This way if you need quick funding for something, it'll be there. Just let me know how I stand as time goes by." The men then emerged in the early afternoon sun. "This has been a fine day for me, Frank. You've treated me well and I'll never forget it."

"Aren't you coming down to the office to sign the final papers and contracts?"

"No. Not necessary. Your hand on this deal is all I require. Long as we both make a fair living on this arrangement what do we need a signature for?" With that the two extended their palms and clasped them confidently and firmly. "You take care, Frank. And thanks again." Allison went off in the direction of the hotel.

Riding the stage back to Socorro that same day, Allison turned to Dora and said, "This has been the strangest but most interesting day of my life. Honey, I just have to tell you about it."

"Please do. I love hearing you tell of the many experiences you've had. You are a never-ending surprise in all that you relate to me. Better than any novel I've ever read."

"Well, now, don't go giving this old galoot the big head, young lady. It's just that you are the most appreciative audience I've had in my life."

"Oh, bosh, Clay. That isn't true. You're an excellent story teller. Please go on."

"Well, let's see. Where shall I start?"

"At the beginning, of course."

"All right. Once upon a time Lacy and Coleman hired me to collect some debts...."

Returning to Las Vegas the Allisons spent the night, treating Miguel Otero to dinner. The next day Clay arranged to have his rig and horses loaded onto the train for the ride to Springer. From there they buggyed the twenty miles to Cimarron where they dined and spent the night at Lambert's St. James. They made a handsome couple, Dora in one of the stylish dresses she bought in Roswell, Clay in a pearl grey suit and Stetson he likewise purchased there, topped off of course with his ivory-headed stick. A dozen or so old acquaintances intermittently interrupted their dinner throughout the evening to chat, but they were having such a good time they enjoyed the brief visitations and looked upon them as small welcome pleasures instead of annoyances. The proprietor Henri Lambert too dropped by, and with a complimentary bottle of French burgundy which was a pleasant touch to their evening.

The morning after Clay replenished his rye supply with four quarts, they rode off to Elkins and the Youngs, a scenic twenty-five miles under a sunny, delightful day. There they spent a week resting and lolling about after their miles and weeks on the road.

"Clay," commented Jack Young, "I think you made a smart move to Roswell, and struck even a smarter deal there. Damn if you ain't."

"It does feel good, Jack. And I have Otero to thank for helping lead me to it. Namely to Wilburn who set it up."

"Wilburn," chuckled Young. "Who'd a thought?"

"Yessiree. And there he is now, a good friend and my business manager. Beats me to hell, Jack."

"God, yes, and after that run-in with him!"

"But I respect the turn in life, whatever it means, and love it."

"Wish you all the luck down there, Clay."

"Thanks, Jack. I was wondering how it'd be if I hired Dora's brothers to come down there and work for me as cowhands?"

"Well, Tom's not too much for cowmanship, but you couldn't do much better with John. He's only twenty-one yet a natural who loves to work cattle."

"Good. I'll have a talk with him and make the arrangements."

At the end of the week Allison asked young John McCulloch if he would drive them the twenty-five mile run to the stage station at the Clifton House near Otero for their return trek to Mobeetie. "Be glad to, Uncle Clay."

"Also," added Young, "here's a list of stuff you can load up at Clifton's to bring back. Have Tom Stockton put it on my bill."

At the stage stop the vehicle was close to pulling out and fortunately had room for two more. Allison was disappointed in not being able to speak at least a few words with Stockton, one of the early drovers on the first Goodnight drive he came with to New Mexico.

"John, please give my regrets to Tom Stockton, and that I hope to visit next time I come through."

"Sure will. You and Dora have a good trip, now, hear? Bye, Dora. Nice to see you."

John and Dora had a quick embrace before Clay helped her aboard.

"And John, I'm glad that you want to come on down to Roswell and work for me."

"Happy to do it, Clay," he beamed.

Allison handed John a white envelope, saying, "Here's a letter of introduction to Frank Wilburn, and some money to help you along. He'll fix you up. You answer to Frank through me, and the workers on my pasture take orders from you. I'll try and get down there about six months. All set?"

"Yes, sir!"

"And this buggy and horses are yours. Look at them as a sort of bonus. Good bye, John, and good herding."

Clay boarded the stage and in seconds the vehicle lurched away with a whoop and a holler from the driver, leaving John McCulloch standing with his mouth open at his uncle's generosity.

Clay's preparing for his move from the Panhandle elated him. He felt as if he were freeing himself from a shackled state of being. Being fed up with the lock the big ranchers had on the entire Panhandle, and although it was like beating a dead horse, he never stopped complaining of the loss of open range and the ungodly use of barbed wire. But now he had grown cocky about it and antsy to get on his way. One evening he, John, Monroe, and Lou Coleman were in a Mobeetie saloon, and Clay was on a rant, engendered by an excessive intake of alcohol.

"Hell with you people," Clay crowed. "I'm moving on out of here!"

"You really are serious, aren't you?" asked John.

"Damn right. I've grown sick of all this Maxwell Grant atmosphere. Christ, how can you possibly stomach it any longer?"

"What's to stomach?" replied John. "I know I'm never going to be any cattle baron, so I settle for what I can make do with, a small herd and enough profit for a decent living."

"He's right, Clay," agreed Monroe. "None of us, including you, have the money to buy, invest or compete with the big boys, so why make it any tougher on ourselves? Small fish in a big pond is what we are, and as long as we're not in bad straits, why holler for nothing?"

"I can't believe what I'm hearing," angered Clay. "Fish bait is what you all are, by God!"

"Clay," injected Lou, "all you can do is bitch. Ever since the Ring took away your ranch, which was never going to be yours anyway, you been in a perfect snit. Back then, if you'd have tried working as an honest rancher instead of hiring out to them assholes as their thug evictor, maybe you'd have amounted to something."

"Why, Goddamn you, Lou!" snarled Clay. "Why don't you go back to Colfax County since all you can do is cry about leaving there in the first place!"

"Because Saluda won't have it, that's why! I should have stayed and let her move the hell out here. Crappy as it was, for a fair-sized rancher I had a hellova nice setup. Better than now!"

"Don't you go blaming Saluda, Lou! If you were any kind of man you would have stood your ground in the first place!"

"With you breathing down my neck and pushing for me to move also? Crap!"

"Now let's not pick old scabs, you two," refereed John. "We're all here together, so let's make the best of not too good a choice. It ain't the end of the world, you know."

"What in hell you mean, John?" cut Clay. "What bad choice?"

"I didn't say a bad choice. I said not too good a choice. It could have been better, but it ain't the worst choice in the world, considering we have select sections, good water and do pretty well. Monroe's right, we're small fish in a big pond and may as well face it and make do. We ain't starving, although we'll never be a threat to ol' Charlie Goodnight," laughed John lightly, trying to put a jocund lid on the boiling pot.

"Why you fish-bait fuckers!" howled Clay. "I can't believe what I'm hearing! None of you will amount to a damn if you remain here! None of you!"

"Don't you call me fish bait," raged Lou. "Just what in hell you got to show after your dabbling in herding? A few acres of land and a handful of cows, half of which are of questionable purchase!"

Immediately following Lou Coleman's unkind blast of words a

deadly silence descended upon the quartet. Even Lou, bluntly outspoken as was his trait, was sorry for his outburst, for he felt suddenly as if he were standing on his grave.

"Lou," spoke Clay in a tight whisper. "Say another word and you are a dead man. Now get out and away from me this second, and don't ever look back or come this way again, except on official business. Savvy?"

Lou turned without a word and left the room, the bar, and Mobeetie, and hastened back to his ranch twenty miles northeast, grateful to be alive. But disgusted and disillusioned with the way things were turning out he grumbled all the way home, wishing he had remained in New Mexico.

"Clay," spoke John, embarrassed at the entire scene, "I don't think that was called for. You know we three have picked up a few illegal hides now and then. Not too many ranchers haven't."

"I don't give a damn. What we've done in any questionable way is our business, and I don't take kindly to having it discussed in public. Lou sometimes doesn't know when to shut up, and I'm glad to be rid of him."

"Still," continued John. "That's no way to talk to close kin."

"Close kin?" laughed Clay coldly. "He's no close kin of mine. I don't think Saluda looks too closely on him, either."

"Christ, Clay," John mournfully shook his head. "How far are you going with this?"

"This what?"

"Your anger. And spite. Just because the big ranchers have the place all sewed up is no cause to get mad at the people around you. It ain't our fault. We ain't your enemies just because we think different. Like I say, we're just doing what we know best to survive."

"Jesus H. Christ, John. You'll be standing on your knees and walking on your knees before long. It's the Maxwell Grant scheme all over again. They screw the little guy and bleed him to death till they finally run him off. That's the way they play. They have all the rules, cards, chips, and deals on their side, and there's no other way they'll play it."

"Shit, Clay," agreed Monroe quietly, sounding half-bored at his older brother's ancient argument. "We all know that. Hell, like John and me say, we do what we can with what we got, and we're doing pretty good for a small outfit. We'd love to expand, but can't for two reasons. One, there's no open range left to do so; and two, we don't have the millions to buy out any ranchers, or to buy in and invest. You got a third option?"

"You damn rights I do. Move the hell out and find a more suitable atmosphere. And I'm going."

"Going?" continued Monroe. "You're always going. You left New Mexico for here, and now that history repeats, you repeat along with it and run off elsewhere. How many more runs have you got? Give it a chance, Clay. Between the three of us we can do better than change our address every time things don't suit us. Like John says, we're no threat to Goodnight, but we're a long ways from starving. Who knows? After a year or two we might be in one hell of a position to buy off some land around us and make a little elbow room for our outfit."

"That makes more sense than leaving so quick, Clay," spoke John. "Monroe's got something there. What about it?"

"Shit. You're both daft."

"How's Dora taking the move?" queried John.

"Hell, she's happier than hell over it, and was happy all during our trip. Soon I'll sell off my acreage to a fella who's been wanting it. I'll be gone before too long."

"So back to New Mexico?" asked Monroe.

"Southern New Mexico. Seven Rivers."

"Oh, yeah, Lincoln County War country."

"That's right. But the shooting's all over with now. That's where Garrett killed the Kid not a month ago."

"In a dark room wasn't it?" mused Monroe.

"Yep," agreed Clay. "The Kid walked in the door with the moon at his back. Perfect target," he critiqued. "Even for a blind man."

But as usual in so many plans, there was a delay of a few months, and impatient Clay grumbled and did what he could to stem his agitation and anxiety. One thing he did which helped calm his impetuosity at such times was hunting. Although deer was rarely seen in the area any longer, cattle, horses and bipods having greatly replaced the indigenous animals, he would head out westward toward the less settled regions of hills and streams hoping to pluck the last deer, always with his trusty hound Rebel loping at his side.

One afternoon on a hunt he spotted a rider approaching from the distant west. Not knowing whom it could be, friend or foe, he drew his Winchester from its leather sheath beneath his right thigh, cranked a round into the chamber, then returned it. Drawing his revolver, he slipped a shell into the empty sixth cylinder with a forty-four slug and reholstered it, leaving the thong off the hammer. As the rider closed up he recognized it was a woman aboard a giant, white jackass, trailed by maybe ten or twelve dogs. Behind her the beast dragged a bundle-laden travois. As she drew closer, in surprised consternation he recognized that it was Tina Menchaca's companion, Princess Bountiful Light. He desired absolutely no confrontation, so made a long looping detour around her, keeping his Stetsoned head down but eyes toward her, praying for invisibility. A hundred-some yards separated them, and they were crossing paths exactly. Allison felt safe.

"Malo!" she suddenly screeched. "Muy malo!"

Damn! Eyes of a hawk!

Allison nudged his mount to move a bit faster while Rebel softly whined nervously, keeping Clay and his horse between him and the strange group passing. Allison threw her a friendly salute and half-smile as he cantered on, keeping a wary eye her way. Her waist-length hair, blowing in the breeze behind her, was all white now, and her face more ashen, leathery and lined. But her eyes were as bright as ever, flashing insanely toward him as she shouted, "Malo! Loco e malo!"

He trotted on with his cohort Rebel tracking closely beside him. The dog peered over his shoulder in a jittery state, tail between his legs. Rebel wanted nothing to do with the odd collection they had come across, although a powerful and deadly fighter of the first order. A quarter of a mile away or so Allison pulled up on a small knoll and turned about. Bountiful Light and her assemblage of yipping canine curs of varied size, color and mix slowly faded northward, toward Kansas he assumed, returning home, and he sincerely wished her luck.

Suddenly several hundred feet away he spotted six wolves skulking through the brush, a male and female and their four young but sturdy pups. They seemed to have been trailing Bountiful Light and her small caravan. Rebel instantly picked up their scent and like a canonshot sped toward them growling for battle, ignoring Allison's order to stay. Clay, angered at the dog's disobedience, joined him, galloping his horse toward the clustered group as Rebel tore into the four offspring. The female watched objectively as her brood and Rebel formed a massive ball of fur, howling, growling and tearing each other to shreds. The male paced back and forth like a bored umpire. Allison reined up and took a shot at the male, dropping him in his tracks. He next hit the female square in the head. Trotting toward the fighting pack in an attempt at pulling Rebel's acorns out of the fire, he saw it was too late. His dog had chewed the throats of three of his deceased foe, but lay dead and bleeding from a dozen open tears which made him look like a blood-soaked rug. The fourth cub scurried limpingly across the field and escaped. "Rebel!" he called as he dismounted. But his hound was too far gone to answer. His one eye blinked, a leg quivered, and he died. Clay dug a grave about fifty feet from the battle site and the three carcasses, buried Rebel, and lay a collection of stones atop him, hoping to frustrate predators from digging him up.

"Goddamn it!" he oathed, hat in hand over the mound of dirt and rocks, eyes wet. "Don't you listen right? I told you to stay! Now how the hell will I ever replace you?"

His heart was out of the hunt now, and he turned eastward toward Mobeetie and home.

Before taking his leave of the Panhandle Allison wished to make a conciliatory gesture toward John and Monroe, feeling sheepish and guilty at his earlier boorish behavior. John was right in his accusal of him talking of kin in such a base manner, distant or no. And although Clay held no closeness to his parents, he still held the family circle in high esteem. Sure, close blood fought like cats and dogs at times, but when the chips are down, who in hell do you really have to go to the line with, to stand and fight against any foe or threat? And so what if he went off in a snit to Texas and angered the old man for not giving a damn about the farm? That was between him and his pop, not the world, or John and Monroe. Hell, he now had the start of what he had looked forward to for years in Dora, a woman and wife whom he loved and wanted to bear his children, the future family he would help nurture, raise and love. First a son for him, then a daughter, then more sons as time fell away, sons to learn and help in the business of raising cattle, to carry on the Allison brand to whatever future they could make of it. It was his way of restructuring his life, recreating the family he wished he had had and felt robbed of. And one bright day in the future he would show them off to his father: his wife, the boys and girls, the ranch and cattle and success he had made of his life despite the last words his father lay on him like a family curse as he rode off to Texas years ago. "You'll never amount to a damn thing!"

Bumping into Monroe in a Mobeetie saloon, he walked over and lay an affectionate arm across his shoulder to pull him against him, saying, "Monroe, I just want to say I didn't mean anything personal by all my jabbering weeks ago. I guess I sometimes twist my anger about in the wrong direction. You know?"

"Well, hell's bells, big brother," grinned Monroe. "I hardly noticed, really. You being a pain in the ass most of the time, anyway."

Laughing together, Clay ordered them another round.

"Where in hell is John?"

Behind him spoke a voice, "Hope to hell you're in a better mood today, big brother." Clay turned and saw John, smiling and standing akimbo.

"You bet I am!" affirmed Clay as he stepped forward to give him a hearty abrazo. "How you doing, young fella?"

"Just fine, how about you?"

"Couldn't be better, except for the delay in moving."

"Yeah, so I hear."

The reunion was a tonic for the brothers, and especially for Clay, knowing he had the unenvied talent of alienating people, especially when imbibing. But the two men he never wanted to estrange himself from were John and Monroe. And of course Saluda, which goes without saying, although married to testy Coleman. So the re-knitting of sibling bonds was a great relief to Clay, both to his conscience and his feelings of culpability.

Buying and selling cows when he could, Clay also continued brokering cattle between Texas and Kansas, both ends of the profession smiling economically upon him. His postal communications from Roswell with Frank Wilburn and young John McCulloch was encouraging too, where he found his herd there had been built up to one thousand head. While Monroe and John were struggling along and seemingly making a small but profitable headway, Lou Coleman in disgust sold his land, ranch and equipment for five hundred dollars and moved off to Kansas City, Missouri with Saluda and their two children. Four months later Clay finally sold his homestead property to an interested party and his range sections to another. A third man picked up his twelve hundred acres along Gageby creek.

Clay and Dora with John, Kate and Monroe spent their last evening together with a small dinner at John and Kate's. It was a convivial gathering filled with nostalgia and family reminisces, and the bitterness Clay held against the grasping cattle association of the Panhandle was dulled by the reality of his ranch coming together.

"Wish you all the best, Clay," saluted John with a small glass of amber. "Sounds like you've got a nice herd started already down in Roswell."

Kate had bowed to John's wish for a touch of liquor to be present this night, but in a tastefully civilized amount. Of course Clay was glad, for his foot was giving him hell the past two days, and he needed his "medicine."

In fact during the evening he made several trips to the privy, ostensibly in answer to nature's call, but in reality for personal relief from his flask of rye. His limping was obvious that night also, but no one made mention of it out of kindness to his limited state.

"Yes," replied Clay with a touch of proudness. "I think maybe I'm finally getting a foot in the door of this profession. I do wish you and Monroe would move on down there. I just know we all could do well together."

"Thanks, Clay," answered John, knowing his wife would not hear of their moving an inch from where they were. "But don't give up on us. Maybe down the road we'll one day show up on your doorstep."

"You'd be welcome anytime, little brother. And you too, Monroe. I don't see why you don't make a move out of here, being single and un-saddled with a helpmate." The last comment Clay wished too late he had not made, catching Kate's burning eyes and grim lips. Attempting to laugh it off he added, "Now there I go, putting my foot in my mouth without thinking. I keep talking like that, Dora for sure will have me sleeping out in the barn with the cows and horses!"

They all laughed at Clay's faux pas, and the tight atmosphere loosened up as Monroe quickly raised his glass.

"John and I are partners, big brother, so I'm stuck with our own marriage contract. But if he ever decides your doorstep is the place to be, set a place at your table for me, also."

"I'll drink to that, by golly!" toasted Clay.

A week later Clay and Dora grabbed a stage for the Clifton House, where he had made arrangements earlier via mail for Jack Young to meet them.

"Well, Jack," began Allison as they were on their way to the Young home. "How's all the land grant fighting holding up?"

"Bad. Tell you about it later. But I got a letter from young John McCulloch saying he's got together twelve hundred cows, and they're getting fat and sassy."

"Twelve-hundred? Last he wrote it was a thousand. That rascal's snuck in two hundred since he wrote last!" laughed Clay. "Hear that, Dora?"

"Yes," she enthused. "And from what he said, he's happy as all get-out down there."

"Yeah. Don't lose that boy, Clay."

"No way. He'd be tough to replace, and that's no lie."

That late afternoon, taking advantage of a chance to be alone, Clay and Jack took a horseback ride into the countryside.

"Didn't care to talk about the grant troubles in front of Dora, Clay. She'll hear soon enough anyway, and I knew it wouldn't please you none."

"To be honest with you, Jack, I don't give a damn what happens here any longer. I got my belly full of it back when I lived here and in the Panhandle both. But I hate to see you and a handful of my old friends in such a bind. What's going on now?"

"The same. Ejection suits. I got mine with a bunch of others. We'll fight them off long as we can."

"I don't suppose McMains is doing much good?"

"Not a twit. He's only one man, but thinks his words are going to make a difference."

"There's but one difference, Jack. Bags of money, slimy lawyers and gassy politicians."

"Amen."

"What about my old buddy, Marion Littrell? He still with you?"

"Naw. He settled with the grant people with a bunch of others. Don't blame him, really."

"What? Of all the men out here I thought he'd have the balls to fight on."

"Hell, a lot of us know the grant's going to win, but I guess some of us are too damn ornery to let those bastards waltz in like it was a Sunday dance."

"What about Mace Bowman? Wasn't he elected sheriff and still fighting the grant?"

"Well, maybe since you been out of town you ain't heard. He's dead."

"Dead? When? I didn't know."

"Just four months ago, in June. Been sheriff only nine months. What happened, was the Red River Cattle Company, a new local outfit, fenced in miles of pasture on the defunct Nolan Grant south of Springer, which had been pronounced public domain by the court. So Mace organized a squatters' group and they cut through the fence and built some cabins in the pasture."

"Sounds just like Bowman, by God. We had a falling out, but I'd go to the line with him any time. So how'd that play out?"

"The Red River people didn't like it of course, claiming they had legally bought the land from a man who in turn had bought it from an heir."

"Sounds like a line of thieves passing on a dead horse."

"Exactly what it was. Anyway, Mace one night was in Trinidad having dinner with County Clerk John Lee the same time their cabins on the Red River claim were burned down. Mace also took sick that night and died a day later. Consumption, it was claimed. And an old lung wound."

"I'll be damned. Smells like a barrel of fish, to me."

"It was, a lot of us think. A hot rumor went around his meal was poisoned, so strong that an inquest was ordered."

"What did they find out?"

"Nothing. It was all talk and no one had the clout to push it. The examiners said he died natural, and that was that."

"Good God, a sheriff yet."

"Something else for you to chew on. You know who was the Red River's range foreman?"

"Who?"

"Marion Littrell."

"Then he would have been in charge of burning down the cabins."

"Right. And let me add that he was also range foreman for the Maxwell Grant."

"Holy shit, Jack. You don't suppose...?"

"I don't know any more than you, Clay. But when I start adding one and one, what am I left with? I can't believe he's just another coolie for the grant, but ambition does funny things to some people, y'know?"

Speechless, Allison could but shake his head in silent disarray, wondering where in hell things were heading, and how much worse things could get. A pair of men he had held in high esteem, regardless his differences with them—Littrell and their quasi-comical duel over pretty Carry Gale, and Bowman facing him down in Schwenk's Saloon—now gone their separate ways: Littrell to the enemy, Bowman to a questionable death. And both fast-draw men. He'd have loved to seen a show-down between them. His money would have been on Mace.

"Christ, I need a drink, Jack. Let's go into Elkins and hoist a few."

"Now don't let all this black news darken your spirits, Clay. And mainly, don't let it lead you on to a crazy bloodletting. Hear?"

Allison laughed. "Ah, Jack, nothing to worry about. Years ago I'd have gotten the boys together and ridden into the Maxwell Grant headquarters and burnt the damn building down around their ears, after first killing every son of a bitch there I laid my eyes on. Especially fat-assed Catron. But I got a future to look forward to. A ranch, cattle business just getting a good start, my Dora. And hopefully a family down the road. Much as I have no use for that collection of land-maggots, I can't let it spoil my life."

"Smart thinking, Clay. And damn if I don't need a drink or two myself!"

Two days later Clay and Dora packed a pair of bags for a visit to Roswell. Jack drove them to Otero where they caught the train. Eight hours later they were in Las Vegas where they deboarded to spend the night and stretch their legs, Clay's limb becoming a problem. Late that morning Allison went along to the bank for a chat with Miguel Otero, and took him out to lunch.

"How's everything going for you down in Roswell, Clay?"

"Perfect. Just like I wrote from Texas before I left. Got a growing herd I hope to send off to market in the future. In fact, Dora and me are on our way down there now."

"That's wonderful. Glad to hear of it."

"I'll probably be dropping you a line in the near future with a little money to add to my account. Won't hurt to keep my options open between here and Roswell, suspecting I'll be shipping some cows to Wyoming."

"Anything I can do for you, don't hesitate to ask."

On the way back to his hotel Allison dropped into a saloon for a touch of painkiller. A double-shot of rye was just what the doctor ordered, so he called for a second prescription with a glass of beer. He relished the taste of his amber in several small sips as he thought in pleasure how his cattle-dream of old was inching in place. Maybe after a few drives the ranch will finally show up, he smiled to himself. Christ, it's been a long haul. While slowly imbibing at his beer a voice at his side asked, "That you, Clay?" Turning, Allison recognized an old Cimarron crony.

"Well, hell, if it isn't Cliff Jackson. How in the world are you?"

"Fine," he smiled. "Fine," shaking Allison's hand.

They spoke for a time recollecting names and places until Cliff said in quiet confidence, "Better let you in on something, Clay."

"What's that?"

"The local marshal, Art Jillson, is looking for an excuse to put a bullet in you. Don't know why, but he's the kind who likes to push his weight, anyway."

"Hell, I don't know the man or have ever met him."

"Just watch your back, Clay. Never know about hombres like him."

"Thanks, Cliff. I'll sure be on the lookout."

Deeply incensed at the news, Allison limped back to his rooms to check out so he and Dora could continue on their journey to the next stop, Socorro. He kept a keen eye up and down both sides of the street, with an occasional glimpse behind him, but saw nothing more suspicious than local pedestrian and horse traffic. Dora sensed his irksome state, but he brushed off her inquiry as nothing more than his pain returning. He was thankful when the train pulled out of the station and wondered whether he should pay the constable a visit next time he was in town. Well, he'd wait and see. Cliff could have picked up a lame rumor or piece of cheap gossip. Then again, Jillson could be a two-bit headhunter looking for a rep. Maybe Otero could find out something.

Along the thirty-six-hour spell to Socorro the pounding in his leg mercifully waned away to a light soreness, and they alighted near nine the next evening.

The Allisons ten-day stay in the Roswell area was a pleasurable time for both. Clay rode about his pasture admiring the growing stock with a feeling of success in his bones, a sense of attaining a good part of his goal, and while Dora was glad to see her brother John once again, she was also happy in her husband's sense of well being. She knew how much he wanted to get a start in the cattle business, how hard he worked toward that direction for years, and now here it was for him, and she enjoyed it to her bones to stand in the reflection of his personal accomplishment.

"Frank," commented Clay one afternoon as the two rode amidst the munching herd. "Them are fine looking cows, although I nervously see now and then slight evidence of a brand change. I do hope they are not alterations and that all is legal and clean here. Not that I question your—"

"No, no," laughed Wilburn. "All is on the up and up. Every calf, cow, steer and horse is pure as the driven snow far as branding is concerned. We are covered completely by legitimate sales contracts and unblemished paperwork."

"Good," answered Allison, knowing from his long experience and knowledge as herder and broker, that many a cattleman had given in to the temptation of shortcuts in order to increase his holdings with the least amount of expense. Many a large ranch had its humble births by way of the crude running iron, a small piece of history that was often overlooked in the self-satisfied recounting of humble beginnings. He just wanted no part of it to touch, taint, endanger or threaten him at this point, where everything could come tumbling down around him.

But Allison's suspicion's were correct, in that Wilburn cut a wide swathe throughout southern New Mexico in fulfilling his contractual obligations, whether cows, horses, sheep or real estate, living by his motto, "One man's misery is another's man's joy." Not that he was the only "entrepreneur" in the region, but he was one of the best with the most influential of connections. For instance, some of Allison's last cows were rustled from Mexico by the Post brothers from Toyah, Texas who were Wilburn's faithful suppliers of cattle from the south, Mexico as well as Texas. And he would always reach out through his "blind," a man he trusted to carry out whatever arrangements were needed, and this way he could remain hidden.

"You're doing a fine job, John," complimented Allison to young McCulloch.

"Thank you, Uncle Clay. This is a healthy collection of cows we got together."

"Yes, they are. When we send them to market you'll be the ramrod. How's that sound?"

"Really? Hey, that would be wonderful! I'll sure try not to disappoint you!"

"I'm not worried a bit. You're a natural with them beasts, young man. One of the best."

Clay and Dora, upon returning to Colfax County stopped overnight in Las Vegas. Clay had not intended to, but the news that Cliff had dropped on him concerning the town marshal gunning for him was disturbing, and so thought he'd have a talk with Otero over it. But Miguel knew nothing of it either, and never met the man to talk to, although he knew by the grapevine that the lawman was a bit on the blustery side. Otero said he'd find out what he could quietly and let him know, either by letter or the next time he was in town.

"Thanks much, Miguel. And whatever the case, I'd like to have you be my escort whenever I drop in town to do any business, if you would? I doubt he'd try anything with you at my side."

"Be a pleasure, Clay. But if it's true, I doubt he'll be our lawman for long."

When Jack Young was waiting for their train to pull into Otero for Clay and Dora, the two were met with a big surprise. John and Kate were there to welcome them.

"What is a nice looking couple like you doing in a county like this?" questioned Clay.

"Well, hell, big brother, we just thought we'd have a little vacation from the oasis of the Panhandle and do some slumming! Wonderful to see you two!" exclaimed John as he gave Clay and Dora a hug hello. "You taking care of this old limping senior, Dora?" he laughed.

"He's tougher than a keg of nails and won't let me, John! Oh, Kate, it's so good to see you two!" she squealed.

"What in hell you mean old?" snarled Clay mockingly. "One more disrespectful word like that, young man, and you'll be the one limping!"

"Oh, my God!"cringed John. "Hide the liquor! I'm in for one hellova thumping!"

The ride back to the Youngs was filled with news back and forth of the Panhandle and of Roswell and of Clay's promising future in cattle. It was a sanguine occasion which elated the spirits of the quartet.

"Got a letter from John in Roswell" commented Young. "He seems to be doing right well."

"Yeah," agreed Clay. "Dora and I left him happier than two hands clapping. What'd he have to say to you?"

"Told me of a cattle deal he made, and how he came out way ahead. Know of that?"

"Sure do. He must have mailed your letter a few days after we got there."

"Seems so. He said he heard of a rancher desperate to sell because of an ailing wife to take back east, and also was being plagued by thieves."

"True enough," answered Clay. "After John strategically exposed a hefty roll of greenbacks that goggled the man's vision, he sold seven hundred of his cows for a piddling. Not a week later John sold them to another rancher for twice what he paid."

"Exactly what he wrote. That boy's liable to be a success if he don't watch out."

"I'll tell you," laughed Clay. "I congratulated him and told him how he shamed me as a broker when it comes to making a deal. But I promised not to scold him if he kept it up. Dora, Kate, I'm really proud of your brother. Right down to my bones."

The plan was for Clay and Dora to rest for a week, then make a return trip south to surprise young McCulloch with John and Kate. He would give his brother John a tour of the area and Kate would have a chance to visit with her brother, whom she hadn't seen in five years. Clay too was looking forward to the journey, but for his own reasons. His foot and leg by turns were giving him fits, first one then the other. That was bad enough, but at times both would beat together like an army of drummers. He had seen doctors a few times, and they all suggested the removal of his foot. The last pulled no punches, saying the limb should be removed from the knee down; that there was danger of it becoming gangrenous. In his opinion the leg was harboring an infection which would wane at times, giving him temporary relief and the false hope of healing. But then it would return inflamed, causing further internal damage. Yet Clay hung on, not relishing the removal of such a prominently important body part. "Hell, doc," he joked dryly at his last sawbones. "What in hell would I look like in an ass-kicking contest?"

The return to Roswell this time was a supreme effort for Clay, in that his limb, while mostly seeming to have subsided torturing him most of the way, returned with a vengeance, causing him to sometimes groan behind gritted teeth, other times to bring a rush of perspiration across his forehead. Having to gulp hefty slugs from his medicine flask helped some, and he was glad to have had the foresight to carry two containers of "Doc Shrub." So he decided that this time his return to the Youngs would be much later, and without Dora, because of a desire to give in to a long repressed thirst. He wished to lock himself in a hotel room for four or five days and nights and soak his brain and body in quarts of alcohol to find some relief from the endless stabbing and burning of his lower extremity. Maybe he could submerge it in enough rye for it to go away, or at least make it dwindle down to a tolerable and acceptable level. The frustration of not finding relief from the constant aching was getting to him, while too, he looked upon a good drunk as a holiday treat and reward for his lengthy abstinence.

In Roswell, while the others checked into the hotel, Clay limped over to Frank Wilburn's office. As he entered, Wilburn looked up from his desk. "Clay! Good to see you!"

"Hello, Frank. Not too busy, are you?"

"No, no. In fact, been slack most of the week. Gives me time to get some of this paperwork done. Just get in?"

"This minute."

Walking over to him and shaking his hand, Wilburn asked, "What can I help you with?"

"Brought my brother John and his wife down for a tour. Be here maybe a week. Mainly wanted to know if you had a rig with a pair of horses we could borrow?"

"Certainly, no trouble. Happen to have one at the blacksmith's with a horse getting shod. Let's take a walk. Only three, four blocks away."

The men trod along in the sun, Clay with his walking stick. Wilburn couldn't help but note the pallor of Clay's face.

"How's that leg doing? Any better?"

"Soreness comes and goes. More often of late."

"I'm sure you've seen enough doctors to make you swear off them, but we have an excellent specialist here might give you some relief."

"No thanks, Frank. They all want to abbreviate me; some the foot, another the leg. I may have to face some physical elimination down the road, but I think I'll fight it off for the time being."

"I'm honestly sorry, Clay. It's a shame. But any time you might want to talk to him, let me know. He's not only an experienced and respected physician, he's a personal friend. Maybe the three of us can have dinner some time."

"Thank you, Frank. Kind of you. I'll certainly give it some thought."

At the blacksmith's Wilburn saluted, "Hello, Carl. Horse done yet?"

"Just a few minutes ago, Mister Wilburn. All set to go."

"Good. I'll take them now. Let's go, Clay.'

Wilburn guided the team to the hotel and pulled in. "She's all yours, Clay. Long as you need them. Saw Young McCulloch a few days ago, and everything's running smooth as silk. He's a good man, let me tell you. Don't ever lose him."

"That I won't, thank you. Listen, Frank. John and his wife Kate, and me and Dora plan to have lunch before we ride out. Why don't you join us?"

"Oh, can't right now, wish I could. You say you plan a week here?"

"About that."

"All right. When you come to return the rig we'll go to lunch, or dinner, whichever, and it'll be on me. And don't argue."

"Fine," smiled Allison. "See you then. Goodbye, and thanks, Frank."

Wilburn left with a wave toward his office as Allison dismounted and entered the hotel. Within the hour the quartet had lunch and were on their way, a four-hour drive.

For five days and five nights Clay bit his teeth behind a benevolent mein that shielded high and low attacks of pain. But he fooled no one. Dora knew, and John and Kate also, of his constant bouts with his foot and leg. Young John McCulloch knew also, and wished he had the magic pill to cure him. John admired and idolized Clay, more so than John, if that were possible. He loved working the herd and the responsibilities his uncle had given him, and vowed to do as good job as humanly possible to win and hold his trust. Clay in return loved him like a son, for he saw in the bright and industrious youth the son he looked forward to having, and one of many. The family thing. Even though not blood relatives, they were as bonded as deep as if they were, and thoroughly enjoyed each other's company. Even their shadows commingled like old kin. "Slick John," his uncle affectionately called him.

"Hey, Slick John, how's it going?" inquired Clay as he and his brother John rode up one afternoon.

"Just fine, Unc. Real fine."

"That's one excellent piece of horseflesh you're riding. New?"

"Yes, sir. Got her with that bunch of bargain cows I bought last month. He threw it in as a bonus. Ain't she a beaut?"

"I'll say. But I'm getting a teeny nervous with you in charge here, you know?"

"Why's that?"

"You're so slick you just might slip this place out from under me one day!"

All three laughed heartily at that. It was the easy laughter of men who respected and trusted each other.

"I'd never do that, Unc."

"You ever do, at least retire me at a decent monthly wage, hear?"

"Well," mused McCulloch, rubbing his chin contemplatingly. "I'd have to ponder on that a bit."

With a wave and a chuckle Clay and John moved slowly through the scattered herd.

"Healthy collection of beef you got, Clay. A lotta dinero on the hoof."

"Why in hell don't you and Monroe get on down here? The three of us could do right well. And with young John as our chief ramrod, we're a cinch."

"Tempting, Clay. Really is. But Kate is too settled in our home and it would take a ton of dynamite to make her even think of moving."

"But, hell, with her brother and sister here it'd be like family, you know? Wouldn't she like that?"

"Sure would, but it's the move from the home she's gotten to love. I've asked. But if things go to hell up there for us, we may join you. Monroe, too. I'll keep you informed."

"Do that, young 'un," he grinned. "And stop stalling."

On the morning of the fifth day as the four visitors climbed aboard Wilburn's wagon for the return to Roswell, one of McCulloch's hired hands rode toward him. He stopped his mount about forty feet away and rudely called, "McCulloch! I'd like a word with you!"

He was one of the three men John had hired to help with the herd, two local teenaged Mexicans and a Texan around thirty who called himself Waco. The Texan bitched a lot, but more so in the last week, especially seeing John's guests make such a to-do over him. But what griped him was his having to take orders from a twenty-two-year-old. He was a lean six-footer with a chip on each shoulder and a sour temper.

"What's the story on your hand there, John," asked Clay quietly.

"Just been complaining a lot lately, and I may have to let him go."

"Sounds like you should do it now, him exposing such unnecessary rudeness like that."

"Wait a minute while I go and see what he wants."

"No, John," insisted Clay. "Make him come to you. You don't take orders from him. Make him understand that."

"You're right, Unc."

McCulloch stepped away from the rig and called to his hand, "You come over here, Waco."

The Texan grudgingly heeled his horse toward McCulloch, then dismounted.

"What is it?" asked McCulloch. "Can't it wait till later?"

"Can't it wait till later?" mimicked Waco sarcastically, dropping his reins and cockily hitching his thumbs in his gunbelt over his slightly growing gut. "No, it can't, damn it!"

"Well, simmer down and watch your mouth before my guests. Now, what's on your mind?"

"I want a raise, that's what!"

"A raise? The three of you get the same wages and are well paid for the area."

"Listen, I gots years of experience over you and I don't savvy taking orders from a young punk kid that's still wet behind the ears!"

Clay debarked slowly and mosseyed over to one side of the ranting Texan. Waco's words burned through him, scorching him to the bone, and his mismanaged mouth toward John rose his internal temperature a thousand degrees, way past boiling point. "Waco?" addressed Clay.

"Huh?" he grunted, as he turned to face the man in black with a walking stick. "What you want, you damn cripple?"

Those were his last spoken words. Clay brought up his stick and buried it nearly a foot into Waco's soft mid-section. His eyes nearly popped out of his head as he forcibly expelled a ton of air. His knees buckled and he bent in horrid agony, unable to talk except to emit a long gasp. Clay raised the stick and pummeled the man about the head and shoulders as he slid to the ground face down in his own vomit.

"Slick John," spoke Clay. "I think I may have disabled your top hand there."

"Top? Looks more like he's hit the bottom, Unc." Bending over the writhing body, John spoke. "Waco, you hear me? Listen good. This is a ten-note, more'n half over what's owed you." He shoved it into the Texan's shirt pocket. "Soon as you're able, get on your horse and ride as far away from here as you can. If I see you again, you won't be so kindly handled. Understand?"

Bleary-eyed, pale and shaken, Waco nodded his head and painfully sat up, gasping for air.

"Everything under control here, Slick John?" inquired Clay.

"Just Jim dandy, Unc." McCulloch leaned over and pulled Waco's gun from his holster, emptied it of its five shells, then stuck the gun back in its sheath. He then inserted the bullets in Waco's front shirt pocket. "You can reload down the road, Waco. Now pull yourself together and ride on out."

"Smart move, John," complimented Clay from the rig.

Waco shakily picked himself up from the ground, vomit-smeared, watery-eyed and still gasping for air, gripped his saddle horn, then shuffled along side of his horse away from the group.

"You be cautious now, John," spoke Clay as he took the reins of the wagon. "Watch your back."

"Yes sir," he replied. "And you take care of yourself too, Uncle Clay."

John and Clay had a good laugh on their return ride, and although the women were in a small state of shock at witnessing the cold-blooded whipping, agreed that Waco had brought it upon himself. The activity for Clay was a wonderful therapeutic release, an exercise that released his need to express himself physically. It was a rush which bolstered his ego, not having had an altercation with man nor beast in years. He feared he was getting rusty, maybe even senile or soft. But when he heard Waco speak to John so demeaningly, that did it. Yessiree! No one, but no one was going to screw with his family. And especially Young John. Feeling elated over it all, Clay laughed uproariously till tears ran down his cheeks.

At their hotel John and the women disembarked and Clay drove on to Wilburn's office. After he thanked him for the use of the rig, Wilburn reminded him of the dinner invite which Clay accepted. "How's seven sound?" asked Wilburn.

"Perfect, Frank. We'll meet you there."

The dinner party was convivial, the food perfect and the wine delicious. It was a two-hour repast they all enjoyed, and they looked forward to many more. Clay's foot and leg took a holiday since after the caning incident, and it brought him to believe that all he needed was a little physical exercise occasionally, an adrenaline rush now and then to clear up his system. Damn if the cane didn't come in handy! In fact, he felt so like his old healthy self that he cancelled his thoughts of remaining behind a few days for his solitary binge. No need, he thought in satisfaction. No need.

The return to Colfax County and the Youngs was quiet and un-eventful. Along the way John and Kate revealed that they aimed to make a trip to Missouri to see Lou and Saluda, whom they had already visited twice, and in fact their third daughter was born there. Although John made no suggestions to Clay that Dora and he join them, recalling his brother's clash with Lou, Clay unhesitatingly asked, "How would you like it if Dora and me joined you?"

"Why, sure, Clay," answered John, slightly taken aback.

"Good. To be honest, I'd like to bury the hatchet between me and Lou."

"I think they would much appreciate that, Clay," encouraged Kate. "Yes, they would."

"Folks, I have to admit I was awful hard on the man, even though his comments were unwelcome. Basically, I like Lou, always have. But like him or not you knew where you stood with him, and he wasn't shy in letting you know, that's for sure!"

Following a two-week stay with the Young's, the Allisons grabbed the two p.m. AT & SF out of Otero for Kansas City, Missouri, a rail-trek of six hundred sixty-five miles. The sleeper fare cost them eight dollars each for the one-way, twenty-seven hour journey, arriving the following morning at eleven a.m.

"How do you like that?" spoke Clay. "Do you realize that if we took a wagon train from Otero to get here, we would probably be just now maybe thirty miles out of there?"

"Yep, that's right," nodded John. "We'd barely be pulling out of Trinidad. Guess it won't be long before we'll be turning in all our horses, mules and oxen to circuses and the glue factory."

The four travelers left the station and hired a conveyance for the ride across town to the Coleman home. Finally alighting with their bags, Clay paid the fare, and in moments they stood before the white-painted wooden house.

"Well," commented Clay, as he withdrew his pocket watch. "It's eleven forty-five, and at least we're in time for lunch."

"Yep," agreed John. "My stomach is in agreement with that."

"Oh, you men!" scolded Kate. "Can't you act a little less than cavemen?"

The door suddenly opened and there stood Saluda, happily grinning. "Clay! John! Lord, what a wonderful surprise!" She flew across the short porch, down the half-dozen steps and into Clay's arms. "Oh, Clay! It's so good to see you!"

"And it's good to see you too, Saluda!" elated Clay.

In the meantime the three Coleman children, Robert Clay's namesake, Edna and Elmer, clambered off the porch and down the stairs to race into John and Kate's arms, squealing like Comanches.

"What in hell's all the racket?" groused Lou Coleman, stepping out on the porch.

"Hello, Lou," greeted John. Kate and me thought we'd drop in for a spell, and brought Clay and Dora along."

Lou braced at Clay's name and the sudden sight of him, not certain what to expect. After a moment he exclaimed, "Well, hell, you all, don't just stand there like a flock of clucking hens, come on in!" As Lou held the screen door open the last to approach was Clay, hat in hand.

"Hello, Lou," he greeted with outstretched palm.

"Welcome to my humble abode, pilgrim," smiled Lou, gripping the extended mitt.

"I, uh, want to apologize for them unkind words back in Mobeetie," muttered Clay quietly.

"Ah, pshaw," minimized Lou over their past unpleasantness with a wave of his free hand. "I'm sorry I practically called you a cow thief in public like that. Right unneighborly of me."

"Sure was, you old rascal," grinned Clay. "I was just nervous some lawman might have overheard you!"

Everybody laughed at that, and the ice was peacefully broken.

After a week of sight-seeing and casually lazing about, Clay and Dora made ready for their departure, Clay anxious to return to his herd and to tie up some loose ends business-wise. John and Kate were staying on a few days more, enjoying the slack time.

"And one more thing, folks," proclaimed Clay across the dining room table over lunch on their last day. "I'd like to make an announcement. Unless you would rather, dear," asked Clay of Dora.

"No, love," she smiled. "Please go on."

"Well, ahem. I have to reveal with pride and joy to you all that my child-bride is in the family way. At last!"

"Good lord!" delighted John. "Another Allison comes forth!"

"Yes!" echoed Lou. "And congratulations to the both of you!"

"Yep," chuckled Clay. "I got a little cowboy to help on the ranch. 'Course it'll be a few years before I can put the rascal to work!"

"A toast, by golly," insisted Lou, as he pulled wine glasses from the cupboard to set before each of the adults. He poured the goblets half full of Chablis, and in raising his asked, "What are you naming the little herder, Clay?"

"Joseph Clay, by God!"

"To the health and good fortune of Joseph Clay Allison!" saluted Lou.

As they all emptied their glasses with uplifted hearts and hearty felicitations, Clay and Dora's faces were covered with beaming smiles. Setting his emptied vessel on the table, Clay took Dora into his arms to give her a warm and gentle caress.

One earlier evening, over a quart of sipping whiskey, the three men began a penny-ante poker game which lasted til the wee hours of the morning.

"How's your leg and side coming along, John?" inquired Lou deep in the game while shuffling, referring to his old shotgun-shooting in Las Animas by Constable Faber.

"Oh, the leg gets a little sore come rain or winter."

"Ain't many men come away alive after a double-dose of buckshot," added Lou. "Lucky."

"He's meaner than hell, you mean," laughed Clay.

"Not quite," chuckled John. "Only half as mean as you."

"True enough, young 'un," agreed his elder, grinning.

"Now and then I pry out a lead pellet or two pushing to the surface. Can't be too many more left in me."

"In fact, Lou," continued Clay, "he was still limping a bit three years later in March of seventy-nine when he strapped on his gunbelt to play deputy to Sheriff Burleson and Mace Bowman to help round up three hard-cases, one who just killed a lawman."

"Really, now?" impressed Lou.

"Hell, weren't much. They had the good sense to surrender, wanting to live. Damn it all."

"That ol' Bowman," mused Lou. "He was something."

"How's that?" queried Clay.

"Kind of a funny story about his wife catching up with him. Left him and refused to live with him any more. So he divorced her, charging abandonment."

"C'mon, Lou," urged John. "What's the story?"

"As I recall this was three years into his first marriage, to Jane Keene. Mace had the gambler's habit, but a gambler's bad luck. Still, he couldn't keep away from the green table. He was also a handsome devil, as you know, and quite a lady's man. Couldn't keep away from them, either. Back then a lot of the fellas would run north to Trinidad, probably the loosest town hereabouts, even wilder than Raton."

John pulled in a pot of pennies with glee. "Hot damn, this is my fourth pot tonight! I'm getting to like this game!"

"Anyway, Mace's wife was alerted by her angry older brother, Bill Keene, that he seen him in Trinidad with a lady of the night he was living with, in a house he rented. So one day the two on a Friday night, after Mace told Jane he was going to be out of town trailing a killer, make the fifty-five mile the train ride from Springer to Trinidad for a house call. Gimme three cards, Clay."

"I'll stand pat, big brother."

"Good grief," moaned Clay. "Not another full-house?"

"Naw," laughed John. "Just bluffing."

"About ten that night Jane and Bill stood nervously on the porch of Mace's adobe abode, not sure what to expect. Bill then knocks hard several times and steps back, his hand next to his holstered gun. After about a minute the door opens, and there stands Mace, drunker than a skunk. He was barefoot and in his long-johns which was unbuttoned all the way down. Over that he had his gun belt strapped on. In his left hand he held a whiskey quart by the neck while his right hung over his holster. He was so drunk his eyes were red and unfocused. In Mace's holster Bill saw that his Colt was in backwards, and while relieved, hoped he wouldn't be foolish enough to try and draw it in anger."

John pulled in another pot of pennies. "Hot damn!"

"So what happened then?" asked Clay of Lou.

"Jane and Bill saw across the room a naked woman sprawled across the divan, drunk also, an arm and a leg hooked on the couch-back to wantonly expose to the world all her fleshy and hirsute attributes. She had waist-length bright red hair spilling over her body and the divan. In her arms was a tiny poodle. But what struck Bill was her eyes, bright and burning. He swore one was blue and the other green, and they didn't look at him but through him, and he got frightened for some reason."

"I fold," announced John, throwing in his hand.

"I'll take two," requested Clay.

"And I'll take one," spoke Lou.

"So what happened next?" asked Clay, intrigued.

"Well, Mace was drunkenly swaying and asked, 'You like what you see?' Bill answers, 'I don't like her at all.' Mace replies, 'Then why you staring at her nakedness?' Bill says, 'I was looking at her eyes. They're weird.' Mace says, 'No they're not. They're only different colored. One's green, one's blue.' Bill says, 'I know. That's what got my attention.' Mace says, 'Well, the Princess don't like to be stared at. It gets her nervous.' Bill says, 'Princess?' Mace says, 'Yep. Princess. She's a half-breed redskin from Kansas. Princess Bountiful Light. They call her that because of her sparkling red hair. I met her not a month ago when she rode into town on a big white-haired jackass called Pete.' Bill says, 'Pretty hair, all right.' Mace asks, 'Who's that behind you?' Bill says, 'My sister.' Mace asks, 'Who?' Bill says, 'My sister. Jane.' Mace says, 'Jane?' Bill says, 'Yep. And she's your wife, Jane, too.' Mace says, 'Both?' Bill says, 'Yep.' Mace squeezes his eyes over and over trying to focus as he looked out into the dark and says, 'I'll be damned!' Bill says, 'Reckon that's so.' Jane yells in a fit, 'Mace, you are double-damned!' Mace says, 'Reckon so.' Then the Princess calls out from the couch, grabbing her hairy part, 'Mascar mi horquilla, gringa!' Bill says, 'That ain't nice, Princess.' Mace says, smiling, 'But she's got a point, Bill. And I'd pay good money to see it.' Jane says, 'Let's go, Bill.' Bill says, 'Goodnight, Mace. Goodnight, Princess.' Mace says, 'Goodnight, all.' And to his wife he says, 'I'll be home a little late for breakfast Monday, dear.'"

John and Clay roared at the last line. "Christ, I'd a loved to seen all that!" howled John.

"Guess the pot's mine this time," commented Clay. "God, it's the first and only one the whole night! Lou, did you say she was a Princess?"

"So Mace told Bill. Saw her once in Cimarron walking in town with a woman friend, Tina somebody. Think they worked for a time across the river from Lambert's in Mexican Town. Good looking women, I'll say that. Sisters of Lesbos, some inferred."

Clay recalled the Princess' eyes now, how strange they looked. That's what it was; one was green, the other blue. How come he never figured that out? And they had that eerie gaze, like they looked right through you. He shivered as a cold finger trailed his spine: someone walking on his grave.

"Did you know them?" asked Lou of Clay.

"Naw. Never did." Strange how she got around. Wonder if she ever made it back to Kansas? He could see her now, astride her giant white-haired jackass, dragging that travois across the plain, trailed by a pack of unruly, unwashed, yipping curs. Her waist-length hair, now white, whipped in the breeze behind her as she screetched back at him insanely, "Malo! Malo, hombre! Malo e loco!"

"Clay, John," exhausted Lou. "It's past three in the morning and I can't muster the strength for another hand or drink. I quit."

"Good idea," agreed Clay.

"Me too," yawned John.

Clay was in seventh heaven all the way back to the Youngs, and was grinning like a child at Christmas opening gifts when he told the Young family of Dora's expecting. "Yessiree," he would happily proclaim. "Young Joseph Clay is on his way!"

"Now, Clay," Dora cautioned. "We don't know if it will be a boy or girl, so you shouldn't set your hopes so high."

"Don't you want it to be a boy, Dora?"

"Of course, dear, because you want one so badly. But it really can't be known until he or she arrives."

"She? Pshaw! I know it's going to be a boy."

Worried he might be disappointed, Dora would gently stroke his cheek, give him a light kiss, and smilingly agree, "Of course, Clay. How could it be otherwise?"

Because of his wife's condition, Clay now wanted to make the trip to Roswell alone.

"Oh, no, Clay. You know I love traveling, and we planned this together. I'm going, too."

"But you're pregnant, dear. The long miles and jostling might not be good for you. I think you should be calm and restful, and having the baby here at the Youngs would be perfect."

"No. I'll return here after the trip. Good lord, honey, it isn't due til late summer, maybe August."

"Oh, all right then. But if you begin feeling poorly, we come right back."

On the way down the Allisons got off the train in Las Vegas so he could have a word with Otero at the bank, then they would take him out to dinner that night.

"McCulloch's been doing quite well, Clay. Looks like you have the beginning of a profitable operation down there, and some good people running it."

"Yeah, McCulloch' s a wonder, and Wilburn' s been nothing short of dependable. By the way, have you been able to find out any more about Marshal Jilson?"

"Yes. Seems all that talk you heard was nothing more than manufactured gossip. He has no interest in hounding you or anyone else, and I'm inclined to believe him."

"Thanks, Miguel. That's good news. We'll be leaving tomorrow, so how about dinner with us? On me, no argument."

Leaving the bank, Clay made for the sheriff's office several blocks away. The aching was pounding a bit, returning again for its usual session. He paused in the shadow of an awning on this bracing afternoon and stepped into the doorway of a closed store. Reaching into the breast pocket of his jacket he withdrew his trusty flask with the disguised label of Shrub's miraculous medicine, and poured a hefty swig down his throat. In moments he stepped along with his walking stick for a talk with Jilson the lawman. For some reason he wanted to talk to the man personally, in a friendly way, and get the feel of the man. The rumor still nagged at him, and he was not one to let sleeping dog's lie. Or even bogus lawmen.

At the office Allison entered and closed the door behind him. As he turned he saw a fat little man behind a badge seated at a desk peering intently at several wanted posters before him. Looking up the lawman greeted, "Howdy."

"And howdy to you. I assume you are the town marshal?"

"The very same. Marshal Arthur Jilson at your service. What can I do for you?"

"I'm looking for a thief. He stole a couple horses from me and I've traced him this far. He might be headed for Roswell."

"What's the fellow's name?"

"Port Stockton. He and his brother Ike are pretty active in the profession. Ever hear of them?"

"No. Can't say that I have."

"They operate mostly around Raton and Trinidad."

"Way up north there, huh?"

"Yep. Another man that works with them is Clay Allison. Hear of him?"

"Nope. And your name, sir?"

"James. Frank James."

"Well, Mister James, best we can do right now is maybe check the blacksmith and stables hereabouts, see if he might have shod or fed his horses on the way through."

"Done that, found nothing. Sure you never heard of Allison? When he drinks he is awful dangerous. Turns into a crazy man. Used to hang around Cimarron a lot."

"No, sir, Mister James. 'Fraid I can't help you there neither."

Allison stared eye-to-eye at the marshal, and as he did so he felt there was nothing to be found behind the man's orbs.

"Where you from, Mister Jilson?"

"Missouri, last. Ohio before that. Born in Michigan."

"Been in law work long?"

"Eight whole months."

"What'd you do before?"

"Hardware clerk. A drummer before that."

"A drummer? What'd you sell?"

"Oh, a little of everything. You know, some of this, some of that."

"Ever pedal Doctor Shrub's medicine? His Spiritual Equalizer?"

"Oh, my, yes. Yes, indeed. A real seller, that. Never cured anything, though."

"Well, Marshal Jilson, thank you for your time. It's been a rare pleasure talking at you."

"And thank you for dropping by, Mister James. Enjoyed your visit. Wished I could have been of help."

"By the way," asked Clay in mid-limp toward the door. "You by chance know a local man by the name of Cliff Jackson?"

"Cliff? Oh, yes sir. See him in the saloons often. Drinks too much, tells a lot of tall tales, but harmless. He give you any trouble?"

"No, not at all. But you might ask him about Mister Allison. I think he used to know him."

"I'll certainly do that."

"And tell him Mister James said 'hello'. We know each other slightly."

"Will do, Mister James."

Clay turned and exited the office while the fat man returned his interest to the posters before him. Quite incensed, Allison was hoping along his way back to the hotel to run into Cliff Jackson. He would have been more than happy to once again put his cane to use. He wasn't sure whether Jackson was merely pulling his leg with the "Jilson rumor," or if he was hoping viciously to set up a shooting. It was like that stupid story which made the rounds over the years and now everybody believed, of him supposedly cutting off Charlie Kennedy's head after they lynched him that night in Elizabethtown, then sticking it up on a pole before Lambert's Hotel. Damn, what an asinine tale! Lambert would surely have shot-gunned him at the very least for putting a dent in his business! And the popular fiction of he and the Red River ferry boatman Zack Colbert having a knife duel on the lip of a grave they dug, in which the winner would cover the loser. That was back when he first crossed the Red River into Texas. All he did was have a fight with Colbert over some snotty remark he made for which he thoroughly whipped him. Someone else's imagination continued the story on from there. When he was young he didn't deny any of the crap people made up about him, in fact loved it that they paled and shook in his company. But now it was downright embarrassing! God, his foot was killing him. He'd give it a hot soak before they went off to dinner.

On the entire journey to and from Roswell Allison catered to Dora's every physical comfort, plying her with overweaning attention in every possible way, and worrying over her incessantly like a mother hen. She found the tender concern in him an irony in contrast to the reputation he had of being a drunken, cold-blooded killer. But in time she sensed the impression was an exterior he didn't mind having and at times perpetuating as a form of self-defense, for he felt it protected his private and personal life, and kept potential troublemakers at bay. There was some truth too, that in certain societies, the closer to the frontier the less the law, and the more likely were the odds that the complaisant man could be a convenient target for the more aggressive predator. When in each other's company Dora couldn't have found or had a more attentive husband, and she did feel completely protected. But this time returning to Colfax County was a relief, and she never thought she would ever look forward to the end of such a pleasing pastime as being on the road. Although she understood and appreciated his concern for her growing condition, and his worry over the health of their future child—and his hoped-for son—he without realizing it was becoming more of an irritating bother. So with quiet patience she put up no resistance to his perpetual attendance but looked forward to returning to the Young's and having the child. And she hoped with all her might he would have the son he had set his heart upon.

Staying in Roswell for a day, and after having a brief confab with Wilburn, Clay and Dora left in Wilburn's rig to pick up John McCulloch for a trip farther south. After a day of rest, the three rode off, and after crossing the Pecos to its east bank continued on until across the New Mexico-Texas state lines. About a half-mile below the border of Texas Allison halted.

"Where in the world are you taking us, Clay?" puzzled John.

"Right here. This is it. Dora, John, you are now on the northeast corner of my ranch. This is the section I'm squatting on until legalities with Texas can be settled upon down the road. In the meantime we'll move on it, cows and all."

Before them in the near distance sat several stone structures in varied conditions of disrepair, the remains of some of Captain John Pope's Eighteen Fifty-Eight military living quarters. More lay farther south.

"Well," smiled Dora, gazing at the ancient buildings while shielding her eyes from the glaring sun. "After killing off the rattlers, plugging up the holes in the walls, putting in a swing for the baby, and hanging doily curtains over the windows, it could be right presentable."

"I knew you'd be impressed," laughed Clay.

There was such pride in Clay's mood and voice Dora felt it would be unnecessarily cruel to dampen his ardor, perhaps even criminal. Desolate and forbidding as the area looked to her, and rundown as the rock houses appeared, she realized she was looking at it with the eyes of a woman, meaning it pointed to a lean, mean and uncomfortable existence for whomever inhabitants desired to compete with indigenous reptiles, coyotes, flies, fleas and mosquitoes—not to mention the cold of winter and the heat of summer while embraced within the hard rock walls. So for now she held back her joyless comments, while on the other hand was genuinely happy for Clay and his land.

"Wow, Clay," exclaimed John. "I think it's terrific! Really. With the river on one side, too. Isn't this where the old Goodnight-Loving Trail cut through, where you first came to New Mexico?"

"Yep, sure is," smiled Clay, proud of the memory and pleased John brought it up. "Eighteen hundred and sixty-six it was. Twenty long years ago."

Clay walked the rig past the few ruins. The river flowed slowly before them, turning south in a wide curve with hardly a ripple. Following it for perhaps a mile Clay reined up, then spoke.

"This is Pope's Crossing where the trail forded the river. The water's wide here but only two and a half feet deep. It's been twenty years and I'd like to celebrate this day by crossing. What say, you two?"

"Let's go, Unc!" enthused John.

"Don't stop now, Mister Allison!" ordered Dora with a smile.

With a hearty laugh Clay urged the horses forward. The team slid cautiously and qualmishly into the Pecos, but once finding their footing smooth and secure, and the river shallow, they confidently stepped out with ease. Mid-stream the passengers felt surrounded and dwarfed by a vast smooth sea, giving them the sensation of being encircled in a blanket of satin. As they slowly advanced to the far shore, the sun strew across its calm waters spangles of glittering diamonds beneath the golden afternoon sky.

A month later Clay and Dora were at the train depot in Socorro where he asked for the umpteenth time if she were certain she wanted to return to Colfax County alone.

"It would truly be no bother to go with you, Dora."

"Heaven's Clay, we've been through this overly much the past two days. Please don't worry. I plan to get off in Springer where I want to visit a spell, then go on to Cimarron for a while. I'll then take the stage to Elkins where it's just a skip and a jump to the Youngs."

"I know, I know, and I hate to fret over it so."

"Well, please don't. You have enough to do now with setting up your range and all, without traipsing back and forth so much."

"It would truly be no bother to go with you, Dora."

"Never you mind. Just sweep out the rabbit poop from our new rock house and see to it that the petunias are decently watered. And make sure there are no pesky Redskins lurking about."

Allison laughed and shook his head, commenting with a grin, "Damn if you haven't a harder head than me."

That's the sweetest thing you've said to me all month," she returned his laughter.

"All right," he acquiesced. "But be sure you wire me from Springer so I don't worry my head off."

"That I will. Now love, if you will lend me a kiss goodbye?"

"Yes, dear. But I want it back next time I see you."

"It's yours," she whispered as she offered her lips. "And safely preserved until I see you again."

Allison returned to his pastures to prepare moving his stock to his Texas section. It was a busy time for him as he threw himself into his work; branding newly purchased cows with his PP brand, familiarizing himself with his property lines as well with his neighbor ranchers, and cleaning, repairing and furnishing a two-room house of rock for he and Dora and their daughter. In between it all he continued adding and subtracting to his herd while brokering on the side when he could. In March he picked up a contract to move fifteen hundred cows to market for the Seven Rivers Cattle Company, a ranch fifteen miles to the south of him. Although headquartered in Colorado City, Texas, one hundred fifty miles east of Pecos, they also ran perhaps twenty thousand cattle on their Pecos-area ranch. Tray Windham was their manager in Pecos, with whom Clay had become acquainted.

The drive began in April for delivery to Wyoming. Seven drovers, a cook with a chuck wagon and a shepherd dog accompanied the bovines. That gave them two men for each flank, one at point, and one at drag, and the trail boss, "slick John," to keep track of whatever problems came their way. The first phase of the run would be to Springer, three hundred miles, to load the herd on rail cars, and where the cook would return south with the chuck wagon. The second lap was to Cheyenne, another three hundred miles, where they would offload. The third and final lap, and shortest, would be for the drovers to push the cattle to the pens on Horse Creek, forty miles northwest.

Allison, with his poorly behaving lower extremity, philosophically accepted his handicap of not being able to travel that long a distance, so took the train. He boarded in Pecos with a round trip ticket to Cheyenne via El Paso. In mid-May along his rail trek north he detrained in Las Vegas to stretch his legs and to put in a PR appearance at the newspaper office of the *Optic*.

CLAY ALLISON IN THE CITY
A MAN WHOSE CAREER IN NEW MEXICO IS WITHOUT
PARALLEL, PAYS A FRIENDLY VISIT TO THE OPTIC OFFICE.

The time was, perhaps, in the early and trying days of New Mexico, when men carried their lives in their hands, juries rendered their verdicts before the cases were heard in court, and men settled their differences at the point of a six-shooter, the above headlines would have struck terror to the hearts of those who were sworn enemies of Clay Allison, and even those who were not, would have feared that his presence was an indication that trouble was to follow; for he was, and is, a brave, determined man, who will sell his life dearly under any circumstances that may come up, fighting at the drop of a hat, and to the bitter end, for a friend, and vindicating his rights at all hazards, none who then knew him, or know him now, can deny.

The laudatory item went on to describe the cowman now as a "quiet, peaceable, well to-do citizen," successful and prosperous in the cattle business.

"What is the occasion of your visit to our city, Mister Allison?"

"I am driving across the country with fifteen hundred of as fine steers as were ever branded. My herd will reach Springer in about twelve days."

"Mister Allison, is it true you have withdrawn from the Lincoln County Stock Association, and are opposed to such organizations generally?"

Clay replied with a long winded, itemized rant which displayed his lack of affection for cattle associations, no doubt additionally fueled by his memory reaching back to his harassment of Fine Ernest and his prompt resignation from a Colfax County cattle group. He ended, "I shall no longer submit to the systematic extortions of these cattle associations in the form of fees, dues, etcetera."

His next point of soreness was to squelch the rumor someone started, and was being prolifically circulated, that he planned to accost the agent for the Maxwell Grant, Harry Whigham, to intimidate him in any way he could. Add to that, he especially disavowed any sympathy with Reverend McMains and his anti-grant agitation.

"I conclude that the law must take its course," he pontificated. "And from present appearances there is no doubt but that the best policy for the settlers on the Maxwell Grant is to make compromises with Mister Whigham, secure their homes and end this eternal litigation and warfare of which old man McMains is the chief promoter and instigator."

He meant these newspapered words to serve as a clarion-call which would precede him resoundingly across Colfax County, to let both the Santa Fe and Colfax Rings and pro-granters of every stripe know he was not interested in their fight. He had made his "deal" with the Santa Feers years ago, and didn't care to pick any scabs. Suicide was not on his agenda. He was a bona fide cattleman now and to hell with them all. And he wondered too, after all his words of wisdom, whether Cruz Vega and Pancho Griego were spinning in their graves?

At Springer he detrained once again to see to the shipping arrangements for the cows which were now making their appearance. It took forty-nine cars to load up all the beef, after which they were on their way again. Running this herd too was no small boon to his ego, showing pointedly, at least in his mind, that the Maxwell Grant Company may have cut him off, but he was still here, alive and kicking, and crossing their precious damned domain with a bunch of "his own" cattle.

At Raton he couldn't resist interrupting his journey once again to drop into the *Comet* office for another spirited interview. Emphasizing his place in society now as a solid citizen, he soap-boxed that "the day for ranikaboo days had passed, that there was no longer a frontier in this country, that hereafter everyone must go for law-and-order."

The cows were finally delivered to J. Dobyns at Horse Creek in early June under a sweaty ninety degree afternoon. They had suffered a tolerable loss of only nineteen head. The yearlings sold for seventeen dollars and fifty cents a head, the two-year-olds for twenty-three dollars and fifty cents and the three-year-olds for twenty seven dollars and fifty cents. Much pleased at the profitable venture, he paid the men off and returned to Cheyenne with John where he wired the money to the Seven Rivers bank account in Pecos.

At Raton he debarked again and made for the newspaper office to report an adventure to his reading public. "Following my return to Cheyenne from Horse Creek, I was gripped with a toothache that persisted too much to ignore. So I trod the streets and entered the first dentist's office that caught my eye. After a cursory exam the ivory merchant saw the problem and swiftly extracted the malignant tooth. Feeling sore but somewhat relieved, I paid the man twenty-five dollars and departed, my mouth stuffed with bloody gauze.

"Soon I was able to cast off the gauze, but within the hour my aching tooth returned, more painful then ever. I went to a second dentist and asked for a re-examination of the crater, and was told the previous doctor had mistakenly yanked a good tooth.

"'Good?' I roared. 'Then what in hell is bad?'"

"With no delay the second dentist extracted the proper ivory after which the pain ceased. After paying another twenty-five dollars, I hastily returned to the scene of the earlier crime. The man was alone so I cursed him, punched him to the floor, grabbed a pair of extractors, and kneeling on him pulled the first tooth I could grab a hold of. Then a second. Trying for another in my irate state, I tore the doctor's lip, who was all the while screaming and kicking like a child in a tantrum. Drawing a crowd, I tossed aside the pliers with, 'Next time I see you I'll get you ready for a complete plate, upper and lower, by God!' As I left in satisfaction I thought I heard several bystanders applaud, possibly a couple of the puller's earlier victims."

Leaving Raton, Clay and John dropped down to Otero where he detrained again for the Youngs to see Dora. Her child had arrived.

Allison peered down at the baby wrapped in a soft blanket.

"Clay," spoke the doctor. "The child has a twisted foot."

"How's that?"

"Look here." The doctor pulled back the coverlet to expose its feet, gently taking the flawed one in his hands. It was twisted at the ankle. As he rubbed it lightly he remarked, "She may have settled in the womb long enough for her foot to grow askew. In time it may straighten, although probably not completely, depending on how set the bones have become. It's a rare situation, but occurs occasionally."

The infant cooed and smiled and waved its arms excitedly as the men looked upon her.

"If I massaged it in hot water every day," asked Clay, "would it help?"

"Wouldn't hurt. Probably be a good thing. Nice and easy, though."

"Clay?" spoke Dora, waking.

"Yes, dear. How are you feeling?"

"Fine. Only somewhat tired."

"Just rest, love. Rest and sleep."

"Clay, I'm truly sorry you didn't get your boy."

"But you have a pretty daughter, dear."

"The doctor told me of its foot."

"It's all right, Dora. She'll probably straighten some. Hot water massaging might help."

"That's right, Mrs. Allison," echoed the physician. "The bones are still soft and may be pliable enough to be influenced in correcting them a bit by daily massages in hot water. Just be careful and patient. It may take a little time."

Clay gazed upon his tiny daughter slowly pumping her legs against invisible pedals. Unbelievable how active she was already. He took her angled right foot in his hand, softly kneading it in his palm. So soft, like warm silk. Why was it twisted so? Laying on it, the doc said. And the right one too. Like his own. A twinge of guilt sliced through him. Moral retribution? Pay backs? He groaned at his inner thoughts, wondering if he were crazy to think such things. My son, my son. Where was Joseph? What happened? A girl. Maybe a boy next time. John had three girls. What does Jesse have? His mind thought back, remembering, counting. Seven so far, the first a boy. Then six girls, all in a row. Jesus.

Every night Clay soaked the little foot in a pan of hot water, massaging it lightly, day after day, night after night. Many nights between feedings he would often set the child on his lap, a pan of hot water between his legs, and rub the submerged foot over and over and over until sometimes both he and the baby fell asleep. Awaking, he would refill the pan with hot water and continue on. Once in the early hours of the morning Dora found them asleep. She carefully removed the child to her crib, took the cooled pan of liquid to the kitchen, then returned to bed. A short time later Clay awoke in a shock at finding the baby no longer in his arms. He believed she and the pan had fallen to the floor. Leaping up in panic, groggy and disorientated, he howled out in fear. Dora appeared quickly and explained what she had done. Pale and shaken he turned his anger upon her, a convenient bystander to take the slack from his guilt. "Goddamn it!" he snapped. "Maybe if you'd have stayed at the Youngs like I asked you to this wouldn't have happened!" They didn't speak for days. And regardless of his persistent attention, internal pleadings and silent prayers, Patti Dora's foot remained malformed. His drinking began anew, medicine for his inwit now.

Returning alone to his Texas ranch, to be joined in a few months by Dora, John and the baby, was anti-climatic. He so looked forward to a son, the Joseph he prayed for month after month. He wondered how Martha Matthews and her Joseph was doing now? He'd be what, twenty-five? Was he a college graduate, or maybe cowboying on some ranch out there? Well, hell. He tried not to let his disappointment lead to anger, for what in hell would he be angry for, or at who? Dora? Him? Fate? Damn it all, anyway. He felt he was doomed to forever hire ranch hands while girl after girl was born to them, and not a son to carry on the work or the name. Shit.

Looking out the window he absently gazed at the landscape rolling by. In Springer the train stopped briefly to leave and take on a few passengers, then moved on. To the west twenty miles was Cimarron. He recalled his years there, the blood and turmoil of his shootings and fights, the roster of dead laid to him; Kennedy, Colbert, Cooper, Vega, Griego, Faber. He really liked ol' Pancho, Francisco Griego, for they were one of a kind and so much alike. If things had been different somehow they may have become good drinking buddies, but being on different sides of the same coin of hostility there was only room for one of them in Colfax County. He had balls but was so easily trapped. Tina didn't like the way he was killed, murdered, she called it. Hell, so what? He was dead either way, and it was me or him, and it sure as hell wasn't going to be me.

He snorted as he remembered how he pumped three bullets into him, and from the front, after the poor beaner turned and saw the gun in his hand. Adios, bonito! He was careful about the set-up, not wanting to be labeled a back-shooter. Code of the West? He laughed. Hell, there was no code, except to kill the son of a bitch first who was out to kill you. And who in hell invented that so-called "code" in the first place, anyway? Some chicken-shit scribbler back east inventing cowboy heros with his brains soaked in an inkwell. Love to drag that lamebrain out here and whip his ass to a pulp, promoting bull-shit like that. We were just a bunch of liquored crazies who waited for the other guy to make the first mistake, then nail him. Don't want to play the game? Then leave your gun at home, cousin. And watch your mouth. Lot of the time it was just the matter of getting the drop on your victim. Like Pancho. "How's about a game of pool, Griego?" God, that was easy. Just like the dumb old ploy, "Hey, your shoe's untied." The idiot looks down and you punch his lights out. So much for the Code of the West.

He stretched out and slipped his pint of Shrub's from his jacket, chugging away, relishing the subtle heat of the alcohol sliding down his throat.

Months later he met Dora and baby Patti at the Pecos depot, and they wagoned back to his ranch. He tried to put a happy face on things but it was difficult, his inner disappointment still with him. He also tried to hide it from Dora, but she could read him like a book. There was a lot of cattle grazing about as they drove along.

"Sure is getting crowded, Dora."

"Yes, seems so."

"Available land down here closing up, too."

"Really?"

"Hard to believe. Getting to be more people than cows," he tried a small jest.

"Yes," came her dry answer.

The terrain wasn't much to brag on, and he could see distaste in Dora' s face. He missed her early excitement of travel, being in new places. It hurt. The kid was happy anyway, waving its arms and gurgling like a normal six-month old. Soon the variety of Dora living in a rock house gave way to requests for a home perhaps in Pecos. His drinking was more frequent although he held it well, but his personality was taking on a hard edge, like brittle granite. She had to put distance between them.

In December of eighty-six he bought a lot in Pecos and had a one-bedroom house built upon it. In January eighty-seven Clay moved her and Patti to their new home, and Dora couldn't help but feel more alive in the more civilized environment; a nice, new, clean house to call home.

"Oh, Clay, thank you so much. You don't know how much this means to me."

"Dora, you and the child had no business living in such a primitive state, and with no neighbors to speak of up there. I'm happy to do this, really."

"I know, but again I thank you. It's sounds silly, but I missed a stove so much, and now I can cook and bake to my heart's content!"

"To be honest, that's exactly why I got this for you. I want a bunch more of them tasty apple cinnamon pies," he laughed.

"Oh, Clay, Clay," she smiled moving toward him and into his arms. "I do love you so very much."

"And I you, my sweet."

Their old feelings for each other re-mended here and there one stitch at a time, for the distance between home and ranch allowed Clay visits of one, sometimes two a month as he came in for supplies, and gave them needed breathing space. In Pecos he would dress in his black suit, hat and boots and they would have dinner out, or sometimes dine at home by candle light. Yet, since his limb was worsening his imbibing increased, and although he hardly drank while in the presence of Dora and Patti, the reek of alcohol would unmistakingly exude from his pores. It was a sore point with Dora because of little Patti being exposed to the stench, but she held back making an issue of it because of his infirmity. Earlier a year before they had discussed amputation, after doctors Clay had seen suggested it, but he balked, so she never brought it up again. In May Dora became pregnant again. She told him the news in June.

"Really?" his eyes lit up.

"It's true. It is."

"Well," he grinned broadly. "Tell you what. Let's have twins this time. A girl for you and a boy for me."

"All right, Mister Allison," she smiled. You're on. You'll get your Joseph yet!"

"By God, Dora, let's celebrate! Tonight a dinner with whatever wine they can rustle up!"

"Oh, yes, Clay! I'd love that!"

It was mid-morning July second and Allison was in Sol Pace's Saloon hoisting a few. Earlier he had claimed his wagon loaded with goods and supplies as he did every month, then normally left for his ranch right after, the first hours of day being coolest for summer travel. But this day he was in a cantankerous mood because of a small disagreement with Dora, and felt a few toddies would be just the thing to raise his spirits. What set him off was the mention of him in a column of the local paper by the editor which he took as a personal affront. Then, just before leaving he had words with Dora concerning it.

"Oh, for heavens sake, Clay. It's a comical comment and not an insult, so get off your high-horse."

"Dora, it's the principle of the thing. He's taken unethical liberty with me without asking my permission to even mention my name in his rag. And I'm going to tell him so!"

"There is simply no talking to you whenever you feel someone has stepped on your toes, no matter what. I don't want to hear any more about such foolishness, and that's that!"

With a grumble about not understanding women he turned and left, stepping into the light of the early rising sun and climbing aboard his vehicle.

Now at Pace's, after three belts of rye and a glass of beer, he waved a hand at Sol, saying, "Guess I'd better get my butt going and hit the road. Got a two-day trip to my ranch."

"Gonna be a hot one, Clay. You be careful."

Exiting the saloon he met an acquaintance on the sidewalk, the lawyer R.D. Gage. "Good morning, Mister Gage," he greeted, extending his hand.

"Why, hello, Clay. I see your wagon there is all loaded up for your usual haul. I don't envy you your trip."

"Gets easier every time," replied Allison lightly. "Getting used to it."

"I suppose it does. But it takes a hardier man then me to make that journey in this summer heat."

"By the way, Gage, have you seen editor Frank Antrim hereabouts of late?"

"No, not for a few days. Why?"

"Well, he made scurrilous mention of me in his rag which I take great exception to. So I want to hunt him down to give him a good solid beating."

"Oh, Clay, I know Frank fairly well, and I doubt he meant anything mean toward you."

"Have you read it?"

"Well, yes, and to be honest it was all in light fun, like he says about a lot of the locals. In fact, he made a little fun of me over losing a case last month, and we all had a big laugh over it."

"Laugh? I want to find him and see if he can laugh while I whup his ass."

"Aw, Clay," smiled Gage nervously. "He meant no harm, really."

"I plan to look him up, and now."

"Ummm, I heard he's out of town, Clay. Gone to El Paso on a business trip."

"Damn the luck. Well, I'll settle with him on my next trip. I'll have my laughs then."

With that Allison limped to his loaded vehicle and climbed aboard. "See you, Gage!"

"You have a safe trip now, Clay."

As the vehicle rolled off, Gage swiftly made his way to Antrim's office to warn him of Allison's threat.

"Christ, R.D. You mean over a silly quip of good-natured joshing he is hot to whip my ass?"

"He surely is, Frank, and you can be certain he will look you up. So you better lay low for a time when he returns."

"Where's he now?"

"He was at Pace's Saloon, but has just driven off for his ranch. He said on his next trip he plans to hunt you down."

"Damn it. He's just crazy enough to do that, too."

Antrim shakily lit another cigarette with the butt of his last. A high-strung man and chain smoker, he was aware of Allison's reputation, and especially of his violent past.

"Thanks much for the warning, R.D. I'll certainly be on the lookout."

"Just you be careful, Frank. Sober, he's as kind and considerate as can be, but when he drinks he's as dangerous as a cornered panther."

Upon Gage's exit editor Antrim put up a sign on the door, "Closed for the Day." Striding home quickly, he all the while peered nervously over his shoulder, becoming more frightened by the minute that Allison would come boring down on him like an enraged beast. He had never met the man, had only seen him from a distance perhaps a half dozen times, riding a wagon or limping about town, knowing he was too crippled to ride a horse. Something about a self-shot foot. He had a deep terror of him and never liked him the first he lay eyes upon him, one of those hate-at-first-sight kind of things. Damn it! He wished he never spoke of him in the paper now. Yet in a subtle, vicious way he wanted to test the man's humor, have a light joke at his expense, and now it became a monkey on his back. Fear of confrontation ate at him; it was a searing acid that chewed its way down to his bones, into the very marrow. He'd have to get him first, that's all there was to it!

Antrim pulled three hundred dollars from his hidden stash, shoved it into an envelope and into his jacket pocket. He then mounted his horse for a seventeen-mile gallop westward to Toyah, a small but growing village of sixty-some people.

It was early afternoon when he reined his tired horse before the Fields Hotel and trod his way to a second floor room. Knocking, a harsh voice yelled, "Come on in!" With no hesitation he did.

"Lordy, lordy," grinned the bearded beefy man playing solitaire at a table, facing him. "If it ain't little Frank. You look peaked and tuckered out as if you run barefoot all the way from Pecos. What's eating you, cousin?"

Catching his breath, Frank threw his dusty jacket across the bed and sprawled across a sofa chair. "Where's Whitey, Jed?"

"Out grabbing a bite to eat. Should be back any minute."

"I got a job for you fellas.'

"That's good news. We can sure use some money. Thievin's been kind of puny lately."

Jed and Whitey Post were Frank's cousins. The two for years practiced a fairly successful career in robbery, rustling on both sides of the border, and gambling. Occasionally they killed a man for a reasonable fee, and their chosen "assignment" merely disappeared and was never seen again. For many miles the region was filled with vacant desert, which they looked upon as a natural graveyard. Just then through the door in walked the oldest of the three, Whitey, so-called because in his teens his hair of a sudden turned white. The two men were stout six-footers, while thin Frank was a brittle five-six. But of the three Frank was the brightest, however that was measured.

"Frank!" hailed Whitey. "I thought that was your horse out front. Hope you have a job for us."

"That I have. And you'll have to work fast. Before a day or two."

"Well, hell, let's hear it so we can move."

"You've no doubt heard of Clay Allison?"

"Who ain't? Don't know him, but saw him a few times in Pecos. Has a bad limp, right?"

"Yes, a foot crippled so bad he can no longer ride a horse."

"Still likes to brag on being a shootist, too. A 'Gentleman Gunfighter' some call him. Now ain't that a stupid moniker?"

"I agree, but don't sell him short. He's a dangerous man, cripple or no."

"So what's the deal?"

"You two know the road between Pecos and the New Mexico line?"

"Like the back of our hands."

"Good. I want Allison killed. But it's got to look like an accident."

"Accident?" spoke Jed. "Why in hell can't we just shoot him and bury him?"

"Whitey, I'm talking to you because you're the only one of you two with brains. Now shut up, Jed. We got no time to lose. An obvious killing would bring up too many questions, and I don't want to waste time going into it. Allison is now on his way back to his ranch with a loaded wagon. His place is in northwest Loving County, against the New Mexico line just north of the Pecos River. It's about fifty miles and will take him two days to get there. I understand he stops about halfway for a few hours sleep and rest, someplace just north of Horsehead Draw. He'll be on the Pecos-Roswell Road, and finally turn off to cross the Pecos to his ranch at Pope's Crossing. It's got to happen on the second day somewhere, before Pope's Crossing. You figure out what you have to do, maybe spook his horses, whatever. But I want him dead, and of an accident. Got it?"

Frank reached into his jacket which still lay across the bed and withdrew the envelope. "Here's three hundred dollars in twenties and fifties." He handed it to Whitey, who whistled appreciatively. "There's another three hundred when you get the job done, and if it's right. An accident, understand?"

"You got that right, Frank. It'll be just like you want it."

"Then get going. You can pull ahead of him cross-country tonight, and set up your play for the accident sometime tomorrow. This has got to be good, Whitey. I'm counting on you."

"Good as done, Frank."

"Fine. When you do it, head quick and unseen back for Toyah and stay here. If all works out I'll see you in a week with another three hundred."

"Nice doing business with you, Frank."

"Make it a good job, Whitey."

"Allison don't know it, cuz, but he's the most accident-prone man on the Pecos-Roswell Road tonight."

Late in the evening on his first day out of Pecos, Allison pulled his wagon off the side of the road about halfway to his destination for a few hours sleep. He hung a lantern on the sideboard to alert any other traffic which might trundle by. Tired and half-bagged, he removed himself to the ground with the intent of shuffling off into the chamisa and salt cedar to relieve himself, fore and aft. Looking about, he could barely discern the landscape about him in the pale light of the quarter-moon through the scattered clouds. Even the stars weren't much through the overcast, and it was another hot night in the upper eighties. Reaching into the wagon he took the freshly opened quart for a long sweet slug. Corking it with a throaty sigh, he lay it back on the seat and limped off into the brush to do his duty. He could hear a pack of coyotes yipping in the far distance as he made his way across the sandy ground, their echoes lending a haunting quality to the near-inky night.

After thirty feet or so he approached the twisted cedar he would use as a brace. It was familiar ground where he had often stopped in his midway point to rest, and many times thought it would be appropriate if he put up a sign signifying, "Off Limits: Allison's Dump Spot." After urinating near the base of the tree, he went to the other side and unbuckled his gunbelt and holster to hang on the short broken limb. He next unbuttoned his britches and shorts, lowered them both to his ankles, gripped the stout lower branch and clung to it in a leaning half-backward position, then squatted and grunted away. He loved the feeling of evacuation, the great purging exudation of bodily waste that made him feel physically lighter after it was over. His entire system celebrated feeling the better for it, a thorough cleansing ritual of excreting old crap. Ahhh, there goes that steak dinner he had earlier, and the potatoes, and the bread, and the vegetables. God, he sighed. It felt almost as good as sex. Why couldn't he do the same with his mind? Why couldn't he also empty himself selectively of old useless thoughts, uncomfortable memories and mental clutterings? Still hanging onto the branch, half-bent and spread-legged, he suddenly realized in shock he had forgotten to bring some wiping paper and let out a curse in frustration. Still frozen in a semi-crouch, he wondered what to do? Damn it! Helpless as a babe in the bush.

He bent and grabbed his bunched-up shorts and pants in both hands and shuffled in half-steps back to the wagon. Literally butt-naked, he leaned over the sideboard and scratched around in a sack for the pack of relief paper. Ahhh, there it is. A pack of Gayetty's medicated paper for the water closet. Clutching it, he shuffled back to the tree, grabbed his safety branch, spread his shanks and proceeded to clean his after-quarters. Done wiping, he redressed, strapped on his gunbelt, and returned to the wagon. Feeling weary and looking forward to some sleep, he stretched out over several blankets placed across sacks of oats, took another heavy dose of rye, and soon fell into a deep slumber.

Waking a few hours past dawn, Allison felt somewhat refreshed although slightly hung over. But no headache bothered him and his leg and foot felt as if they had given up complaining, so he thought for a change he was way ahead of the game. After taking a touch of the hair of the dog, he pried open a can of beans and devoured them ravenously without the benefit of heating, accompanied with chunks of dried beef jerky. In a rage of thirst he half-emptied his water canteen in one long swilling. Now greatly revived, he was ready to meet the day. He fed and watered his horses, climbed aboard, took another belt of liquor, then urged the beasts into their customary walk. Twisting the reins around a small post before him, he settled back and lit up a cheroot. King of the hill, by God. But soon the King began sweating like a hog in an oven beneath the glaring midmorning sun, and like the proverbial copper coin, his leg returned to pay his body its cruel throbbing visit. Hoping to head off the coming bout he grabbed mister rye by the neck and gulped liberally.

He was perhaps fifteen miles from his ranch, just a stone's throw across and northeast of the bank of the Pecos. It was an irony he ended up ranching there, right on the original Goodnight-Loving Trail over which he himself had herded over a half-dozen times. Back in eighteen hundred and fifty-five Captain John Pope had been assigned by the army to drill for water, during which he had seen to the construction of perhaps a dozen stone structures as a small fortress against Indian attacks. But the drilling was an unsuccessful venture and they left in eighteen hundred and fifty-eight. The Butterfield Overland Mail Company immediately took over the location as a stage station, its route running from San Francisco to St. Louis, Missouri and back twice a week, two thousand seven-hundred and ninety-five miles one-way. At the commencement of the Civil War in eighteen hundred and sixty-one, they left. Clay, soon after moving on his section, settled in one of the rock houses. Although in slight disrepair, but one of the better of the group, he made it as comfortable as he could for Dora and their half-year-old daughter, until building a house in Pecos. He knew it was no picnic for them to live in such primitive conditions, surrounded by rock in icy winter and practically freezing, then to roast within the same walls in the summer. While he and his hands took it as a natural acceptance, they of course now and then would pair off and take turns running up to Roswell and the settlements for recreation and loosen up a bit.

Yet here he was, unsatisfied and dissatisfied, not much happy with the way things had turned out. Hell, he finally had the ranch and cattle he had always wanted. True, he was no Charles Goodnight, never would be, he accepted that. He still had a good spread, a good crew and was his own boss. He did wish John and Monroe would come join him though, make it more a family atmosphere. Young John McCulloch would like that, too. But he knew it was because of his imbibing Kate wouldn't have anything to do with him. Jesus H. Christ, didn't she know it was for his foot and leg? Couldn't she cut him some slack? He knew she blamed him for John's shotgunning too, nearly getting him killed, and he himself suffered enough over it as it was. Still carried the damn endless guilt about that every day, still seeing him on the floor in a puddle of blood. Of course his continuous drinking made him meaner than a snake, even though he hadn't killed or beaten anyone up because of it in years. Not since Faber had he killed a man, nor since caning Waco had he whipped anyone. And both sure as hell deserved what he'd given them. His leg. His goddamned rotting-away leg is what it all comes down to. Because of it he drank too much, and now in turn the booze makes him hard to get along with, and that makes everybody around him standoffish. Shit. What a vicious circle. He upended the quart and poured a long stream down his throat. It was warm from the heat of the day, and the bottle hot to his touch.

He lit up another cheroot and gazed about the frying landscape slowly passing him by. He must be stupid being out in the sun like this, even the coyotes were smarter than him. Colfax County, he muttered for the dozenth time with a snarl. Wish I never heard of the goddamned place. So why didn't he leave it alone, where so much of his life started and ended? Why dredge it up again and again like old vomit? It only infuriated him and raised his bile level to spillover. Shit. He tried over and over to blame those Santa Fe Ring bastards for all his troubles, even his shot foot, but knew in his twisted heart he was just turning out to be a cantankerous old fart with a sack of endless bitches and complaints. My God, leave it alone! he nearly shouted to the heat-swirling landscape around him. You made your own lousy choices! Sick of his sourness, weary of his pain, he drank down a bit more of the warm whiskey.

Damn foot. It was really throbbing and burning now. Should have had Frank set up an appointment with that doc friend of his. But hell, it would have been the same news: off with the leg. Should have done that years ago and gotten it over with, but kept hoping it would heal. He was disgusted with himself, all these years clinging to his dying limb like a vain bull holding on to his limp dick. Well.... The decision came to him then, sudden and lightening-like, like one of those clear and final biblical epiphanies that clobbered one of them raging, complaining prophets: let the son of a bitch go, dummy! Hot damn! Why the hell not? It's about time!

Yes, his mind was made up, he would do it! It gave him a burst of satisfaction to have finally, after all the past years of agonized limping, to self-agree in ridding himself of his leg. He was so glad, so thoroughly relieved, so happy at his decision, he saw himself in the days ahead moving about on his peg leg, painless and free. He could ride a horse again, even dance if he cared to. But most of all he would stop being such a pain in the ass around Dora, whom he embarrassingly knew had had her fill of him and his grousing. She didn't deserve his dark moods, especially when drinking, regardless of his usage of alcohol to numb his aching. Her patience was wearing thin, if not already plumb gone. But the pain was always there anyway, and increasing, despite the ample doses of rye. Yes, away with it! It was like he was being born again. Off with the old and on with the new! Yes, he laughed aloud. A brand new leg!

He emptied the last fingers from his quart, grabbed it by the neck, then flung it in a high arc over the brushy desert, watching it tumble and sparkle and flash beneath the sun in its aerial journey. In moments he heard the distant breakage of glass as it descended upon a rock. And he'd lay off the damn booze, too! And by God he'd have his Joseph yet!

Yessiree! Soon as he got to his ranch he'd take a bath, trim his beard, put on a clean set of clothes, pack a small bag, leave McCulloch in charge, and tell him where he was going, to El Paso to get legally butchered. He'd leave his rig at Dora's, whom he was certain would share in the elation of his decision (maybe she'd agree to come along—at least he hoped she would), but either way off to El Paso he'd go on the very next train. Christ! He felt like a kid at Christmas! He never felt more free in his entire life. It was like the unburdening of a long unbearable weight.

As the wagon was about to descend the downslope of Salt Creek crossing the world about Allison exploded into a deafening roar of thunder. Startled, he nearly leaped from the vehicle as it suddenly shot forward. It took him to the Civil War a split second: was it a cannon? An air burst? No, it was the simultaneous blast of a pair of shotguns detonating its four shells practically in his and the horses' ears, instantly thrusting the equines into headlong panic. They shot forward in an effort to escape the unspeakable threat they were suddenly accosted by, zooming down the slope like a speeding cannonball. Allison, adrenaline pumped, tried to hold on to his seat, knowing he'd best grab the reins from the post in order to regain control of the terror-stricken beasts. But he was physically helpless, being thrown about like a child's toy. His alcohol be-fogged brain hampered decision-making, slowing whatever thought processes he was trying to organize, hardly knowing where he was or what was happening. He grasped that he was on a runaway wagon, but what in hell for? What was that explosion? He was still in shock and couldn't quite grasp the situation. Should he try and jump to safety?

As the wagon rolled in swift velocity downward and hit the bottom of the dry creek bed, the resolution was rudely taken out of his hands and made for him. When the horses began their galloping stride up the grade he was thrust from the bouncing, swaying vehicle as he tried stomping on the brake, forgetting about his weak foot and leg. As a result hot slashes of pain ripped through his limb. Completely off balance now, he was flung from the seat and hit head and shoulders-first onto a mound of earth, the result of someone grading the entire slope some days before to ironically make for smoother travel, leaving a hill of dirt along both sides of the road. His body then twisted and slid feet-first under the wagon between the front and rear wheels. In a flash the right rear wheel ran across his neck, crushing and breaking it, killing him instantly. The wagon continued rumbling northward, the pair of wide-eyed equines fleeing in blind terror as fast as possible.

Jed and Whitey Post stood with empty shotguns amazed at the destruction they had wrought, and at how easy it was. They stared at the speeding vehicle as it faded into the distance. Then all became deathly quiet.

"Christ," oathed Jed. "Did you see that?"

"Sure did," replied Whitey, stunned at the swift scenario.

They stared at Allison sprawled on his back on the upslope. With his arms and legs akimbo, he appeared as a felled giant crab. His neck was crushed and askew, his tongue protruded grotesquely, his eyes were hugely agape and rolled upward. Cold-blooded as the cousins were, the dark event gave them nervous pause.

"Do you think he's dead?" whispered Jed.

"He's dead all right."

"Should we check?"

"Go ahead."

"Naw. You go."

They stood staring, neither desiring to go near the corpse. The afternoon was silent and time stood still, its heat weighty and ponderous. The blinding sun roasted the two as they remained as statues, gazing at their work. Jed happened to look up at the far horizon toward the Pecos River, hardly two miles east. Waves of heat shimmered before his eyes in the ninety plus oven. What he saw puzzled him.

"What's that?" he asked quietly.

"What's what?"

"That. Out there beyond. Toward the Pecos. See?"

"I don't see nothing."

"Sure. Way out toward the river."

Whitey stared but could see nothing. "I don't see a thing. Heat's getting to your pea-sized brain."

"Naw. C'mon, look."

"Your eyes are just playing tricks, Jed. Mirages. I don't see a blamed thing."

As Jed squinted toward the east he saw a tiny woman riding north pell-mell on a giant white jackass pulling a travois. Her long grey hair streamed behind her in the breeze, and after her trailed a pack of unbathed, unbrushed, shaggy poodles, bounding joyfully in the bountiful light.

"Sure, Whitey, see? Good God Almighty."

"Ain't nothing out there, dummy."

"Good God Almighty," he whispered in awe. He wondered if she and the dogs were going to Roswell.

"You're heat-struck, Jed. Let's get the hell back to our horses and outta here."

Jed continued gazing at his distant vision disappearing on the dancing horizon, wondering if it were real. He was certain it were no mirage. "God Almighty."

"C'mon, dummy. Let's git. We sure as hell don't want no one seeing us out here."

"Huh? Oh, yeah."

The two trod through the sand and underbrush and cedar, the broken corpse of Allison still in their eyes. "God Almighty" was all Jed could continuously whisper over and over in puzzlement as he followed Whitey, for with Allison in his visual memory was coupled the mysterious mirage of the mule-riding woman and pack of curs. "Good God!"

To the south of the accident site maybe six, seven miles, John Coalson was riding horseback from Roswell. A ranch hand for the Johnson brothers of Pecos, he was on his way to Toyah to visit his brother Doug for a time, a Texas Ranger. Up ahead through the wavering furnace of heat he thought he made out a horse-drawn wagon. He hoped it was someone he knew who would stop for a bit of conversation. It would be a most welcome treat and break the monotony of the ride.

It wasn't too long before he could make out that the vehicle was driverless. He saw it was loaded down with supplies, and the pair of horses drawing it, now slightly blown out, appeared to have had a hasty run. He then recognized the rig as Allison's.

Stopping the team, he dismounted, tied his own mount to the backboard, got aboard, then turned it about to retrace its steps. Three miles later at Salt Creek he found Allison's splayed body on the upslope, cold and dead. "Good God Almighty!" He dismounted and walked to him. "Clay?" he spoke, feeling foolish, knowing he was dead. "Clay?" He reached with his fingers and drew the cadaver's eyes shut. The protruding tongue was purple and huge, his neck horribly twisted and crushed. "Good God, Clay. I'm sorry." It was a terrible way to die, thought Coalson.

CODA

ROBERT CLAY ALLISON, two months short of his forty-sixth year, was buried in Pecos, on July fourth, eighteen hundred and eighty-seven, Independence Day. Seven months later, on February tenth, eighteen hundred and eighty-eight, Dora gave birth to their second daughter in Pecos, whom she named Clay Pearl.

His two thousand five hundred head of cattle, valued at seventeen thousand dollars, was sold at a private auction to W.D. and W.F. Johnson.

On October twenty-third, eighteen hundred and ninety, Dora married the third of the Johnson brothers, Jesse Lee. Soon they relocated to Fort Worth, Texas. On January eighteenth, nineteen hundred and twenty-six, Dora, sixty-three, died while undergoing an operation in Baltimore, Maryland. Her husband Jesse died December twelfth, nineteen hundred and thirty-seven at Fort Worth at seventy-five.

Monroe Allison died August fifth, eighteen hundred and eighty-seven in the Panhandle at forty-three, a few days over a month after Clay. It was said he had ridden his horse to a water well on the Gageby Creek ranch, probably to fetch both a drink, when he suffered a fatal heart attack. He was found on the ground next to his horse, and was buried in the Ellom Cemetery nearby.

In September John moved his family back to Clifton, Tennessee, taking the body of Monroe with them to be reinterred in the family cemetery. In December John and Kate became the parents of their fourth and last daughter, Tina Willie. Some time after Clay's demise, John's wife was said to have had to talk John out of returning to Texas "to take care of Lee Johnson," believing that Johnson was behind or somehow responsible for Clay's death. Jesse Lee Johnson was the man Dora married in eighteen hundred and ninety. Where or how John picked up the story is unknown. Perhaps it was malicious gossip by a Johnson enemy, or a foe of Clay's. Possibly an antagonist of both. Clay Allison was not a man to mince words, right or wrong, especially when imbibing, and undoubtedly created hard enemies here and there. In turn, Jesse and his two brothers were financial powers in the region as bankers and merchants, a profession not kind to economic losers and may have created a few foes themselves. But Jesse Lee's reputation seems to have been that of a decent man of good character, as testified to by several Allison relatives. Thus John may have been the victim of well-placed loose talk. Yet, besides editor Antrim, it was said Clay also had had a disagreement with a local rancher and was looking to settle his hash.

The final months of John's life was spent in physical agony, ironically echoing Clay's bullet-damaged foot. It appears John's leg, and perhaps body, became infected with lead poisoning from pellets he was still carrying from Constable Faber's double load of buckshot back in December eighteen hundred and seventy-six. From November first, eighteen hundred and ninety-seven through January fifth, eighteen hundred and ninety-eight, Doctor J.K. Cook made thirty-four visits, including four "staying all night," and performed one operation on John's leg on December eighth. A second physician, doctor Hardin, also attended November nineteenth. After two months and seven days his suffering came to an end, and he expired at two thirty in the morning, January seventh, not quite forty-four years old.

To prove there was longevity in the Allison clan, their parents Jeremiah and Mariah lived to a ripe old age. Jeremiah died in eighteen hundred and ninety-two, shortly after his eighty-first birthday, and Mariah in eighteen hundred and ninety-four at eighty.

Their oldest son Jesse Alonzo died April nineteenth, nineteen hundred and four, three months after his sixty-fifth birthday. He and his wife Frances Katherine had raised ten girls and four boys, and the only individual of that generation to carry on the Allison family surname appears to have been their son John Monroe, eighteen hundred and eighty-nine to nineteen hundred and thirty-three. John's son, Charles E., was born in nineteen hundred and twenty-two.

Allison grave marker in Pecos, Texas. Courtesy James S. Peters.

Samuel B. Axtell (1819-1891), the governor who did what
he could to repay Allison for his break with the Santa Fe Ring.
Courtesy Museum of New Mexico, negative #8787.

Manly Mortimer Chase (1842-1915), Cimarron rancher.
Courtesy Denver Public Library, Western History Department.

Stephen ("Smoothe Steve") B. Elkins (1841-1911),
supposed leader of the Santa Fe Ring.
Courtesy Museum of New Mexico, negative #91328.

Henry M. Porter (1838-1937), speculator, banker and cattleman, and strong supporter
of the Colfax faction. Courtesy Denver Public Library, Western History Department.

Frank Springer (1848-1927), attorney, cattleman and pro-land granter of the Colfax faction who successfully argued before the Supreme Court for the validity of the Maxwell Land Grant.
Courtesy Museum of New Mexico, negative #45483.

F. J. Tolby grave marker in Cimarron, New Mexico. The original broken marker is leaning behind.
Courtesy James S. Peters.

Possible grave site of Cruz Vega, as pointed out by Fred Lambert, circa 1967. Courtesy James S. Peters.

Allison flanked by Adie and Joseph Matthews shortly after breaking his leg. The photograph was reportedly printed backwards since it was his right foot that was injured, circa Fall, 1871(?). Courtesy Robert J. Matthews.

Allison's unpaid bar tab, St. James Hotel, Cimarron, New Mexico, November 1876 and January 1877, $27.50. Courtesy Denver Public Library, Western History Department.

Mason T. Bowman (1844-1883), Colfax County Sheriff, 1882-1883. Courtesy Mary Lail.

St. James Hotel-Bar-Restaurant, circa 1875. From a painting by James S. Peters.

John Allison ranch section, Gageby Creek, Texas. Courtesy James S. Peters.

www.ingramcontent.com/pod-product-compliance
Lightning Source LLC
Chambersburg PA
CBHW030536030726
47495CB00004B/1018